T0365689

Living the Dream

Living the
Dream

BONNE PARISH

LIVING THE DREAM

This is a work of fiction. All of the characters, names, incidents, organizations, and dialogue in this novel are either the products of the author's imagination or are used fictitiously.

iUniverse books may be ordered through booksellers or by contacting:

iUniverse
1663 Liberty Drive
Bloomington, IN 47403
www.iuniverse.com
1-800-Authors (1-800-288-4677)

ISBN: 978-1-5320-1731-5 (sc)
ISBN: 978-1-5320-1730-8 (e)

Library of Congress Control Number: 2017904369

Print information available on the last page.

iUniverse rev. date: 08/16/2019

To my other mother, Mrs. Murray.

Thanks Jean for your love and support.

And to my husband Dar...

Together we're living dream.

1

Of all days to tell your boyfriend you're pregnant, the Ides of March isn't the best choice. A touch of gloom settles over me as I contemplate my lover's reaction to the news. But after missing my period for three weeks he insisted we do a home pregnancy test and go together to see my gynecologist. A sense of dread washes over me as I contemplate having to tell the man he will be a father, but I'm ecstatic with the news. I always dreamed of this moment…well, maybe a slightly different version but I've always known I wanted a family of my own. As the doctor leaves the examination room I try to remember those deep breathing exercises from my free trial yoga class last month and try to still my racing heart. A sly part of my brain knows that no amount of deep breathing will help the soon to be father in the next room.

The procrastinating part of me stalls for time as I walk into the small restroom and wash my hands. The pensive face in mirror showcases the inner turmoil I'm experiencing now. I take stock at the reflection in front of me showing shoulder length, shiny dark brown hair… my best feature, a slight flush on my high cheekbones, and a decided unattractive white ring circling my full lips now void of the pink lip gloss

I applied this morning. I smile trying to ease the tension around my mouth and grin when I remember how often Pax would swear he noticed my blue eyes first, then my smile, and finally my 'smoking hot' body as he calls it. He is a physical guy, usually the life of the party but as I turn to leave the restroom and walk out into the waiting area I can tell he's not in a partying mood.

Paxton Barrett doesn't like change and especially changes he feels are being thrust upon him. He loves his fast-paced lifestyle, devil-may-care attitude, and most especially, his freedom. Sometimes I'm amazed we've been together for two years this past October. Even though he is a tad spoiled, I still tingle when I think about how much I love the man and usually overlook his lesser qualities as I'm sure he does with mine.

My damp palms remind me of the task before me so I wipe their sweaty residue down the sides of my burgundy pencil skirt and force myself to walk out to the waiting room. Pax looks so out of place sitting on the navy colored hard plastic formed chairs, flipping through an outdated lady's magazine. His charcoal gray pinstriped suit, pale gray shirt and lavender silk tie are top of the line in the corporate world but appear over dressed for the rest of the waiting patients and one look on his face reveals his patience is at an end.

"Well? What did Doctor Phelps say?" he quickly whispers when I walk over and stand in front of him, anxiety written all over his face.

Taking his strong, left hand I place it gently over my belly and smile down at him.

"You're going to be a daddy in about seven and a half

months," I can't stop the giggle that escapes my lips as I rush on to say, "I know this is a shock, but we love each other and intended to get married eventually, right?"

The stunned look on his handsome face is a dead giveaway he wasn't thinking along those lines, at least not soon. Hiding my disappointment, I tug him to his feet and hug him before whispering in his ear, "It will be alright sweetie, I promise. You're just a little scared, that's all."

It takes two seconds before he wraps his arms around me, but when he does I feel a thousand times better, because being in his arms is where I belong. He lets out a hard sigh of resignation before kissing my temple and turning us towards the exit. Pax slips into a semi-depressive state and frowns down at our joined hands.

"Yeah, it'll be alright," he murmurs and guides us over to the elevators. "Let's go for a ride since we don't have to be back at the office."

We took the afternoon off, anticipating the need to be alone after we received the verdict as he called it. I smile at him and nod my head in agreement. When we reach the parking lot he opens the door of my 1969 black stingray Corvette my father and I lovingly restored. Pax loves this car so much I'd be hard pressed to ask him to choose between the two of us. Once he's behind the wheel he turns the key and the mighty beast roars to life and he settles into a quiet mood. Quickly we're heading towards Lake Sinclaire, a small town situated around a peaceful lake suited for a family and my self-confessed ideal spot to think.

I've always dreamed of living on *Lake Sinclaire*, a great body of water just above Albany, New York. There are mountains all around the serene water with dense forests helping seclude it from the ever-encroaching urbanites. It would be the ultimate place to live. We both work in the city for a magazine called *Viva La Femme* owned by a multi-media outfit out of Ontario Canada. Pax is in sales quickly climbing the infra-structure of the company and I'm an executive assistant to the Editor in Chief, Star Bridges. Neither of us mentioned to co-workers why we took off today not even our best friends Ginger Simmons and Jim Wiley, both employees of the magazine. That we all work for the same company makes keeping a secret near impossible, but so far, we've done just that. They'll both be mad at us for not sharing this life-altering bit of news beforehand, especially Ginger who isn't all that crazy about my choice of mate.

Pax takes the Lake Sinclaire exit knowing exactly where I want to go without being told. He knows just seeing the lake will sooth my nerves and hopefully his own. We're both silent not willing to share our thoughts just yet. I settle deeper into the bucket seat and reflect on having Pax's child; the greatest gift he could have given me. My own childhood was wonderful, so very normal and carefree that I want to recreate the joy and great times I experienced with my own children. Staring out the side window it dawns on me Pax and I have never discussed how many kids we each would like. Hopefully this pregnancy will be easy for both of us because I know I want at least three if not four kids, spaced out a couple years apart.

From the small bits and pieces, I've dragged out of the man his own childhood was less than idyllic. His father was a workaholic and an alcoholic, a deadly combination. The man dropped dead at his desk in his library at forty-two. Paxton discovered his father and being only seven years old it had a lingering effect on him both as a child and as an adult. He doesn't like responsibility and insists on living in the here and now. I suppose his mother remarrying only a year later increased his insecurities and lack of desire to grow up.

His mother Beth married a wealthy business man out of Albany named Stanley Carmichael. Stanley tried his best to help Paxton adjust to losing his parent and having a new man to answer to, and even Pax admitted he was a terror for most of his formidable years; then throw in an older step-sister with a chip on her shoulder, I guess things were dicey in that household. I can't imagine my life without my one and only sibling Vic. We fought like cats and dogs but that's normal, I think…Pax and his stepfather have a good relationship now making our bi-monthly trip to their house a pleasant experience and his sister Terrie works in the Sales Department of Viva La Femme at the home office in Ontario. I've seen her a handful of times and like her immensely.

"Let's go for a walk on the beach," Pax says breaking the silence and shaking me out of my own thoughts as he pulls off the highway and onto the shoulder where a public access staircase is conveniently located. The small town of Lake Sinclaire is a couple miles further down the two-lane highway. There are a handful of great houses along the rocky shore, some new, some old, and a couple needing repair, but it's an affluent place to settle down without being pretentious.

"Sounds good," I reply loving walking hand in hand with him, hoping to discuss our future.

But he's still quiet as I remove my wine-colored pumps from my feet and slip on the black ballet slippers I carry in my over-sized bag and walk around the hood of the 'Vette' and stand next to him. He's been churning his own fears in his head but when he reaches for my hand and threads our fingers together I feel the previous chill leave my body. Pressing his strong arm into my side I rest my head on his shoulder and wait for him to begin.

He takes a deep breath and says rather unenthusiastically, "I guess we'd better get married."

Wow; as far as wedding proposals go that was the most depressing one I've ever heard. Trying to understand his reluctance I look up at him and smile, waiting on the crooked grin I love to appear on his face, but the boyish smile remains hidden behind the gloomy frown. He isn't looking at me either but out across the lake, avoiding eye contact. He narrows his eyes against the bright March sun reflecting off the water. The sexiest feature on the man is his near black eyes and thick lashes under straight dark brown brows. His long narrow bridged nose has a slight bump from a high school sports injury keeping his gorgeous face from being too 'pretty' as his mother calls him.

"What's wrong Pax?" I ask and instantly regret the question when he blows up.

"What's wrong? Are you nuts?" he barks in a chilling tone and drops my hand from his. I hear the facetiousness creep into his next words. "We're about to become parents, you know 'Mom and Dad'?" he snorts down at me letting me see the anger snapping in his dark eyes. Now that he's said the words out loud, he lets loose his temper. "What the hell could possibly be wrong Harper? Our lives are about to change drastically, and not for the better in my opinion." He runs his trembling fingers through his hair and continues his spiel, "neither of us are ready for the responsibility of taking care of another human being and that's not counting the financial burden of raising a child." He glances back towards the horizon and mumbles, "Yeah, what could possibly be wrong?"

It's no surprise I'm getting the blame for this unexpected pregnancy, it's written across his face and I hear it in his snide and sarcastic response. My patience wears thin at his attitude so I stop walking making him stop. He turns towards me, hands on his hips and lets me speak.

"First off, don't talk to me in that tone," I tell him hating this spoiled brat attitude he adopts when things don't go his way. "You're just as much to blame for our lack of protection that night and you know it."

He stares down at me for a couple seconds then pulls me to his chest hugging me closely in unspoken defeat.

"I know," he whispers in resignation. "I'm sorry it's not your fault, we're both to blame."

This fateful night flashes through my mind. We were celebrating his new promotion as Vice President of Sales, the youngest in the history of the magazine. A group of us went out to dinner. I was so proud of him and how far he'd come with the company in such a short time span. We drank Champagne and got caught up in the moment. As the dinner party ended and a taxi was called the two of us were all over each other. By the time, we reached our apartment we were past restraint. We barely made it up to our second story apartment before he picked me up and tossed me on the sofa in the living room. I can never seem to think straight when he's making love and I failed to notice we were without protection. He quickly remembered too and pulled out of me but by then the damage apparently had already been done. The next morning, we were both so hung over we swore off champagne drunks and vowed to always have a spare condom on both our persons. Now we must pay the piper for our sensual dance but it appears one of us is less enthusiastic at the solution to the problem.

"I botched that proposal, didn't I?" he laughs then turns to face me; placing his hands on my shoulders he rests his forehead on mine. "I love you Harper, will you marry me?"

Tears well up in my eyes at his revised proposal and as I reach up to touch my lips to his I breathe in his mouth, "I love you Paxton, yes, I'll marry you."

We seal our bargain with a deep and sensual kiss then break apart when we hear a couple little kids from down the pebbled beach shouting at us.

"Get the ball Mister," a young boy of maybe six years of age hollers standing beside a smaller version of himself. "Don't let it go in the water or we'll get in trouble."

Quick as lightning Pax shoots out his foot and traps the ball underneath the sole of his black leather wingtip. He releases me and stoops down to pick up the black and white sphere just before the two little guys reach him.

"Thanks!" they yell in unison. "Mom would have taken the ball away from us for sure," the older boy laughs. "She said not to play near the lake but it just got away from us."

Smiling down at the blonde-haired boy Pax holds out the ball and says, "I totally understand, but you better head on down to that flatter area if you want to play soccer."

"We can't, that place is for sale and the mean lady that put the sign in the yard told us to stay away because she has work to do," he informs us looking over his slight shoulder towards this empty house. "She already told on us to Mom when we accidently knocked over the flower pot by the mail box."

"Well, be careful okay?" Pax says reaching out and ruffling the tow-headed kid's hair.

"We will," he says laughing over his shoulder and grabbing the hand of his younger brother before heading back to his playmates.

I can't help myself but hug the man making him laugh when I squeeze his waist.

"You're going to make a wonderful father," I vow and suddenly the light and easy look on his face is gone and he simply shrugs his shoulders.

"I guess we'll see, won't we?" he says in a skeptical tone and heads us back down the beach, just like that the special moment is gone.

We walk past the house the boys told us was for sale. For a split second, I imagine it's our home, complete with little kids playing in the front yard. The house is a beach house with the two-story main structure and an observation tower as the third floor. The weathered cedar shingles are stained a dark shade of teal, the color of the lake as the sun sparkles across the water. White trim outlines the entire structure with mullioned paned windows; multiple sets of French doors; dual upstairs balconies on either end as well a huge screened in front porch that wraps around the side of the place. The property has a white picket fence surrounding a large rectangle of grass in dire need of cutting. There's even a small boat house, well more like a large tool shed in miniature to the main house closer to the lake. I love the place and feel as if it's beckoning me home.

Even if I could convince Pax to consider buying it with me we'd still be hard pressed to make a sizable down payment on the property because his money is always 'tied up' or so he claims. Honestly, the man is high maintenance. The silver Jaguar he bought last year, the perfect sailboat he rents during the summer, and his wardrobe and high rolling ways always leave him strapped for cash; he's constantly bumming a twenty here or fifty there. Plus, he loves his rented townhouse or frat house as I refer to the home we share. His friends regularly crash there or drop by for a free meal, whenever I have time to fix one.

The love of cooking runs in my family. My parents are partners in a very successful restaurant in the city called Draper's. My older brother Victor and I were taught by the master chef and since my mother is domestically challenged as she refers to herself their marriage is made in heaven. Mom is no slacker however, she is a brilliant financial advisor for several large corporations and institutions and often is a guest speaker for company seminars.

"Hey, where'd you go?" Pax asks waving his hand in front of my face to bring me back to the present. "Stop worrying about the baby," he tells me miss-reading my day dreams. "We're getting married so our parents can't say anything. Let's go get you a ring and then we'll break the news to Mom and Stan."

Get me a ring? Like he's never considered buying me one before? Something tells me I've let our relationship slide in our joined futures. Not wanting to discuss our situation anymore I simply nod my head and slip back into my dream home, my dream children, praying my dream husband doesn't turn into a nightmare.

2

His mother is beside herself with joy at the news of her first grandchild. Beth Carmichael and her husband Stan are good, kind people always seeing the silver lining behind even the darkest cloud namely their son. Pax immediately tells his parents we aren't interested in a big wedding, no fanfare, he even suggests we go to the courthouse for a civil ceremony causing Beth to gasp in disappointment. He is acting as if I'm not in the room so I smile apologetically at my soon to be in-laws and turn to face the father of my child leaning sulkily against the traditional white mantel on the living room fireplace. The Carmichael house is a lovely, typical two story brick colonial home in an older neighborhood in Albany. The place is designer perfect from the matching cream and rose floral sofas to the muted toned Aubusson rug covering the lovely oak floors. Nothing out of place in the immaculate dwelling except my toad-like prince looking like he swallowed a handful of glass.

"Paxton, you and I haven't discussed the particulars of the ceremony. Let's not commit to anything until we've talked things through, in private," I tell him in an obviously condescending tone of voice and giving him the look I know

11

he understands to be 'you're pissing me off' because he stares at me for a couple seconds then drops his chin to his chest and holds out his arms to his side in defeat.

"Fine, you're the one calling the shots," he says in a snide manner making me wish his parents weren't in the room so I could throw something at him, possibly the antique Windsor side chair I'm using.

"Glad you're seeing it my way," I reply in the same tone making him raise his normally straight brow into a disapproving arch, which I ignore as I wind up our visit. "We still have to tell my folks so we'll be heading out, thanks for being so supportive. I can't tell you how much that means to me, well to us."

Beth gives me a sympathetic nod and holds out her arms to hug me. Her silvery champagne colored bob shifts when she tilts her head and smiles. Pax's midnight gaze must have come from his father's side because the hazel sparkle in Beth's eyes makes her appear almost angelic. She is so classy and gracious that I love her like my own mother but she has one flaw, she continues to make excuses for her self-absorbed child. A thought keeps flashing in my head of future temper tantrums but not from my child; Love is not blind, I know he's not perfect, but I'm not either... Suddenly it dawns on me Paxton must grow up, and fast because I will not raise two children.

"Forgive him sweetie," she whispers in my ear as she walks me towards the foyer of the magnificent home. "He's scared he's going to have to take responsibility for someone, or something."

"He's thirty in two months Beth," I reply in a hushed

tone letting her know I'm not buying what she's selling. "He's way past due."

She laughs and releases me holding my face in both her hands.

"Amen," is all she says then reaches for her son standing behind me. "You behave young man," she tells him as he reaches down to kiss her still-smooth cheek. "Treat her with kid gloves and lose the attitude."

"Yes ma'am," he mumbles chucking his softly reproachful mother under her chin. "Just so you know her father will probably come after me with one of his chef's knives. Don't be surprised if this is the only grandchild you get from me."

The three laugh at his silly joke as they walk us out onto the front porch but I wish Daddy would do just that and cut out his tongue while he's lopping off the man's other appendage. We promise to have a 'sit down' with my parent's as Beth called it to discuss the ceremony and to make it soon as she can't wait to get started on the affair.

Once we're back in my car he turns the ignition and pulls away from the curb all without looking at me or saying anything about his rude behavior. Since Mom and Dad's place is about twenty minutes away I vent my anger at his treatment of me.

"Pax why are you so angry with me?" I demand feeling him mentally slip away from me and go into pout mode while he manipulates us through the light suburban traffic and then back onto the main thoroughfare.

"Don't start Harper," he warns not bothering to look my way and fueling my anger.

"Pull over," I tell him refusing to be in the same vehicle with him for a second longer. "Now Paxton, I mean it."

He signals to turn and pulls the car into an empty parking lot, turns off the motor and stares straight ahead still refusing to look at me.

"Get out," I tell him opening my car door and climbing out of the car as I feel myself reach the end of my emotional tether.

He steps out of the low-slung vehicle and waits for me to join him. Instead I push him out of the way and slide behind the wheel slamming the door and locking it. I adjust the seat for my height and turn the key in the ignition and tremble with anguish as the powerful motor roars to life once again.

"What are you doing?" he sighs sliding his hands in his trouser pockets, clearly showing his agitation and his impatience.

"Leaving your ass behind," I reply and put the car in reverse when he leans through the open window and turns off the engine pocketing the keys.

"What the hell is your problem?" he demands obviously forgetting his earlier petulant mood. "Let's go tell your folks, get read the riot act and then go buy you a damn ring."

"You're the problem and I don't want your damn ring. Give me the keys and I'll drop you off at the townhouse, then I'll see my folks alone," I snap feeling such anger and resentment at his attitude. "You, in this mood will probably have to be rushed to the hospital when Dad finishes with you."

For the first time since we walked out of the doctor's office he laughs a genuine, smile breaking chuckle. His laughter always makes me smile and even now, when I can't stand the sight of him his laughter soothes my frazzled nerves. Pax reaches inside the window and releases the lock of the door before I place my hand in his extended palm as he helps me out of the car. But instead of moving out of the way he presses his hips into mine pushing me against the rear panel of the sporty car. Needing his contact I push my body into his space.

"I'm sorry for earlier," he murmurs placing my arms around his neck. "I know this isn't easy for you either, and if I could I'd kick my own ass for you, satisfied?"

"Not by a long shot," I reply letting him nuzzle his chin between my shoulder and neck. "I just need to know you're going to be there for me and the baby, no matter what Pax."

"Harpo..." he sighs his dreaded nickname for me in my hair. "I'll be there, I promise. Now let's go see Chez Draper and your mother, then maybe I'll take you out to eat at Lombardo's later, how does that sound?" he asks suggesting we go to my second favorite restaurant and making me believe we're back on an even keel.

"Like the nicest thing, you've said to me all day," I retort making him realize he's been taking out his anger, fear, and disappointment on me.

"Harper you're going to have to bear with me on this," he lets me hear the uncertainty in his voice. "I don't know anything about being a dad... I'm no role model, I'm out of my element, okay."

That makes me laugh and puts a frown on the handsome devil's face. Leaning over I kiss his cheek and rub the line between his eyebrows with my index finger until he relaxes and smiles at me.

"That's better," I sigh feeling the tension ease out of his body. "We'll get through this together, you and me, no matter what, okay?"

"Okay, I really am sorry for being a colossal ass earlier," he apologizes again. "But I don't want a huge wedding, no matter what."

"Now you're talking," I laugh since I don't want a huge drawn out affair either. "But keep an open mind and a closed mouth when dealing with our mothers. They're going to throw out some wild, dramatic ideas believe me. But we have the final say, remember that."

"Don't worry," he laughs back. "If my mother wants to release doves, your father gets to cook them."

His easy-going manner lasts until he walks into my parents' study of their mid-century modern home. As Pax takes in his surroundings of a much used blue and tan plaid sofa, bookcase lined knotty pine walls filled with best-selling novels, financial journals my mother has written, and hundreds of cook books some penned by my father, framed photographs of my family, retro looking table lamps taller than a small child, heavily draped windows, worn russet colored leather chairs, a large chrome and glass desk complete with enough household bills to make even the stoutest of bachelors cringe I imagine he's looking into our future and hating what he sees...single dwelling in the suburbs, a thirty year mortgage, several kids, a dog, regular lawn-work, PTA meetings, Tuesday night meatloaf...all too predictable for his liking and mine too. I feel his anxiety level rise but there's nothing I can do about any of that right now. Shaking my head to clear our morosely identical thoughts I share our news with my folks and they take it well I guess. Dad is standoffish but Mom is thrilled, just like Beth.

"I'm so happy for you both," she says not picking up on

the tension Pax keeps emitting, however my dad senses it and sends Mom off for a bottle of champagne to celebrate while my fiancé continues to pace the floor of my parent's favorite room.

"Are you alright Paxton?" he asks sitting down beside me on the much-loved sofa, hugging me around the shoulders. "You look a little green around the gills. Something tells me you're not thrilled about your upcoming fatherhood."

Licking my suddenly dry lips I reply for Pax but he beats me to it making my father tense up at his response.

"No sir I'm not exactly thrilled," he admits breaking my heart at his reluctance to embrace our future as he picks up a small silver picture frame holding a school photo of me in the first grade. "Neither of us is thrilled, but it's a done deal so we're taking the necessary steps and accepting our responsibility." Pax stares down at my father while he strokes the photo of me with his index finger and smirks before he continues, "You can't ask for more than that, can you?"

To say my father is displeased is an understatement. Draper Mead is a family man. He put his own career on hold when he and my mother got married, helping put her through college and then concentrated on his own career after my brother and I were toddlers. To say a man isn't thrilled about becoming a father doesn't sit well with Dad.

"You do know how babies are conceived, right?" Dad snaps, his normally sparkling blues eyes flashing in disdain as I feel his body tremble with silent outrage. "I mean now days, everybody knows how to prevent pregnancies, am I right?"

I shake my head at Pax silently warning him not to respond but he is bristling at the tone of voice my father is using. The younger man stiffens his spine and uses my father's derogatory question as an excuse to vent again while he pours fuel on the fire with his retort.

"Yes sir, but sometimes, when you're both drunk, things get out of hand, you know how it is…" he baits my father as he slides the picture frame back on the crowded shelf before placing his hands on his hips in a provoking manner. "But don't worry, I'll never be without birth control again, neither of us will right Harper?"

My father turns to look down at me and I can feel his icy blue gaze demanding me to look at him but I refuse; instead I continue staring at my knuckles now turning white as I fiercely clench them on my lap. Before Dad can reply Mom walks in carrying a tray of fluted champagne glasses, an uncorked magnum of sparkling wine, and a smile that could out shine the sun.

"Here we go," she says setting the tray on the coffee table and bending over to kiss the top of my head. "I'm so excited, another grandbaby… Our baby is having a baby."

Mom ducks her head as the tears of joy start to well up in her green eyes. She is a beautiful woman at fifty-one having always been health conscious and it shows; now she's in better shape than I am. She and Dad have a wonderful marriage too, a real partnership; one I'd always assumed would be replicated in my own union but now I'm unsure. She nods at my father to raise a glass and give a toast to the parent's to be and reluctantly he does, in his own way.

"I wish you the best of luck," he says making my mother frown at the less than stellar sentiment, "You're certainly going to need it. Congratulations to you both on your upcoming marriage and becoming parents."

I watch as Pax empties his flute and helps himself to a refill from the heavy green glass bottle on the tray resting on top of several large books on the glass and steel coffee table. I myself barely touch the rim of the glass to my lips knowing I will not leave here with my father's true blessing. We stay about a half hour and then promise to meet with both sets of parents the first chance we get to plan the wedding. Walking outside with the two of us Mom and Dad wave at the front door as we pull away from the curb and head back to our place in the city. Things are not right between us and I'm waiting for the explosion to occur the entire trip home but he's sulkily silent. I'm the pregnant one but he's having the mood swings.

He pulls up to the curb of the townhouse he shares with Wiley and quickly turns off the engine. Pax is already walking up the front steps as I climb out of the car but he waits on me to join him at the front door and holds it open for me to enter first. But instead of going up to our second-floor apartment to discuss today's events and rehash the pitfalls we will be dealing with he stops in the common foyer and turns towards his roommate's living room leaving me tired, bitter, and ready to scream at his refusal to deal with the issue at hand. Paxton flops down on Wiley's hideous yellow vinyl sofa joining his friend and landlord engrossed in yet another baseball game on the huge flat screen TV attached to the wall. The room belongs in a frat house I think to myself as I look around the unkempt room with disgust.

There are no curtains or blinds on the grungy floor to ceiling windows. A month's worth of discarded deli wrappers and used coffee cups from the café down the street fight for space on top of old, mix-matched end tables. Garish lamps of different heights and decorating styles illuminate the messy man-cave. In the center of the spacious room sits a large rectangular glass and brass coffee table loaded down with sports magazines, a couple remote control devices for the TV attached to the opposite wall of a working fireplace. A small statue of St. Francis of Assisi is hiding behind a great number of empty dark brown beer bottles stacked in an impressive pyramid. Besides the bottle tower there are also a six-pack of empty crushed beer cans scattered across the table with empty peanut shells from a large antique glass dish precariously hanging over the edge of the tabletop. The burdened table is flanked by the afore mentioned monstrosity of a sofa and two matching black leather and chrome cube chairs covered with discarded items of clothing. Shoes are strewn across the weathered hardwood floor and a massive burgundy oriental rug covers the width of the room, both needing a thorough sweeping. It's a pig sty and I refuse to step further into the room.

"Hey where'd you run off to today?" Wiley asks offering his best bud a cold beer from the small cooler stationed at the end of the ugly yellow sofa and practically ignoring me standing in the doorway. "Melanie was looking for you and she wasn't too happy when Simmons told her you left for the day."

"Simmons needs to keep her mouth shut," Pax mumbles taking out his anger and aggression on my best friend Ginger Simmons. He kicks off his shoes and props up his feet on the coffee table, causing a landslide of magazines to add to the debris on the rug and twists the cap off the brown bottle before taking a healthy swig. "How mad was Mel?"

"Let's just say I'd show up early Monday morning with a couple warm bagels, some smear, and that awful Turkish coffee she enjoys…" he laughs at Pax nodding his head at the suggestion.

Having had a stressful day, I'm not in the mood for these Frat boys. I walk over to stand in front of the screen and say, "Pax, we need to talk."

"Cut the man some slack," Wiley says barely looking over at me. He's a classical tall, dark, and handsome sort but self-absorbed; a true bachelor at heart… we do not get along. "You had him to yourself all afternoon, let him unwind and not have to listen to any more nagging."

Instead of standing up for me Pax grins and bumps knuckles with his friend in solidarity. I reach down to pick up one of the sacred remote controls barely visible in the pile of peanut shells, turn off the game, and throw the device out of the room and down the hall on my way out. Shouts of anger reach me as I climb the stairs to our apartment, but instead of Pax coming after me Wiley appears in the foyer and reaches over to pick up his cherished controller then sneers up at me. I always thought Jim Wiley was immature but I never noticed until now how the two men appear to be cut from the same flawed cloth.

"What the hell is wrong with you, having your period?" he jeers checking out the remote devise for possible damage. Shaking his handsome head, he continues. "My man needs to rethink this 'living together' situation," his brown eyes blazing with righteous indignation over my rough-handling his precious remote control. I give into the desire to vent and lose my temper at the stupid jerk.

"Get used to it you bumbling clod," I lean down

gripping the bannister and hiss at him. "He's about to get married and become a father all in one fell swoop." I motion with my index finger in a circular motion to encompass the townhouse and finish with, "so this 'living together' situation is about to end. There will be a change address for Paxton because there's no way in hell I'm living under this roof one second longer than necessary."

I storm up the rest of the stairs and barely hear Wiley asking his best friend 'what the hell is going on' before I slam the door to our place shut. I drop my bag on Pax's own horrific black leather sofa with the ratty faux brown fur draped over the back and kick off my heels before I sit down and try to calm my nerves. Pax not following me upstairs makes me want to cry… but then again everything makes me want to cry… stupid hormones. Focusing my energy on the positive I bend over and pick up my shoes then must hold on to the arm of the sofa to brace myself as a wave of dizziness washes over me.

"Are you alright?" Pax asks from the doorway, startling me since I didn't hear him on the stairs.

"I will be in a moment," I reply tucking my hair behind my ears and stand up once more, "Nothing for you to concern yourself with."

I walk past him and head down the corridor to the kitchen, the only room in the place I like. When I moved in it was about the size of a closet but with the help of my father and my brother Vic, the kitchen became the best room in the joint. I told Pax and Wiley I wanted to redo the room and they told me to go for it and I did. They bitched and moaned about the noise, the mess, and both almost blew a gasket when they had to lug the old appliances down the flight of stairs but they've enjoyed countless meals I've prepared on my new stove and always help themselves to the groceries in the stainless-steel side by side refrigerator and freezer. The cabinets were in great shape so I sanded and painted them a rich chocolate brown, replaced the cracked glass and the door knobs, changed out the Formica countertops with Carrera marble and had the floors in the entire apartment refinished. It took about six weeks to complete it but I enjoyed every minute I spent on my hands and knees, elbows and arms covered in paint and varnish.

Refurbishing the place was fun too. I was thrilled when Ginger and I found the four matching kitchen chairs at a local flea market on one shopping trip. I had them stripped and taken to a man across town that canes seats. I ordered out of a mail order catalog reproduction old school house light fixtures and hung them over the peninsula cabinet. I love the beautiful light pattern they cast across the newly painted tin ceiling. That was only five months ago, just after Halloween when I agreed to move in with Pax...it seems longer than that somehow.

Opening the fridge, I take out a jug of orange juice, pour myself a glass, and take a big gulp of the cold, refreshing drink. Pax walks into the room and helps himself to another beer from the fridge then pulls out one chair and sits down with a heavy sigh.

"Let's get this over with," he says taking a swig of his drink.

"What are you talking about?" I ask feeling clueless at his willingness to discuss the situation.

"I know you're upset, angry, and disappointed with me over today," He looks down at his hand holding the bottle.

"Get it out of your system so we can make plans for getting married."

The tone of voice he's using sets my back teeth on edge. He's acting like he's been handed a life sentence, doing hard time instead of having his plans expedited. Now I know for sure he was never thinking about our future, at least not one we would be sharing on a permanent basis. I walk around to sit down across the table from him and lick my dry lips, trying not to let him see how much his attitude is killing me inside.

"I won't marry you," I tell him making his head shoot up and his mouth drop open first in surprise, then anger.

"What the hell are you talking about?" he demands scooting up from his lounging position in the chair. "I've just spent the last four and a half hours letting you convince me we're going to be fine as husband and wife, mom and dad… now you're refusing to go through with marrying me?"

"Paxton, I love you with all my heart, but you don't feel the same way," I try to explain to him fighting back the tears collecting in my throat. "I thought we were always going to be married, have a family… grow old together but I guess that was my dream, not yours."

"Cut the crap Harper," He barks at me going back on the offensive. "You're an amateur on the guilt trip circuit; I lived with the world's greatest professional guilt monger, my mother; so, stop with the martyr bit. We're getting married, we're having a baby, and then we're going to grow old. There, that sums up our futures quite nicely I think."

"I can't believe you," I whisper wiping the tears now free flowing down my cheeks. "I didn't trap you; I didn't set out to get pregnant. You're acting like this is entirely my fault, that I'm ruining your life..."

He looks up at me then guiltily averts his eyes letting me know that is what he thinks. The man I fell in love with is nowhere in sight, just this angry, asinine jerk who seems determined to end our relationship one hateful word at a time.

"That's it," I tell him emptying my juice glass. "I wouldn't marry you if you were the last man on the face of the earth. I'll move out of here this weekend then you can go back to your 'glory days'. Don't worry, I'll let you know when your son or daughter arrives, until then, drop dead."

I carry my glass to the sink and start to walk out of the room when he reaches out and wraps his arms around my waist, pulling me backwards into his chest and dropping his chin on my shoulder.

"I'm sorry," he whispers burying his face in my hair. "I love you, you know that...it's just I'm not ready to be somebody's dad."

"I've already told you you'll do fine, but I can't make you see we'll be a team, a pair, partners..." I cry and he turns me around to hug me hard. "I love you so much Pax, but apparently, you don't feel the same way or want the same things, so I'm leaving."

"No, you're not," he whispers and presses a kiss on my forehead. "We'll muddle through this somehow," he laughs and says, "I apologize again for hurting you. Every time you say it will be alright cold chills race down my spine at the thought of screwing up." Pax takes a deep breath before finishing his apology, "we're not the first couple that's found themselves in this position and we certainly won't be the last, right? We can do this, I hope."

He bends down and kisses me on the lips, lightly at first, then drawing a deep, heart-felt response from me. I hate myself for succumbing to his charm but I let myself be drawn back into his embrace. Before the kiss can progress into more he scoops me up and carries me into our bedroom where he gently lies me down on the white duvet covered bed and starts unbuttoning his dress shirt. By the time, he's standing naked in front of me I've stripped down to my bra and panties suddenly dying to join with him, at least we'll be connecting on some level. Dropping his knee on the bed he climbs on top of me and kisses my belly, my abdomen, my breasts, and then my lips.

"I need you baby," he whispers on my skin. "I need to be inside you, where I belong…" and he removes the last of my clothing making me tremble with anticipation.

Pax is a thorough lover, always making sure we're both at fever pitch. The second his lips touch my breasts I become ultra-sensitive and imagine sparks flying off me. His touch sets me on fire creating a need so strong I whimper when he's taking too long. Reaching for his hips I guide him between my open legs, pressing my fingers into his taunt buttocks and finally, I feel the head of his engorged penis at my gate, waiting to slide home.

"Look at me," he whispers making me open my eyes and stare into his near black orbs. "I love you and together we'll see this through, I promise."

I can only nod my head in response, tears of joy and relief clog my throat robbing me of speech then I feel him slip past my naturally resisting inner muscles. I lose myself in the myriad of sensation he always creates when we come together. The steady give and take of our bodies is a comforting yet exciting process and one we've always found thrilling even when we spice up our course of action. Tonight, all I want is to feel his body ramming mine, filling me to the top with his essence, his drive, and his assurance we will be together forever. The tale tail signs of my own climax rush upon me. He slips his fingers between my folds and sends me off the map when he presses my exposed nerve center. His own cries echo off the twelve-foot ceiling then his weight crashes down on top of me, holding me prisoner beneath his sweaty body.

"You always amaze me," he pants turning his damp head and kissing my neck. "Don't ever stop loving me Harpo, I need you so much."

I wrap my arms around his back and hold him tightly loving the way he always surrenders to his passion and enjoying how I can drain him of all energy after we make love. He always gives me a hundred ten percent when we're in each other's arms. Minutes later he rolls over on his side of the bed and gathers me to his body, my back to his front. Just before we fall asleep I feel his hand creep around my front and he covers my flat belly in a loving, protective manner and my heart swells with joy… he's accepting our child and for the first time today I feel confident everything will be all right.

3

Three weeks later I'm exhausted but happy. The wedding plans are complete, the invitations sent, the reception will be held in Beth's back yard per her request. Dad has the meal ready to go and I've bought my dress helped by Ginger and my sister in law Shawna. The only drawback in my perfect wedding is the engagement ring Pax chose for me; it's huge, almost unsightly but it's what he wants me to have so I wear it proudly. The 4.6 carat emerald cut diamond is set in a platinum setting and covers the entire first knuckle on my finger. The minute my parents' saw it they pretended to need help raising my hand up for inspection implying it was too heavy for one person to lift.

Pax has stepped up to the plate as my father says and has been the perfect fiancé. He even helped choose the music and what he'd prefer my father prepare for the menu. The two men have rubbed off on each other it appears; even Wiley has come around and stopped being so hateful. He's even asked my advice on fixing up his place. Unfortunately, work has picked up for both of us, we're spending longer hours at the office and less time together. Pax has traveled a great deal for his job but he assures me it's temporary. He's constantly on his phone texting or taking a call into the other room. But at least he's not complaining any longer.

Ginger and some girls in the office are planning a bridal shower and bachelorette combination party tonight and I was told both mine and Pax's mothers will be attending since I refused to have a traditional bridal shower. Mom threw a fit telling me I was breaking tradition by not allowing her to throw me one but I had the perfect counter argument.

"Mother, I've been living with Pax for over six months, I don't need anything, besides, we've already 'broke tradition' by shopping for my dress in the maternity section," I teased making her and Beth both laugh at my logic even though I bought my gown off the rack in my usual size and didn't have to have it altered. The two women finally relented and agreed to join the girls for a Saturday night out on the town. Pax urged me to go have a good time; actually, he said the guys were coming over anyway for his last poker night as a free man and for me to live it up while I still could.

The party started great with a limousine picking up Ginger, Mom, Shawna, Beth, her stepdaughter Terrie, and I at Beth's house. From there we drove to our first stop, a swank restaurant that features barely clad men as waiters. My mother insisted we not tell my father where we were going or she'd never live it down. We looked amazing in our evening clothes; even my mother let her hair down and dressed in a tight black dress with a leather jacket and boots. Beth was graceful as ever in her navy sleeveless sheath dress and pearls but after one drink she was cutting up with the rest of us. My soon-to-be-step-sister-in-law Terrie and I have always gotten along; she normally is reserved but like her stepmother after two drinks she was telling tales on a pubescent Paxton making all of us cry from laughter. I wondered how the office girls would react the next time they saw Pax. Just the thought of him being the butt of a couple jokes was enough to send Terrie off on another round of stories.

Later the bar the girls took me to was a male stripper club but our parents refused to go inside and after much teasing I agreed with the elders and vetoed the naughty side of the evening. Soon yawns appeared and I told the girls I was done for the night but they insisted the night was still young even though it was after midnight. I explained little Pax was as taxing on me as big Pax and I'd had enough. Laughing at me they all wished me a good night and I made them promise to call it a night, but from the looks and sounds of the group, especially from Ginger and Terri I doubted they were heading straight home.

It was after one in the morning before I stumbled up the stairs to my apartment, dead on my feet. I tried to be quiet so I didn't wake Pax but it sounded like a herd of elephants were traipsing around the room but it was only me dropping my shoe, bumping into the chair on my way to the bathroom. I tip toed across the dark bedroom trying not to step on a creaking board and quietly closed the bathroom door. My stomach became queasy but after brushing my teeth and removing my make-up it eased up. I slipped into bed and rolled over onto his side of the mattress only to find it empty. Wiley must have made good on his threat to keep the man out all night, drinking with his buddies from work. Pax vetoed Wiley's plans for a traditional bachelor party but I guess he got roped into going with the gang anyway. My father and brother weren't invited I'm sure. My body was screaming from exhaustion and I was fast asleep before my head hit the pillow.

I wake to severe cramping and know something isn't right. My side of the bed is wet and as I lean over to turn on the lamp on the nightstand a sharp pain stops me from moving. Breathing through the agony I reach for the lamp again when I note the time, 4:35a.m. Pax is still not home. Picking up my phone I call his number and hear it ringing in the distance. I slide out of bed and crumble to the floor as a gush of warm blood oozes down my leg.

"Paxton! Help me!" I shout at the top of my lungs feeling afraid and scared at what's happening. A couple seconds later I can hear heavy footsteps on the stairs and the front door is slammed open. Thank God Pax heard me.

"Harper what's wrong?" Wiley shouts running into the bedroom dressed in a pair of low riding jeans and nothing else. "Oh my God, what happened? Are you alright?" he asks when he sees me sitting on the floor, my nightgown bloody below my waist. Quickly he runs into the bathroom and returns with a couple bath towels.

"No, I'm losing the baby, where's Pax?" I groan pushing the towel he hands me between my legs but I know it's too late, I've lost the baby.

"He's passed out downstairs," he admits and then reaches for my phone. "Let me call the ambulance and then I'll get Pax up."

"No, I don't want an ambulance; just get me to the hospital, please." I tell him hating having to depend on this man who earlier this evening called me a wrecking ball and chain to my face as I left with Ginger.

"I'm so sorry," he says making me look up into his face and see genuine regret.

"Don't start being nice to me now," I cry and a wave of dizziness washes over me as I try with all my might not to pass out.

"Hold on baby sister, I've got you," Wiley assures me and quickly picks me up sending my head crashing onto his bare shoulder before he carries me down the stairs into the living room where Pax is sitting on the sofa holding his head in his hands.

"What the hell is going on?" he snaps at being roused from his sleep then sees all the blood on the towels and jumps up to take me from his best friend's arms. "Hang on Harpo," he whispers reeking of whiskey and cloying perfume making my stomach roll. "You're still the designated driver buddy," he tells Wiley over my head. "Let's go man, grab my shirt and shoes while I carry her to my car."

They rush me to the hospital but it's too late. The ER doctor on call is explaining it was more than likely a chromosomal issue and my body aborted the baby naturally. He drones on and on but I stopped listening. The loss is devastating and I'm feeling sorely abused by life's turn of events. Lying on a stiff gurney waiting on the procedure suction curettage to be performed I feel the tears sliding down my cheeks and anguish fills my aching heart. Paxton is holding my right hand; my mother is holding my left but I feel no comfort from their touch. The doctor sedated me earlier but I felt nothing before he injected the IV. The cramps were the last physical sensation I felt.

"Baby, it's going to be alright," my mother croons

stroking the damp hair off my forehead. "Don't cry sweetheart, you'll have more babies, right Paxton?"

His slight hesitation speaks volumes but I'm too tired to retaliate.

"Sure Harper, we're young, healthy… it just wasn't meant to be, for now." He says in what I'm sure he thinks is a sympathetic manner but all I can think about is I lost my child not our child.

"It's not fair," I whisper as I feel a rush of warmth spreading through my body. The drugs are kicking in. "I did everything right Mommy," I whisper unsure if I'm at fault or not no matter what I was told earlier.

"I know you did honey," she is telling me but she sounds so far away. "You and Pax will have more children, now just relax and let the doctors clean you up. Come on Pax let's go outside and let them tend to her."

I close my eyes and let my brain slide sideways no longer caring if anyone can hear me or I can hear them. The next time I open my eyes I see Paxton sitting beside my bed. He's texting someone. A nurse walks in and startles him when she notices I'm awake.

"How are you feeling dear," she inquires making my fiancé put his phone away and pay attention.

"I'm fine," I tell her unable to take me eyes off the man. "When can I leave?"

"We were just waiting on you to come out of the anesthesia," she says removing the IV from my hand. "Once you've got your balance you can get dressed and your fiancé can take you home."

"Thank you," I reply waiting on Pax to say something.

He waits until the nurse pulls the curtain and leans over and kisses my dry lips.

"Are you okay?" he asks a touch of genuine concern in his voice that acts like a balm to my strung-out nerves. "You scared the crap out of me. Mom, Stan, Terrie, and your folks are waiting to see if you're alright."

"Is that whom you were texting?" I ask and I know from the look on his face it wasn't.

"No, I was texting Wiley telling him what was going on," he says making me feel bad about doubting him. "He didn't want to upset you by hanging around whatever that means."

Over the last three weeks Paxton has been on his phone texting or emailing when he thinks I'm not watching. Our parents have stuck by our wishes for a small ceremony and I thought Pax was getting into the whole marriage idea, but now that the baby is no longer motivating him, I wonder if he still wants to go through with the ceremony scheduled next weekend. He continues to stare at me waiting for me to say something I guess.

"What's the matter Harpo?" he gently asks rubbing my bare arm lying on top of the sheet.

Using his nickname for me makes the tears flow again. Carefully he wraps his strong arms around me and holds me tightly, swaying back and forth.

"I'm sorry I lost the baby," I cry into his faded navy blue T-shirt that still reeks of booze and someone else's perfume but now has a touch of manly sweat indicating he was worried and upset over this evening's drama.

He kisses the top of my head and says, "I'm sorry too but it wasn't because of anything you did, remember what

34

the doctor told you? It was a critical time and our baby just wasn't ready. Please don't cry."

I know in my heart he's relieved but I also think he's sad too. He had talked about becoming a father in a more positive light, even thinking about names and laughing at the baby photos our parents produced of each of us. I kiss his neck and pull back to stare up at him praying the concern I see is genuine.

"Let's go home," I tell him not wanting to speak my fears out loud just yet.

"Do you need some help?" he offers and together we dress me and only must wait a couple minutes for the orderly to bring the wheelchair to take me out of here.

"Get ready for our parents," my fiancé turned chauffer bends down to whisper in my ear bringing a smile to my lips when he pretends to cringe but stops the wheel chair so our families can tell us goodbye.

"How are you feeling Princess?" my father asks hating to see the distress on my face as he bends down to offer his condolences.

"Okay Poppy," I assure him using my old childhood nickname for him and accept his hug.

"You go home and rest," Beth tells me hugging her son and lovingly pats me on my shoulder.

"We'll see you at the rehearsal dinner Friday and then our place Saturday for the ceremony," Stan reminds me as if I'd forget my wedding day. "We've even got the boxers an outfit, right Bethy?"

His wife smiles and nods her head making Pax groan at his mother and stepfather's antics of including their three full size boxer dogs in the ceremony. Their house, their rules he said.

"Call me later," my mother whispers as she hugs me tightly to her chest.

She bends down to give me the once over and I see the worry in her face. Normally she looks young and vivacious but right now she looks every day of her age and then some. Worrying does age a person. Her sparkling green eyes are cloudy now and the fine lines fanning from the corners of her eyes are more pronounced but she is still the most beautiful woman I know. Her shoulder length blonde hair is pulled back into a ponytail, she is wearing no makeup and her yoga pants and top are stained and wrinkled attesting to the fact she grabbed whatever was available and flew down here to join me when she got the call.

"Goodnight kids, Beth, Stan," my father says pulling Mom away from me. "Let's get home; Victor will be waiting on news," as he herds the well-wishers through the main lobby of the facility.

The night air feels cool and clean on my face as Pax wheels me to the waiting Jaguar. It's going to rain and somehow the early morning sky reflects my inner turmoil. After buckling me inside the car he climbs behind the wheel.

"All set?" he asks and turns the key allowing his powerful car to growl to life and take us home. "Wiley said he'd talk to us tomorrow not wanting to upset you further with questions. He called Ginger so she'll let Star know you won't be at the office on Monday. The doctor said for you to stay in bed and rest."

I'm shocked at the concern and thoughtfulness coming from his best friend and amazed Ginger didn't show up at the hospital but it's for the best. Right now, all I want is to lie down and be left alone. As we pull up to the curb I wait for Pax to open my door and assist me up the steps. It feels good to have his undivided attention. Gently we walk upstairs to our apartment and while I get ready for bed he pulls the covers back and undresses.

Our bedroom is dark even with all the lamps and ceiling light turned on. The guys painted the room and I've always hated their choice of colors. The walls are a chocolate brown; the molding and the ceiling are painted the same color. The hardwood floors are stained dark too. The only brightness in the entire room comes from the white duvet covering the antique black four poster bed and the white marble fireplace on the opposite wall. Two huge floor to ceiling windows let in the morning sun, but now they are black rectangles void of any light since our bedroom is at the back of the house and the yard lamps don't cast enough light this high up to affect the room.

"Come on sweetie, let's get you in bed," he says having changed into his black silk pajama bottoms. "Wiley cleaned up the room for us and removed the mattress cover pad," he smiles at me and notices I'm shocked again at the man's thoughtfulness. Pax runs his fingers through is thick, dark hair while he waits on me.

"You look worn out yourself," I reply holding out my hand to him.

"Exhausted as a matter of fact," he smiles and turns me towards the bed. "Be careful climbing up on the mattress," he warns recalling I hate how far off the floor his bed sets.

After quick kiss goodnight, he turns off the bedside lamp which is a rusted looking wrought iron contraption with a dark linen drum shade. This place is a male dominated room I think to myself as my brain refuses to relax. I wonder how long we'll be staying here after we get married. We didn't even have time to think about a nursery before tonight. Snuggling into his arms I rest my head on his chest and soon his even breathing tells me he's out and I feel myself drift off to sleep.

4

The wedding rehearsal at Stan and Beth's house took all of ten minutes since we're not having an elaborate ceremony. My father had me in stitches the entire time we were supposed to be solemnly walking down the aisle in the Carmichael's back yard. Beth and Stan had marked off the space with two garden hoses since the chairs wouldn't be delivered until tomorrow morning but the dogs kept playing tug of war with our boundary markers that Dad and I looked like a couple drunks staggering down the ever-changing corridor. Officiating the quick but lovely ceremony will be Judge Patrick Horne, a friend of Stan's. His Honor reminded me of the actor Gene Wilder with his wiry reddish brown hair, large blue eyes and infectious smile and had everyone laughing and having a good time. Even the flower girl, my niece Cassie was behaving like a pro as she pretended to drop her rose petals from the dainty white basket in her tightly clenched fist.

Before we left Pax's parent's place Beth stopped us and took both her son's and my hand and nodded her head toward her husband holding a small plain black lacquer box in his bear like paw of a hand. As he opened the antique box a hush fell on the four of us. Lying on a small bed of black velvet worn smooth and shiny in places was the most stunning piece of artwork I had ever seen. The delicate and intricately carved piece of aged ivory in the motif of two love birds on a single branch with leaves and vines intertwined around the edges brought tears to my eyes. It looked so fragile but I knew was stronger than it looked since it endured multiple generations of Beth's family.

"This brooch has been in my family since God was a boy," Beth said smiling at the two of us. "It's supposed to be handed down to each bride on her wedding day, but since Terrie refuses to get married, you're the only daughter I'm going to have," she laughed making me smile at that thought she continued, "Please wear this brooch tonight and tomorrow pin it under the skirt of your wedding gown, as your something old."

I hugged the woman then Stan and told her as I gently slipped the sharp pin through the fabric of my dress and fastened the clasp, "It would be an honor to wear such an heirloom."

"Thanks Mom, Stan," Pax murmured and hugged them both before he reached for my hand and helped me into the Jaguar. "See you there," he said as they turned back towards the house. "Thanks for humoring my mother like that," he whispered before leaning over and kissing me.

"I meant what I said," I replied placing my hand over the keepsake. "I'm not always big on tradition but this one seems nice."

Now sitting in traffic as we head over to Draper's Restaurant I wonder if I've been experiencing bridal jitters and Pax is happy about our upcoming wedding. Glancing over at his profile I honestly believe we will be all right. Perhaps I've been reading more into Pax's ever-shifting moods. Since last Saturday we've been inseparable. Losing the baby has brought us closer than I ever dreamed possible. Pax kept staring at me at odd times and then smiled and said I'm beautiful, or he's so lucky to have me... many compliments have been bestowed on me and I must say I've loved every minute. My thoughts shift back to the present and looking over at him I can't help but feel proud this gorgeous man will become my husband tomorrow. He's dressed in a sharp black suit, shirt, and tie, all new and custom fit to his frame. He looks so handsome I can't stop looking over at him.

"What's wrong?" he asks not taking his eyes off the road but feeling me staring at him. "Did I miss a spot shaving?"

"No," I laugh having gotten caught ogling him. "I was just thanking my lucky stars I'm going to be marrying such a hot, sexy man tomorrow."

He flinches at the mention of tomorrow but covers it up with a wink and a slow perusal of my outfit. I know he likes my dress since he was very complimentary about it and the new black lace underwear I modeled for him earlier this evening. The berry colored knit dress is classy, understated, and elegant. The black suede pumps I'm wearing make me feel sexy. I left my hair down. I'm wearing the pair of diamond stud earrings he bought me as a wedding gift. He gifted them the day after I lost the baby. I was sitting at the kitchen counter, reading the morning newspaper when he held the red jeweler's box out towards me.

"I love you Harper and I'm sorry we lost the baby, but we've still got each other, we're a pair, a good team; partners just like you said," he kissed me and opened the hinged lid making me gasp out loud at the beautifully sparkling diamond earrings resting in the black velvet lined box.

"Thank you so much," I whispered wiping the tears from my cheeks. "Your words are the true gift…" I sniffled then smiled up at him and teasingly said, "But I'm keeping the diamonds too."

I thought we were on the same page concerning our plans but having seen the painful expression whip across his face just now I'm feeling anxious again. I will drive myself crazy with this roller coaster ride of emotions if I don't square things away with the man. Before I can say anything, we arrive at Draper's Restaurant and as Pax assists me from the car he appears to be genuinely happy so I chalk it up to bridal and groomsman jitters again. The second we walk into the eatery we're ensconced amongst our friends and family and barely see each other until we're seated at the table and the best man and maid of honor are seated at our sides.

"You look lovely," Wiley says pushing his friend out of the way he can kiss my cheek. "I hope you're feeling well."

Smiling at the handsome man I nod my head hating that I still tear up at the mention of the baby but Ginger's palm rubbing up and down my back offers me sympathy but also strength. I don't know what I'd do without her. She is so strong and the best friend I could have. Even now she understands how to deal with my stress levels; she pushes me when I need it, holds me back when I'm going too fast, and shows me her strength and solidarity by a simple touch of her hand. The only reason she wasn't with me in the ER last weekend was because Wiley never called her…even though she admitted to going home and passing out. The two had a knock down drag out fight in the office that Monday. Thankfully our bosses were out of the building or they'd both have been called on the carpet for the tirade they subjected my co-workers to witness. She and the best man are not speaking which is a good thing since nobody wants to hear their verbal sparring again. Thankfully all negative thoughts fly out of my head as I smell the tantalizing aroma of dinner being set forth as everyone takes their seats at the table.

My father prepared a crown roast of pork with lemon-herb stuffing, buttered peas, and salad of mixed greens with herbed French dressing. Soon the only sounds heard are silver touching china and a low murmur of conversation. After the meal is over, the dessert of Baba Au Rhum and rich French roast coffee has been polished off, I sit back and sip on a glass of chilled Chardonnay until I hear someone calling my name. I glance around and see the photographer motioning for me to join my two bridesmaids standing off to the side. The nervous, older man is pointing at his wrist watch silently telling me I must hurry. Pax is nowhere in sight so I set off to locate the missing groom. Accepting hugs and well wishes from my father's staff as I pass through the kitchen it's a good ten minutes before I find him in the cloak room, talking on the phone.

"I know but there's nothing I can do at this point," he softly says slurring his words; "I can't do that. Listen, I've got to go, I'll talk to you tomorrow," he says then I can hear the smile in his voice as he says, "…yeah, me too, until then goodnight."

He ends the call and turns around startled to see me standing in the doorway.

"What the hell?" he demands guiltily letting me know I startled him with my presences and I can smell the whiskey on his breath. "Were you eavesdropping on my phone conversation?"

"No I wasn't, but who were you talking to?" I ask getting angry at his defensiveness and letting my frayed nerves cause me to sound harsh.

"It's called a private conversation for a reason," he leans heavily against the counter top. We're interrupted by his mother who apparently was sent to find the two of us.

"I thought I'd find you two hiding out someplace, but a cloak room?" she laughs noting the strained look on both our faces. "Come on children, a couple more shots then you can call it a day."

Smiling at his mother in relief he holds out his hand for me to go before him and then drapes his arm around my neck like we weren't about to have another argument over his phone call. We join the others waiting on us and rest of the evening is a fog and I can't even blame the alcohol. I simply can't get past his secretiveness even when he's acting normal now. By the time we make it back to our place he's drunk and incapable of carrying on a conversation so I help him to bed and slip between the covers, hoping and praying this is only nerves making me doubt my betrothed. Sleep evades me and I'm forced to relive tonight's strange behavior repeatedly until I finally reach the point of mental exhaustion and fall asleep.

5

The next morning, my wedding day starts off to a less than stellar beginning. The groom is hung over and won't get out of bed, I have a splitting headache and upset stomach, and my cell phone won't stop ringing. Everybody needs something or has a question only I can answer. I hang up the phone for the third time in ten minutes and walk over to refill my traveler coffee mug when Pax walks into the kitchen wearing only his jockey shorts.

"Is there any coffee left?" he asks walking over to the cupboard and taking down a mug.

I stand there amazed he doesn't have his act together yet. Granted he has only to shower, shave, and put on his tuxedo but he seems to walk in a daze. I feel my temper rise when he doesn't acknowledge me standing there waiting on him… to say something or do something groom-like, but I can't for the life of me remember what I want from him now. Mentally shrugging my shoulders, I put the cap on my cup and turn to walk out of the room when he growls as I pass by him, grabbing me around the waist and nuzzle my neck with his chin.

"Stop, Pax," I laugh suddenly feeling lighter. I wrap my

arms around his neck and he twirls me around the room kissing my lips with great fervor.

"Let's runaway," he whispers kissing my eyelids, cheeks and forehead. "Come on, let's take off, borrow Victor's motorcycle and drive off, just you and me."

Pulling back to see his face I'm shocked at the sincerity in his eyes. He really would leave, take off and not give a thought to all those hours spent organizing, renting, and plus all the food my father had his staff prepare for today's reception. But before I can comment he grins and spins me around and laughs.

"Got-cha," he jokes and tries to make me believe he was only kidding, but I saw his eyes and know he meant it which scares me to the core. "Come on Harpo, I was just pulling your leg. You need to hurry if you're going to meet the girls for your salon appointment."

I continue to stare at him even after he hands me my stainless-steel mug. He kisses me deeply, drawing a response from me and pulls me tightly to his chest.

"I love you Harper," he whispers and I hear pain and a touch of regret but I don't understand where he's coming from.

"Are you alright Pax?" I ask praying I'm misreading the past couple of minutes of his mercurial swift mood swings. "Is there something wrong?"

"No baby but you better hurry or your phone is going to start ringing again," he assures.

No sooner than he said that the phone does just that. He laughs as he picks up his cup and takes a sip watching me over the rim of the white ceramic cup.

"I love you," I tell him and he nods his head as I walk out of the room answering my Mother's call.

"Honey we're out front," she says in my ear. "Hurry up or we'll miss the time slot."

"I'm on my way out the door now," I assure her. "Have the flowers arrived at Beth's yet?"

I'm out the front door running a mile a minute as I climb into the town car Beth rented for my wedding party's use. We make our time slot and once we're all made up and have the best up-do imaginable we head over to my future in-law's house and get dressed for the big event. All my doubts and fears disappear as I stand in front of the antique cherry cheval mirror in the guest room filled to over-flowing with priceless antiques and heirlooms. My mother and bride's maids tuck a stray hair back into place, spritz me with perfume, and slide the most gorgeous white long sleeved gown over my head and begin buttoning the twenty satin covered buttons running down my spine and over my lower back. The heavy cut ivory brooch brushes my ankle reminding me of its silent witness to this all-important day. The veil I chose will hang down from the lovely chignon Enrique whipped up for me. I'm wearing the diamond stud earrings I received from Pax as my something new. Stepping into my white satin pumps I can't believe the transformation shimmering before me.

"You look breathtaking," Mom tells me with a tear in her voice. "Thank God the weather is holding out for us. It's gorgeous like you. Everything is working out perfectly," She clears her throat and continues. "I know things didn't go the way you'd always dreamed they would, but you're marrying a man you love to distraction, and he loves you the same way. I want you to be happy daughter, trust in him to always be there for you, and he'll do the same. You'll see, some men take a little longer to warm up to the idea of Happily Ever After with the same woman, but I think Paxton is just a bit scared of having to grow up. Give him time and he'll turn out to be the man of your dreams."

I hug her softly and whisper, "Thanks Mom, you sound just like Beth and I know you're both right. I love him so much, and together we can do anything, just like you and Poppy. I can't wait to start living that dream."

She pats me on the bare shoulder and then ushers everyone out of the room giving me time to collect myself before my father comes to get me. Walking over to the bedroom window I gaze down at the budding Maple tree lined backyard transformed into a natural cathedral with a hundred white wooden chairs creating an aisle in the lush green lawn, small hanging lanterns with sprigs of ferns, blue hydrangeas and white roses suspended from a shepherd's hook at each row. The chairs are quickly filling up with friends, family, co-workers, and even some folks I've never seen before. My bridesmaids are standing off to the side dressed in royal blue long sleeved day dresses for warmth, each a different style but in the same color. My brother and Wiley are standing on the opposite side dressed in black vested suits and royal blue ties. The judge is talking to Stan while my flower girl is twirling in her royal blue tulle gown with matching blue tights on her legs, chomping at the bit to do her part in the program.

On the other side of the lawn an L-shaped row of white linen covered rectangular tables are loaded down with Poppy's chafing dishes filled with delicious prime rib, duchess potatoes, several sides and large bowls of salad with china, glasses, beverage dispensers, and a huge wedding cake of French vanilla with orange curd between the layers his pastry chef Raul made just for me. A bar is set up next to the food while the diners will be sitting at one of the ten round tables accommodating the hundred guests waiting on the ceremony to begin. Stan is adjusting the outdoor heaters he insisted we needed just encase the nip in the air became a chill.

A knock on the door signals my father's arrival to take me downstairs so I take a deep breath and turn to face the man that I've worshiped for twenty-seven years. But my smile quickly dies on my face when it's Pax that opens the door and steps inside the room.

"Oh, my God you look beautiful," he whispers and closes the door then takes a couple steps to reach me. He's dressed in his beautiful black tuxedo suit and white tie but he's not smiling...he looks distraught.

"Pax what's wrong? Why aren't you down there in your place?" I ask panicking.

He takes a deep breath and says, "I can't go through with it."

I take a second or two to absorb what he's saying then I laugh at his silly prank, but unlike this morning, I'm prepared for his crazy joke.

"Fine, let's go back to our place, put on our sweats and watch some old movies," I tease but when he doesn't smile back I feel my heart break. "Paxton, sweetie what's the matter?"

"I don't want to get married, not today anyway," he says

reaching for my clammy hands where I notice his palms are damp too.

"You better be preparing me for the world's biggest prank," I whisper feeling the tears clog my throat and fill my eyes. "Are you serious?" I ask hearing the shrillness of my voice.

"Yes, I can't marry you today," he begins and I know the next words out of his mouth will devastate me but like a train wreck I can't turn away. "I've been seeing someone for the last couple of months, nothing serious, just lunch, hanging out at her place… she's going through a divorce and at first it was just a flirtation, but then…"

"No! Tell me you're lying," I shout at him pulling my hands out of his grip and placing them over my ears, as I feel my world shift on its axis.

"Harper, please listen to me," he says reaching for me again but I evade his grasp and walk over to the window, gazing at the attendants and guests fidgeting due to the delay. "Fine, I'm going to say it and then I'll go. I cheated on you, even after I found out you were pregnant. I only slept with her once but I can't go through with today and have this on my conscience."

"Why?" I ask turning to face the man I would never have expected to cheat on me.

"I told you I wasn't ready to settle down," he explains staring down at his black patent leather dress shoes like a little boy having been caught being naughty. "I liked being with this woman, even though I love being with you…I'm sorry. I'm a shit and a coward when it comes to facing you, but you deserve better than what I can offer."

A knock sounds on the door and then my father's voice penetrates the oak panel making me aware this is happening.

"Everything alright Princess?" he asks making me bite my lower lip thinking of having to explain I'm being left at the altar. "Your bridesmaids are here if you need help with something."

"Give me a minute Poppy," I tell him unable to take my eyes off the guilty looking stranger standing in front of me.

"Okay, but hurry it up," he says chuckling. "The natives are getting restless."

I sit down on the bed unmindful of the damage I'm doing to my beautiful satin gown. Paxton kneels before me and takes my hands in his, twisting the large engagement ring on my finger.

"Please forgive me Harper," he whispers with genuine sorrow and remorse in his eyes before he takes a deep breath and continues to knock me for another loop. "I'm taking a position at the Ontario office. I accepted the offer two days ago, but couldn't bring myself to destroy your dreams, but I can't do this to you or to me. I hope one day you'll understand."

He kisses my knuckle and I feel my mind and heart warring over how to deal with this news. It's as if my psyche fractures and I'm straddling the fissure until I feel my temper draw me back. I pull my hand slowly from his grasp and then back hand him with all the pent of fear, frustration and downright anger I've repressed for the last six weeks. I feel the air whoosh past me as I connect with his flesh, splitting his lip with the sharp edges of the atrocious ring he gave me.

"God dammit," he shouts falling over backwards holding his hands to his bruised flesh and glaring up at me in shock and anger, wiping the blood off his mouth with a linen handkerchief he takes out of his coat pocket. "Are you crazy? I'm going to need stitches."

"Good, that way we'll have matching scars, only you'll see your betrayal every day when you look in the mirror," I shout back at him causing my father, brother, and the best man to barge into the room followed by Shawna and Ginger looking ready to kill my betrothed.

"What the hell is going on?" my father demands looking at the two of us ready to tear into each other. "Answer me!"

"Sir, I'm not going to marry your daughter," Pax says standing up assisted by Wiley shocked to the core at his best friend's reply. Shawna covers her mouth but not before a gasp escapes from between her lips. She reaches for Ginger trying to get ahold of Paxton but holds the feisty redhead back.

"You're not going to marry her?" Poppy asks wearing his black formal suit; his voice getting softer and more deadly while his face becomes a cold, hard mask, his eyes now a frosty steel blue.

"No, I'm sorry for doing things this way, and God knows I tried to explain how I felt over the last couple of weeks, but ... anyway I'm leaving but I want you to know I love her," he says turning to face me again. "I'm sorry for doing this to you Harper, but I'm not ready to settle down."

"You son of a bitch!" Vic shouts reaching around my father to get at Pax. "You'll pay for this insult to my sister."

"Victor settle down," Dad tells his hot-headed son, barely holding my incensed brother back from reaching my former fiancé and points at Shawna to keep her husband still. "This is between the two of them. But Paxton, if you do this, hurt my girl like you're doing, you'll regret it for the rest of your life."

"Maybe, but at least she won't be tied down to the wrong man for the rest of her life," he replies staring at me, silently pleading with me to understand. But all I can hear is I'm being jilted, on my wedding day, in front of my family, with a yard full of guests…

"I hate you," I whisper making him close his eyes for a second or two as he absorbs the venom in my words before he nods his head.

"I know, but I love you," he answers then turns to leave the room with his best man just staring at me in shock then pity, something I will never abide.

"Get him out of here," I whisper feeling the tears start to well up in my eyes as Wiley slowly nods his head and closes the door behind the others. "Please, everybody leave."

Poppy walks over towards me as I hear the shouts of anger from Victor and Ginger out in the hall before my father sits on the bed pulling me down next to him wrapping his arms around me and swaying us back and forth, humming a soft lullaby he used to sing whenever I was upset. My mother walks into the room, a waft of her lily-of-the-valley perfume reminds me of her unconditional love, adds her arms to the hug and hums with him. Finally, after a couple minutes of absorbing their strength I raise my head and smile up at them.

"I have to go tell the guests there's no groom," I sniff and accept the linen handkerchief my father offers me. "I'm sorry about the time and trouble you and Mom went through, not to mention the expense…"

"Hush," Poppy says wiping the tears from my face with

his finger. "Why don't you let me handle the non-wedding while you and your Mom slip out the back door?"

Smiling up at him and his kind offer I shake my head and reply, "No Poppy, I'm not running away from this fiasco of a non-wedding, I did nothing wrong. I have nothing to be ashamed of and I won't let anyone coat me with pity either."

"That's my girl," Mom says standing up and holding out her hands towards me. "Besides, it's best to be remembered as the stoic, noble one, not the cowardly jackass leaving the country with his ears down and his tail tucked between his legs, right Poppy?"

He nods his head and smiles at the two of us, "Did you see the split lip she gave him? He won't need stitches but that's going to leave a mark on him for the rest of his life."

I know I should feel bad about striking the errant groom but he had that and so much more coming; I regret I didn't knock him unconscious until I see his parents. Beth and Stan are waiting for me at the foot of the stairs with such shame and embarrassment on both their faces it pains me to join them but I know I must face them and the rest of the sympathetic guests.

"Honey, I'm so sorry, but try to understand he's just afraid to grow up, give him some time, you'll see, things will all work out," the delusional woman tells me.

Stan walks across the marble tiled foyer into the library and pours himself a stout drink, tossing it back in one gulp, slamming the on-the-rocks crystal tumbler on the oak built-in shelves before he walks back towards me and says, "You deserve better than that little shit."

As his wife tries to shush her angry husband he hugs me to his barrel chest and whispers, "You're a tough little lady, don't let this get you down, I promise he'll pay for hurting you, maybe not today, or next week, but he'll regret today I guarantee it."

I smile up at him and kiss his deeply lined cheek then hug Beth before I walk arm in arm with my parents and face the guests sure the wedding is a bust. Standing alongside my family I address the mingling crowd.

"I'm sure most of you have figured out the wedding has been called off due to a missing groom," I tell them hearing the whispers of sympathy, the gasps of indignation, and then the angry jibes coming from the mob. "But since the food and drink is here, and I can't get the caterer to take any of it back…" which makes the crowd laugh at the joke and Poppy to wrap his black suited arm around my neck and kiss the top of my head, I press on. "I want to thank you all for showing up, for the love and patience you've shown to me and my family, Beth and Stan included, but as the groom informed me not twenty minutes ago, it's better not to be bound to the wrong person, even for a minute of your life. So, let's loosen your ties, take off your shoes, and fill up the plates. I love you all for understanding, but let's have a party…"

As I walk through the crowd carrying my disappointed flower girl on the ruined hip of my faux bridal gown I see the looks of sympathy and compassion I'm receiving so I keep Paxton Barrett's split lip in the fore front of my mind, helping me to endure the well wishes, the condolences, and the jokes. At six o'clock I'm spent, done in and ready to break bricks in two with my head. I leave the clean up to the Carmichaels and Poppy's staff and accept the ride home back to my parent's house since my luggage is waiting for me there. The three-week honeymoon is a bust but I know I'll take the time off from work to recuperate and reprioritize my life.

Later that night, my face scrubbed clean of the Hollywood glam makeup, the ruined wedding gown draped over the student desk chair in my former bedroom I tell my concerned parents goodnight. Lying in my childhood bed I let the tears of remorse fall, wondering what happened to the little girl's dreams I carried deep inside me. I'm void of emotion. Losing the baby was difficult, but losing Paxton seems unbearable until I remember his confession of infidelity. Something inside me mends my broken heart, almost like cement seeping between the broken pieces like glue, encasing the vulnerable part of me from further hurt… Cold, unfeeling, and without regret I roll over on my side and refuse to cry any more tears over Paxton Joseph Barrett. It's time for me to build a better dream…

6

Since I wasn't expected back at the office for several weeks I started looking for a place to call my own. I knew of several apartments I could have moved into immediately but my heart was set on owning a house, a place I could call home and since my checking and saving account are both healthy I felt like buying was the right thing for me. So began the search for a new dream. I spent the first couple of days certain I could find my dream home but after countless viewings of home on a realtor's website I got depressed. I couldn't imagine living in a house without Paxton which depressed me even further that I could still feel that way about him. So, I switched gears and browsed apartments with little interest.

Sipping coffee at my parent's kitchen table a week after the non-wedding I'm hit with an epiphany. An image of the teal cedar shingled home on Lake Sinclaire pops into my head and I get a compelling urge to drive out to the lake and see the house again. But first on my list of jobs to accomplish today is to return the ivory heirloom brooch to Pax's mother. I haven't spoken with her since the fiasco. Pulling into her drive and turning off the engine of my black

Corvette I notice the three boxer dogs are in the front yard warning me Beth is already outside and now I won't have to go indoors, which is a relief since I planned on making this visit short and sweet. I wrap my khaki jacket closer to my perpetually chilled body and walk up the Oak and Maple tree lined driveway.

The dogs bark and race over towards me, their little stubbed tails wagging when they recognize a friend. Bending down to pet them I get trampled by twelve large paws. My worn jeans, white t-shirt, and black ballet slippers are taking a beating from the canine welcoming committee until Beth comes around from the back of the house and calls them off.

"Hi sweetheart," she calls out spreading wide her arms for a hug surprised at my dropping by to see her.

"Hi Beth how are you?" I ask going through the niceties and accepting her hug.

She holds me at arm's length and asks, "Have you heard from Pax yet?"

Laughing at such a silly question I reply, "Has hell frozen over?"

She grins and says, "Honey don't give up on the boy please," she wraps her arm around my waist and walks over towards the front porch to sit down on the brick steps. "He did a stupid thing calling off the wedding like that, and well, that little slip… can happen to anybody; Everybody makes mistakes, even you."

"I'm not perfect that's for sure," I reply refusing to be lobbed into the same category as her scoundrel of a son. "But I never cheated on him; he can't say that. But that's old news and I've moved on. The reason for my stopping by is to return the heirloom brooch you loaned me. Since I'm not going to be a member of your family, I wanted to return it to your safe keeping."

I reach in my coat pocket and remove the lovely piece of jewelry hating to part with it but it's a tradition that doesn't include me so I place it in Beth's upturned palm and wrap my fingers around hers and kiss the knuckles of her hand before I stand up to leave.

"I'm going to miss you and Stan but a clean break is what's needed so I wish you both the best and hope the next woman your son asks to marry will appreciate you for a mother-in-law like I did," I tell her before she jumps up and hugs me to her bosom letting her tears of regret flow down her cheeks.

"I love you like a daughter," she whispers then releases me and turns her back towards me to hide her breakdown. "Take care of yourself honey and don't hesitate to call if you need anything, okay?"

Knowing I'd do without before I called on this family again I pat her on the back and walk towards my car. A feeling of remorse washes over me and once again I let my temper seep to the surface and lay the blame at Paxton's feet for hurting his mother like this.

Next on my list of to do items is to drive over to the apartment and drop off the key after I pick up the rest of my belongings. My dad and brother already helped me take the large items I wanted to keep and even though I've no need for them yet, I had them take the professional grade appliances I bought and the gorgeous mirror hanging over the bath room vanity and the wall sconces I purchased. Victor wanted to take up the new flooring we installed but with help from Dad we talked him out of destroying the apartment. With a box truck, full of my clothes, dishes, lamps, and appliances I rented a storage unit and put those items except for my spring and summer wardrobe in limbo.

I've been lucky so far today not running into people I'd just as soon forget existed, namely Paxton's best friend. Ginger left me a voice mail saying Paxton was out of the country so I didn't need to worry about running into him. She and I have spoken a couple times but she is swamped at work and we've not gotten together to hash out the faux nuptial yet. As I let myself into the apartment for the last time I walk through the place, exorcising the ghosts of this dead relationship. Today I can smile at the large chunk of wood missing on the newel post leading upstairs. Pax and Wiley were chasing each other and Pax slammed his best friend into the rail, knocking the ornate ball off the top of the post and splitting the wood. They repaired it as best as they could but I always noticed the damaged trim, all because they were acting like children. Next I walk through the dining area and see the massive table he and I argued about buying. He insisted we needed the large table to seat all his friends when his turn to host poker night. The stupid piece of furniture is so large when you're sitting at the table; no one can get around you, which created an interesting holiday get together at Christmas last year.

I take the small original artwork I fought long and hard for the right to hang on the kitchen wall even though Paxton hated it. I received it as a Christmas gift from Ginger who knew the artist, but he protested when I told him I wanted to hang it in a place where I could see it every morning. He said my niece could have done a better job but the artist is now much in demand and together we couldn't afford one of her paintings. Next I packed up all my books from the built-in shelves in the living room leaving him the sports magazines, the computer games and the war picture books he loves. I took only the photographs of my family and friends whether he was in them or not. Several photos of his were in my picture frames so I left the photos and took my cherished silver frames I plan on filling with new memories later.

The coffee maker is tucked under my arm since it was a wedding gift from Ginger and he never made the coffee anyway. Finally, as I walk through the rest of the place I feel like my entire existence of living here has been removed, leaving no trace of me. I've moved on. My heart will always ache missing him and the way he made me feel, but my head won't miss the frustration of his selfish ways, his immature antics, and lack of vision for the future. My body will miss him for obvious reasons...

I turn and lock up the place feeling someone else lived here, not me. I drop my set of keys in the mail slot of Wiley's closed apartment door and lightly walk down the front stoop steps and climb into my car. Needing to feel the wind in my face I lower the windows of the car and head towards Lake Sinclaire not expecting the house to still be on the market but needing to see the place anyway. As I pull up in front of the lovely two story structure I see a 'reduced price' sign covering the 'for sale' sign and decide it's a good omen and worth a look. Climbing out of my car I see the three little boys playing outside in the neighbor's yard. They wave at me and as I return the salute I hear a woman's voice address me.

"Are you here for the house?" a plump middle aged lady

dressed in an orange blazer over black shirt and polyester dress slacks inquires. My first thought is she looks like a jack o lantern but her earnest smile makes me crank up the wattage on my own grin and I hold out my hand towards her.

"Yes, I'd love a tour if it's still for sale," I confess knowing it will be a pleasure and a heartache walking through the unattainable house I've strangely come to love.

"Oh, honey let me show you the potential of this place," the woman introduces herself as Pauline Naples. She begins with a sales pitch that wins me over the moment my right shoe lands on the first step of the screened in porch.

The house is amazing. It needs a lot of work done on the inside but nothing I can't do or have done for me. The open floor plan is perfect with the French door entries on all sides of the first floor. Walking into the kitchen area I can imagine a fresh coat of white paint on the wood planked walls, the floors need sanding and re-stained, maybe a couple boards replaced. The ceiling has exposed beams and the plaster has some water stains illuminating a leak somewhere but since Dad's business partner's son is a contractor I think I can get that fixed easily enough.

Next, we walk into the living space with two separate French doors leading to the back yard and from there I can see the lake and it's gorgeous, breathtaking. There is a balcony leading off hopefully the master bedroom. I practically race up the creaking stairs and sure enough the lake front view is majestic from this room, my room… I'm in deep trouble thinking of this place as my own and I haven't even heard the asking price yet. There's a guest room in the front of the house with its own balcony facing the street, two separate full baths and a spiraling staircase that leads to the watch tower. By the time my chubby, out of breath realtor joins me in the loft I'm sold on the place.

"What's the original asking price?" I inquire praying she doesn't list off an exorbitant amount.

Thankfully the price isn't too steep but when she reminds me of the dropped price I'm ecstatic knowing if I'm careful, and okay with clearing out my savings account, I can swing the place. I'll be eating hamburger and macaroni and cheese for the next thirty years, but I'll be eating them in my dream home...

I excuse myself and call my mother needing to hear her opinion and to see if she can join me out here, and as my luck continues to hold out she says both she and my father can swing by and check out the place acting like she's not shocked at my request. We talk for a couple more minutes then I return to the realtor and smile at her cherubic face.

"I've called my parents and they'll be right out," I tell her and she beams with pleasure.

"Perfect, your daddy can explain the pricing and how everything works," she says assuming I asked my folks out here for financial reasons.

"Well to be truthful, Dad leaves all the finances to my mother," I tell her bending down to check the lovely sea blue green subway tiles of the back splash in the kitchen. "She is the financial advisor for Keenan Contracting, you've heard of them before?" I ask knowing she has since she must deal with companies in the new construction and pre-owned homes and Keenan Contracting has been in the news lately having won a large and lucrative contract for a new subdivision just outside of the City.

"Of course, your mother is Deidre Mead?" she asks

laughing and clapping her hands together in delight. "I recently met her at seminar she spoke at in Albany. It's a small world, isn't it?"

We chat for another half hour as we walk through the house's first floor again. By the time my parent's walk up on the porch I feel like the place is mine.

"Mom, Dad what do you think?" I ask unable to contain my excitement any longer when we're out of hearing range from Mrs. Naples, still excited over meeting my mother.

"It's charming sweetheart," my mother begins but says, "Can you afford this place?"

"They've recently reduced the price," I tell her and once she hears how much they dropped the asking price my father looks around for defects.

We leave Mom alone with the realtor and together Dad and I walk through the house, nitpicking it to death until we join the women in the kitchen and my father turns and says, "It's a sound structure, at least from what I can tell. Let's call Marc Keenan, do a walk through before you sign on the dotted line, okay?"

I nod my head at Dad's voice of reason and wait for him to call his silent partner's son. Unfortunately, Mr. Keenan is tied up this afternoon but can be out here first thing tomorrow morning, so we make an appointment with the realtor and I tell her I'll have an offer after my contractor scopes out the place. Mrs. Naples is thrilled, practically giddy from the sparkle in her eyes and hands she keeps clasping together. The plump realtor doesn't bother hiding her elation at finally getting an offer on the house.

"There aren't a lot of people that want this big of place so far out of the city. There are a couple of full time residents on this end of the lake but since it's a good forty five minutes to the next city, well, some folks just find it inconvenient I guess." She says locking up the place then joins us on the front porch steps. "Is it just you?" she asks and for the first time in almost a week I don't tear up at the mention of my relationship status.

"Yep, just me, and maybe a nice size dog or two," I think out loud making my father nod his head in approval and my mother sigh in relief. "I love the peace and quiet out here, and I've already met the neighbor's kids when I was here earlier this spring."

"And you still came back?" the realtor teases. "They're not bad kids, just boys. That means dirty hands, loud noises, and broken flower pots."

I laugh out loud knowing the boys and I will get along famously. We talk for a couple minutes more but she has another appointment and vigorously shakes my hand before she walks over to her little red compact.

"See you tomorrow, nine o'clock sharp," she reminds me and I laugh as I wave goodbye.

"So, am I crazy or what?" I ask the two people in the world I can trust for an honest answer.

They look at one another and smile, nod their heads and hug me to them.

"Certifiable, but we love you anyway," Dad tells me then looks behind him and says, "At least you've got your appliances already," making me and Mom burst out laughing.

"And don't forget the master bathroom mirror and sconces," Mom reminds us. "I'm so glad you're able to laugh about things again. I don't mind telling you I was afraid for your well-being this week."

Looking down at my scuffed ballet slippers I smile at her concern before I reply, "I love him still," I tell them both feeling their silent dread at hearing that. "But I want a grown up to spend the rest of my life with not some frat boy, emphasis on the word 'boy'."

Dad smiles and nods his head in agreement but doesn't comment. I know he liked Paxton very much even though you'd never know it from the last six weeks. I rest my head on his shoulder as he and Mom map out the best plan of action about my finances. I trust my mother implicitly and know she'll find loop holes for me to use and get me the best interest loan out there while my father is already figuring what it will cost me to refurbish the place.

"Lake Sinclaire is a lovely town dear," my mother says. "I'm sure there are a lot of local craftsman and merchants that would love to help you furnish this place plus you don't have to do it all at once, right?"

Dad laughs and says, "Well I don't see our little girl waiting thirty years before she makes her mark on this place, am I right Princess?" He nudges my shoulder and makes me grin.

"No, but I was thinking of asking Star Bridges if she had a designer up her sleeve, that would have some freebies or knock offs or even outdated pieces, I'm not picky," I reply. "Except in my choice of men that is… well starting now."

We laugh at the joke and soon the sun is setting so we head back to their place and spend a lovely, peaceful evening as Dad never works on Mondays. He fixes us a wonderful meal of Cornish hens, wild long grain rice, bacon wrapped green beans, and a wonderful hazelnut torte he whipped up. I could get used to eating like this, but I know once I've signed on the dotted line, I will start putting down roots in my own neck of the woods, and I can't wait.

My dad decides to come with me the next day and speak with the contractor Marc Keenan. Together we drive to the lake. Dad parks his yellow 1972 Cuda in front of the house while I eagerly race up the walk and open the screen door and smile at Mrs. Naples who is speaking with the contractor.

"Sorry we're late but Poppy drives like an old woman," I laugh as my father walks up behind me and wraps his strong arm around my neck and pretends to pummel me with his fist.

"Hey Marc, good of you to meet with us," he says and shakes hands with the realtor as well. She grins at having two good looking men standing so close to her.

Marc is around forty, average height and build but he is a knock out. There is a spattering of silver running through his dark curly hair, black brows and lashes frame crystal blue eyes that I'm sure are laser sharp. He has a crooked front tooth and deep brackets on either side of his mouth hopefully from laughing so much. The skin at the corner of his eyes crinkles when my dad introduces us.

"This brat is my one and only daughter, Harper," he

says and I shake the hand Marc Keenan extends to me and love the power I feel in his calloused palm. "This is Ken's youngest son Marc," he finishes introductions and we both grin at one another.

Something about the man makes me smile, puts me at ease. I'd describe him as...comfortable. He turns to look at the porch and balances all his weight on one leg trying to test the strength of the floorboards. Not a squeak or a give does he find which makes me feel good. The realtor opens the house and excuses herself to answer her cell which appears to go off every couple of minutes. Business is either good or the buyers are more anxious than she's letting on. I hope for the latter because all night long I dreamed of this place finished out the way I pictured it yesterday but with two dogs, three kids, and a husband that reminded me of Paxton... they're called dreams for a reason I guess.

"What do you think about that Harper?" my father asks then rolls his eyes when I bite my lower lip, letting him know I wasn't paying attention. "Girl, if you're serious about buying this place you better listen to the man," Dad admonishes me but I can't take offense because I wasn't paying attention and I do want this house so I buckle down and get into the conversation.

"The floors are sound, and so are the foundation blocks,"

"There is a slight leak from the upstairs guest room bath,"

"No mold found anywhere which is good, especially up here on the lake,"

"Recommend a new roof, gutters, and flashing, windows are new and so is the furnace and air conditioner."

"I can have her moved in by the end of June if she's willing to do a lot of the work herself."

I hug the man and start laughing at the thought of being in here by the 4th of July.

"Tell me what I have to do first and I'll see that it's done," I tell him making him laugh along with my father at my enthusiasm.

"First you need to buy the place," he teases making me giggle at the assumption I already own the property. "Then I'll recommend some high school kids that are looking for summer jobs who happen to be nephews of mine, they'll work cheaply and I'll make sure they do a good job. How does that sound?"

I hug him again then jump up into my father's arms and he twirls me around like I was still his little girl. We're both breathless when he sets me on my feet and kisses my forehead.

"Now that's how a man's little girl is supposed to behave," he laughs and shakes hands with Marc Keenan. "I know you're a busy man so we'll let you go and we'll be in touch as soon as she's got the keys in her hand."

"Sounds good," he says and shakes my hand again. "It's been a pleasure meeting you Harper Mead. I look forward to hearing from you soon."

I watch the man charm the realtor on his way down the drive and then she's standing beside me with a proposal in her hand.

"Are you ready to put in a bid?" she asks with a huge grin on her round face, all excited about closing the deal on this place.

"Yes, I am," I tell her and she and I start laughing while Dad makes a phone call on his cell.

"Let's fill out this form and then I'll call the owners, who are anxious to sell so we shouldn't have any delays. Now let's begin, okay?" she asks and together we fill out the appropriate forms and just as I'm making my bid my father joins us.

"Wait, don't put anything down yet," he says then nods his head for me to join him for a private discussion.

"Excuse us," I tell her and stand up from where we were sitting on the front step and follow my dad around to the back of the garage. "What's wrong?" I ask worried he's changed his mind about the place. "Is there something wrong with the house?"

He smiles at me and says, "Not at all, but I spoke with your mother and she agrees with me. Because of the horrible last two weeks we want to gift you with the down payment for this place, that way you have a little more fixer-upper money at your disposal."

Sighing at how sweet an offer that is I can't let them do that.

"Thanks Poppy but I can't take your money," I begin only to have him interrupt me.

"This is money I received from Paxton on your non-wedding reception. I sent him the bill and he wired me the entire amount plus he paid for the rehearsal dinner as well," he laughs and then hugs me to his chest, resting his cheek on the top of my head. "Take the money, and I want you to sell that God-awful engagement ring too. That would cover the cost of the new gutters and flashing plus leave you some money for porch furniture."

Laughing at my old man and his craftiness I decide to accept his gift and together we walk back to the realtor and place the bid. She calls the sellers and within minutes they've agreed to my offer and we decide to meet at the bank tomorrow afternoon. And just like that, I'm a first-time home owner.

"Thanks Poppy," I whisper to him as we're driving back to his house. "I love you and Mom so much. I promise not to let you down. I'm going to spend all my time and energy on this new place and by the fourth of July, I'll have a big house warming celebration. And you can do the cooking."

He laughs as we pull into the driveway of my childhood home, "How is that a party for me?"

Rolling my eyes, I laugh at the man, "I'd bet you three mortgage payments if I started fixing the food you'd butt in and take over within a ten minutes."

Opening his door, he laughs and draws his long frame out of the vehicle before he points his finger at me over the roof of his car and replies, "I'm not taking that bet."

"See I told you," I laugh and we spend the rest of the afternoon going over my budget until it's time for him to head over to his restaurant.

I call Ginger and let her know I'm now a home owner and she insists on coming over for a tour. With her son, Fabian, the three of us make the forty five minute trip back out to the house and she is sold on the place as soon as she pulls into the driveway.

"It is perfectly suited for you," she begins. "Oh, look at those adorable little boys watching us from next door."

I wave them over and the four brothers introduce themselves to us and to Fabian.

"We're the Hutchins, I'm Travis, this is my twin brother Trevor, my younger brother Silas, and the baby is Joey," the handsome seven-year-old says. "Did you buy the Greenburg's house? This is our vacation house, is this going to be your vacation house too?"

"I did buy the house and it is my only house." I smile and shake their extended hands. "My name is Harper Mead, this is my best friend Ginger Simmons, and that strapping young man is her son Fabian," I introduce us to our little welcoming committee. "I saw you guys several months ago, down on the beach, do you remember that?"

"Yeah, your husband saved our ball from going into the lake while we were here on spring break," Travis recalls making Ginger glance over at me to see how I'm doing with the mere mention of a husband but I'm fine and smile at her.

"That wasn't my husband, just a friend," I explain. "I just wanted to tell you I'm your new neighbor and maybe to invite you and your parents over for a meal once I've moved in."

"Mom will love that," Trevor says. "She's always complaining she never gets to go any place when we're here, right Silas?"

"Right," The light blonde haired boy named Silas replies. "Do you have any kids?"

"No stupid she just said she wasn't married," Travis teases his younger brother and scuffs him on the back of his head.

"Well maybe she was married but now she isn't," Trevor defends his brother who is rubbing the back of his head. "You know like Randy doesn't live with his Dad anymore cause his mom bought a divorce and married that new man."

I smile at the arguing Hutchins and soon Fabian and the boys run down to the short sandy beach with a warning of not getting wet.

"This is the perfect place for you," Ginger sighs as we sit on the porch step.

"And have I got the perfect man for you," I tell her not realizing until now how perfect Ginger and Marc Keenan would be for one another.

I tell her about my contractor and she agrees he sounds divine. She's even willing to help me paint the interior just so she can meet him. After an hour, we round up Fabian and tell the Hutchins goodbye heading back towards the city. Fabian is asleep in the back seat of Ginger's SUV so we discuss what's been happening at work. She finally brings up Pax and the owner of the magazine.

"Well, Melanie and the worm left for Ontario the Monday after the non-wedding and I haven't' heard when they're returning," she tells me making me flinch inside at the thought of him cheating on me with our boss.

"Was he really seeing the dragon lady?" I ask calling Melanie Swann our personal nickname for the dynamic woman we both secretly envy.

"He admitted to cheating on you," she says. "Per Wiley she's the only woman he's spent any time with, that he's aware of. Of course, Candace Whitaker, Melanie's personal assistant says they're not seeing each other and I guess she'd know."

Candace Whitaker has recently been through a nasty divorce herself and I feel such sympathy towards the woman. There's nothing worse than finding out your spouse has been cheating on you and you really are the last to know. I shake my head to clear those thoughts and listen to the rest of the inter office gossip Ginger is sharing. Soon we turn into my driveway and I tell her goodnight as I lean into the open driver's side window of her car as she prepares to head back to her place.

"I'm happy for you," she sighs. "Enjoy the rest of this week and we'll make plans to start work on the house as soon as you sign the paperwork. I can't believe you've moved so quickly on this place. But call me when you get the keys and we'll make plans, okay?"

I agree and smile as she pulls out of the drive and heads back to her townhouse on the other side of town. Turning around I walk onto the porch and sit down on the porch swing, enjoying the peace and quiet of the moment until my cell phone starts ringing in my back pocket. Glancing down at the caller ID screen I see Marc Keenan flash on the screen. Smiling I answer the phone with a lilt in my voice.

"Hello Mr. Keenan," I begin only to have him correct me.

"None of that," he laughs a deep throaty chuckle, "call me Marc. I just wanted to let you know I lined up the work detail and they can start the first of June, if that works for you."

"Isn't that the first Saturday of their summer vacation?" I ask knowing it is since I've been mapping payments and recall the next two month's dates.

"It is," he says, "That will give you time to move in, plus keep them on the right track. They need to work as much as they can this summer if they expect to have jobs when they graduate next year."

"No free rides, huh?" I tease but he takes me seriously.

"Never, everyone is responsible for his and her own

futures," he says in a tone of voice I'm sure he's used once or twice while talking to the younger crowd. "Well, I just wanted to give you a head's up we're good to go. Did they accept your offer?"

"They did, I close tomorrow afternoon. I can't believe how quickly this all came about," I laugh making him join in too.

"Well, after what you've been through you deserve a break," he says letting me know my father has filled him in on my personal life.

"Did Poppy go into detail about the non-wedding?" I ask praying he did not.

"Not at all," he says smiling into the receiver. "Your mother told my father who told me about it... I'm really sorry it didn't work out."

"Thanks, I guess everything happens for a reason," I wax philosophically.

"Bullshit," he replies making me laugh even harder than before. "Your guy screwed up, end of story. But what I was referring to was the miscarriage. My wife and I went through two of them, and never did have any kids. Then she was diagnosed with uterine cancer and that was it. She's been gone six years this coming December."

"Oh, Marc I'm so sorry," I tell him feeling his loss after six years. "I guess there's always someone worse off than you."

"Thanks a lot kiddo," he laughs making me smile at how that last statement sounded.

"I didn't mean anything by that," I assure him but he keeps laughing at me.

"Honey you need to stop beating yourself," he says. "Anyway, I need to go but I'll be in touch with you in a week or so. We'll decide when to install the gutters and flashings as we put on the new roof. Other than that, you're on your own with the painting and sprucing up of the place."

"Thanks, that's the stuff I love. I can't wait to get started," I tell him and then we end the call as if we'd been friends for ages.

8

Three and half weeks later I'm filled with a sense of wonder as I pull the large moving van into the drive of my new house. Oh, my God I own this beautiful place. I glance over and smile at my sister in law Shawna sitting across from me on the bench seat as she checks out the place with her look-a-like daughter Cassie sitting between us in her child safety seat.

"It perfectly suits you," she says making me laugh out loud in agreement.

"I know," I tell her not bothering to hide the excitement in my voice and put the truck in park before stepping down and walking around to the back of the van and unlocking the sliding door leaving her to deal with Cassie and her non-stop questions.

The house has seen some major changes in the last four weeks. The floors have been refinished, the walls and ceilings have two coats of fresh white paint, the tiles have all been re-grouted and the plumbing has been checked out and deemed perfect by Marc Keenan himself. All this work has been accomplished mostly within the second and third day of my ownership. I've been back to work for three weeks now and had to cut back on the workload taking in the extra time to get to and from work, but the commute is worth it. Ginger and Fabian have spent the last couple of evenings out here with me but I'm not sure if it's the peace and quiet of the beautiful surroundings, that I'm feeding them for their labors, or time spent with my newest friend Marc Keenan.

I can't stop the grin as I recall how taken he was with Ginger a week ago, when he called to say he needed to get measurements for the new gutters and would it be all right if he came out that Saturday. Luckily Fabian was with his father and Ginger was spending the weekend with me and would be painting. It worked out beautifully. He stayed the entire day and left late that evening after talking to Ginger for hours. The painting was slow, but their friendship blossomed and he's called me twice asking if I thought she'd like to go out for dinner or a movie. The man finally took the plunge and asked her out and they've been inseparable now for the last six days and counting.

"Harper where do you want to start?" my mother asks as she grabs a load of clothes from the back seat of her car.

"Grab an armload and take them directly to my room, the closets are freshly painted and aired out," I tell her reaching for the first of many boxes I had packed in the storage facility. Next, a barrage of questions is aimed at me that leaves my head spinning…

"Harper, where does this go?"

"Harper does this chair go in here?"

"Harper where's your cleaning supplies?"

"Harper…where'd you put my tool box?"

"Somebody grab a fly swatter there's a huge spider on the porch!"

"Harper… Harper… Harper!"

I swear I'm hating the sound of my own name but thankfully we're almost finished unloading and then I'll be able to start unboxing the items at my leisure and placing things where I want them to go.

"Who's hungry?" I hear my father ask and the entire cast and crew chimes in they're famished.

"Papaw can I have a Coney dog?"

"Pizza and beer sounds good to me."

"There's plenty of groceries here, fix whatever you like,"

"Take out would be quickest,"

"Let's fire up the brazier and roast hotdogs and marshmallows!"

Just then my neighbors come over bearing submarine sandwiches, bowls of homemade potato salad, chips and dips and the best smelling chocolate chip cookies.

"Hi there," a lovely brunette woman in her late thirties says as she directs each of her four boys to deposit their dish on the front porch. "I'm Pam Hutchins and these boys are my sons Trevor, Travis, Silas, and Joey. That's my husband coming across the yard, his name is Darrell and we'd like to welcome you to the neighborhood."

I laugh and wipe my dirty palms on the backs of my jeans and hold out my hand in greeting.

"Hello, I'm Harper Mead, your new neighbor," I smile as she places the platter of sandwiches in my hands instead of shaking hands with me. "This is so nice of you, please come on inside and help yourself to a beverage, there's bottled water, sodas, and beer in the red cooler."

Darrell Hutchins finally reaches us carrying a couple bags of potato chips and frowns at his wife before saying,

"Sorry I'm late but I had to catch the end of the mystery movie I was watching, I'm Darrell and I know you've already had the pleasure of meeting the boys, but we're a lot easier to take on a full stomach." He is about forty-five, dark hair with a sprinkling of gray at the temples. A middle-aged paunch is forming around his waist but his chocolate brown eyes sparkle with good humor. Everyone laughs, except for his harried wife so I place the platter of subs on the island and soon everyone is getting to know each other. We break for an impromptu supper. The gift of food is such a nice touch I tell them to stop in anytime. The boys take off after having eaten their weight in food asking if Cassie can play with them, leaving the grownups to enjoy the peace and quiet and dessert and coffee.

"I'm so glad somebody bought this place," Pam says accepting the hot cup of coffee from my mother. "I hated seeing this place just sort of die. I can't wait for the summer now that I have someone to visit with. We come up on the weekends after spring break until the fourth of July then we're here for the entire summer, right honey."

Darrell looks almost apologetic before he replies, "right you are dear. We'd love to live here year-round and are working on doing just that."

Mrs. Hutchins shoots her husband a withering look but pretends like he didn't answer in such a condescending manner. "Darrell and I are both teachers and we look forward to the school breaks. So, we'll be seeing a great deal of each other looks like."

I can't help but laugh at her enthusiasm and so does the rest of my family. Soon the sun sets and a breeze picks up heralding a nice rainstorm is on its way. My moving crew is spending the night, sort of camping out in the living room. We can hear the distant thunder and see flashes of lightning so Darrell calls the kids indoors. Soon our peaceful reprieve becomes a shouting match, even little Cassie acts up.

Pam smiles at me and says, "Sorry about the noise explosion but I think it's time we left for home anyway, come on boys tell the nice folks goodnight."

On cue, they shout 'goodnight' to the room and after agreeing to drop off their dishes tomorrow after I wash them the Hutchins leave and take the ungodly racket with them and we can enjoy the soft sounds of the night on the screened in porch.

"Oh, my God," Victor turns to his wife sharing his lounge chair and laughs when the Hutchins are out of hearing range. "And you want to have another child? What if we end up with the likes of those monsters?"

Shawna calmly smiles and says, "Our children wouldn't act like that, would they Papaw?"

"Not while I'm around," is Dad's reply as he reaches for his granddaughter's hand. "Just look at how sweet little Cassie is behaving now that those hellions are gone… maybe there's something in the water up here," making everyone chuckle.

"Well, since the beds are put together I think I'll turn in," my mother says standing up from her deck chair and stretching the kinks out of her back. "Goodnight Angel," she murmurs to a half sleeping Cassie leaning against my side as we share a chaise lounge.

"'Night Mamaw," she yawns and snuggles deeper behind my back making me appreciate the little one's warmth in the damp night air.

Next my father kisses everyone goodnight and follows Mom indoors and upstairs to the guest room. Since there's only one bed left I insist Vic and Shawna take it leaving Cassie and me to sleep on the roll-a-way bed I bought. After a token argument, the husband and wife team kiss us good night and head upstairs to my room.

"Well Miss Cassie, it's just you and me kiddo," I tell her walking over to the hide-a-bed I stashed in the living room and opening the contraption after I lock up the place and turn off the porch light. "Let me get some pillows and sheets while you brush your teeth, then we'll turn in too, okay?"

"Okay," she sleepily replies. "Where's Uncle Pax?" she asks and her question throws me for a loop when I follow her into the downstairs half bath where I left my toothbrush and paste.

"Pax doesn't live here," I tell her smiling as she brushes her teeth. "He is somewhere in Ontario I think. Why do you miss him?"

"Oh yes, he was always so much fun," she says spitting in the sink after she rinses her mouth before returning to the living room. Next I help remove her shoes, socks, and jeans. "He could sneeze like Donald Duck," she laughs and follows me over to the fireplace hearth where Shawna laid out her daughter's pajamas. "Do you miss him?"

"Oh yes," I whisper thinking about all the times he'd piss me off then cajole me back into a good mood which nine times out of ten ended in mind blowing sex, "God, how I miss him."

"Call him, maybe he'd like to have a sleep over," she says making me smile despite myself as she climbs on the bed and snuggles under the quilts.

"No, I think I like it best when it's just you and me," I reply making her cuddle up next to me.

"Okay, but you might get lonely when I'm not here," she yawns and drifts off to sleep leaving me wondering what the former love of my life is doing now. I slip into an exhausted sleep but dream of Pax standing outside on my deck trying to find a way inside but he can't find the door…

9

Finally June arrives along with my new roof and new roommates. Rolling out of bed at six o'clock in the morning is not my idea of how to spend the weekend. But Marc assured me he'd have his crew on the job by seven o'clock and since I didn't want to greet a truckload of teenage boys in my pajamas I jump in the shower as my coffee maker prepares my jolt of much needed caffeine. I pad over to the guest room to check on Ginger and smile when I see she's still conked out. Fabian is with his father this weekend so I invited Ginger to join me knowing she's dying to spend time with Marc. I close the door to her room and walk back into my bedroom and admire the vast changes I see. My bedroom is perfect with the queen-sized brass bed covered in crisp white linens, the colors of a summer's day are reflected by the green rag rugs strewn across the wood floor. Turquois glass vases are filled with sweet daisies on both nightstands and the bright white sheer curtains are pushed back to reveal the breathtaking view of the lake. No more painting, cleaning, scrubbing…The move is officially over.

Last weekend, Memorial Day Holiday gave me an additional day off and I accomplished a lot. I bought two puppies, two large breed short haired bull mastiffs ten weeks old. The owner of the local pet shop was practically giving them away since they couldn't prove the lineage due to a mishap at the breeders. I looked in the large plate glass window of the pet shop and saw two adorable tan and white puppies and knew I had to have them, both. I agreed to pick them up today and I'm looking forward to the company. It is isolated out here during the week but on the weekends, there are boat traffic, skiers, and sounds of partying on all sides of my home since sound travels well across the lake. I love everything about the house but I still get lonely occasionally.

After I shower and pour myself a cup of coffee I walk outside onto the screened in porch and sit in one of my new white wicker chairs I bought after selling the massive engagement ring. Dad was right; I paid for the gutters, flashing, new porch furniture and even bought custom made cushions in a colorful striped fabric for the tower room. Looking down at my ring less hand I wonder what Pax is doing right now. Ever since Cassie mentioned him, he's been in my thoughts. Work seems like a different place since he's gone, like the light went out somehow. Even when I hear someone talking about him I still can't relate. It seems like he dropped off the face of the earth, just like I wished a couple months ago.

Finishing my first cup of coffee I stand up to get a refill when I hear a large vehicle pull into the drive. Quickly unlocking the screen door, I wave at Marc as he gets out of his white full sized work truck and heads over to join me on the porch.

"Good morning," he says smiling at me when he notices

Ginger's SUV parked in the drive. "Can I get me a cup of coffee?"

"Sure, help yourself, but where's your crew?" I ask seeing no one else so I walk back into the house behind him.

"I gave the boys directions and a time to show up," he says walking over to the coffee pot and refilling my cup before reaching into the cabinet for a cup of his own. "Kids got to learn on their own."

"You're good," I tell him making him laugh and follow me outside onto the porch. "So, tell me how's it going with you and Ginger?"

He grins and looks down into his cup and shyly says, "I was just going to ask you that same question."

Laughing I tease him and say, "Oh, Ginger and I are getting along just fine..."

"Smart ass," he mumbles and takes a sip of his coffee pushing the visor of the baseball cap he is wearing off his weathered brow and running his hardworking hands through his dark hair as I sit there laughing at him.

"Hey you two," Ginger says opening the screen door revealing her cut off jean shorts and red t-shirt before joining us. "Good morning Marc," she whispers before kissing him softly on the lips. "Have you been here long?"

"Nope, just long enough to get me a cup of coffee and to sit down," he says patting his lap for her to join him which she does and snuggles into his neck.

"He had time to call me a bad name," I tattle to my house guest making her look down at Marc in surprise.

"What in the world would possess you to call this paragon of virtue, this untainted saint, this ethereal creature a bad name?" she teases then looks over at me and continues,

"I'll bet she opened her mouth and said something real smart ass like didn't she?"

"You nailed it," he says shifting his legs so she can lay back against his chest. "I should have known she'd be fierce with the comebacks, since her parents are both lightning fast."

Before I can reply I hear a stereo being played way too loudly and the shouts of rowdy laughter as a rusty blue, beat up late model king cab pick-up truck pulls into the driveway announcing the work crew's arrival. One by one five strapping young men climb out of the truck, each dressed in worn jeans, holey T-shirts, and new lace up work boots. Marc lifts Ginger off his lap, stands up straightening the creases out of his jeans, and more than likely repositioning himself from having his 'girlfriend' sitting on his lap and walks over to the screen door and holds it open for Ginger and myself to exit the porch and join the boys at the truck.

"Good timing guys," he says looking at his watch. "Did you have any problems finding the place?"

They all talk at once.

"Brent was reading the map and gave Brian the wrong street name."

"Rob insisted we were heading in the wrong direction but refused to take over reading the map."

"Brad spilt his coffee on the print out you gave us so we had to decipher what was left."

"Willy was ten minutes late getting to the office so we were behind schedule the entire time."

Ginger and I are dying of laughter at the crew assembled in front of us. You can tell they're all related from the dark hair, varying shades of blue to gray eyes, and broad shoulders.

They continue fighting like cats and dogs until Marc lets out a shrill whistle stopping them in their tracks.

"You are on a job site, act like it," he warns them and miraculously the five-man crew turn as one to introduce themselves as if Ginger and I haven't been listening to their moans and groans for the last five minutes.

Once we've shaken hands with each member they turn and open the tool box on the back of the truck loaded down with asphalt shingles, boxes of nails and five brand new tool belts. Brad, the darkest haired boy climbs into the bed of the truck and grabs the roof jacks; Willy is holding the planks while Brian and Brent help Rob carry the cooler, the radio, and a couple safety harnesses.

"Step back ladies and watch the Keenan boys get the job done," Marc says and soon he's removing several ladders from the back of his truck and the boys' vehicle.

I walk back indoors to make another pot of coffee and with Ginger's help, bake six dozen chocolate chip cookies. I stocked up with cold cuts, chips, dips, and lemonade just to have on hand if the workers get hungry. After twenty minutes of shouting orders, and getting them lined up Marc walks back inside to make a bee line for the freshly baked treats.

"Oh Lord, I hope they don't smell these until they've removed all the old roofing first," he says snitching two of the gooey cookies for himself. "Man, these are great," he says as he gobbles another one down.

Ginger laughs at him and reaches over to wipe the smear of chocolate off the corner of his mouth reminding me of when I used to do that to Pax whenever he'd buy his favorite cupcakes at the local bakery. I smile at the memory and try to push thoughts of the man out of my head. Deciding to leave now to pick up the puppies I turn to tell Ginger I'll be right back when I see she's in a serious lip lock with her new beau. Leaving a note, I place it on the counter and head out the side door loving the slam of the screen door as I do so. The boys are working in sync with one another laughing and joking like only teenagers can do.

Ten minutes later I arrive at the small town of Lake Sinclaire which makes me smile at the quaintness of the small burg. The sidewalks are bricked and small ornamental trees have been planted along the main street median area. Large potted petunias cascade over the sides of the concrete pots adding a pop of red, white, and purple colors to the businesses lining the main thoroughfare. Old buildings have fresh coats of paint on their doors and trim, wooden slat benches are placed in front of several establishments and already several older gentlemen are occupying the seats, enjoying a cup of coffee from the local bakery on the corner. Parking my car in front of the pet shop I grab the new collars and leashes I purchased yesterday and smile when the owner of the store is just flipping over his open sign hanging from a string on the front glass window. He unlocks his door and holds it open for me.

"Good morning Miss Harper," the owner Mr. Bolton greets me, his kind grandfatherly face creases into a charming grin as he touches his sparsely covered head with his hand. "You're up bright and early. Are you ready to take your babies home?"

Laughing at calling these soon to be massive dogs' babies I nod my head and smile at the friendly old man as we walk to the back room where he has the pups crated.

"Yes, and I've already picked out their names. York will be the taller one's name and Kirby is the stockier one, how's that?" I ask making Mr. Bolton grin and nod his head.

"Those are fine names Miss Harper," he agrees. "Let me get Dorian to help you load them into your pet carriers."

"I knew I was forgetting to buy something," I groan in dismay at the oversight and he laughs at me when notices my black Corvette parked out front.

"Honey those two pups are going to be all over you in that fancy car of yours. Would you like Dorian to deliver them later this afternoon?" he offers but I hate to wait until they close up shop when he slips on the collars of my new babies.

"I'll chance it," I tell him and he pats me on the back and says, "let me get you a couple of blankets, just in case they're not the best travelers, okay?"

He leaves me to get acquainted with the pups and immediately I fall in love with their soft long haired coats, their wet pink tongues, and their soulful brown eyes. They appear happy to see me. So far so good I tell myself.

"Here we go," he says handing me the clean, worn blankets. "You only live across the lake, right? You should be home in ten minutes, don't worry they'll do fine."

I wonder about what Mr. Bolton meant about good travelers. I was hoping he was worried about their toenails digging into the leather seats but now I'm wondering if they will get car sick, or even worse… A couple minutes later with both pups lying on the passenger floor board with the seat pushed back as far as it can go, the two brothers curl up into one large fur ball and go straight to sleep. I make it home in twenty minutes since I drove extra slowly due to pot holes and not wanting to disturb them. As I pull into the drive I see the crew is taking a break making me wonder how long I've been gone. I wave as I drive past them knowing they're talking about my vehicle but when I pull into the open garage and walk around to the passenger side and open the door the work crew is fascinated by my dogs. The pups stretch and slowly climb out of the vehicle and much to the delight of the boys and their loud shouts of encouragement the puppies race around, jumping on the guys and making me laugh so hard I almost fall over.

"What is going on out here?" Marc says as he opens the French doors leading out to the side porch. "Dear Lord, do you realize how big those dogs are going to get?" Marc is laughing his fool head off when the four legged brothers trot over towards him. "These guys are going to eat you out of house and home," my friend warns me. "But they'll keep you company and scare off any unwanted attention you may get, that's for sure."

York and Kirby are both curious and with their large paws and block heads they appear gangly but I love them. When I sit down, cross-legged on the drive way they wander over to me and sit down beside me already coming to my shoulders. I look forward to their advancing size. They're impressive even without their lineage tracked back to the old country. I don't care about that, I'm just glad the two brothers belong here. Leading the pups to the garage where I bought a chain link kennel for them I watch as they meander into the crate and get the feel of the place. Thank God, they've been spayed otherwise with their size they'd quickly be marking territory on items close to my head. I leave the gate open and walk away wondering if they will follow and sure enough, they walk on either side of me where ever I go. Laughing at their attempts to catch up with me I take them down to the beach and let them run free. They stay clear of the lake at first then roll around on the pebbly beach, chewing on each other's mouths and tails and anything else they can get their teeth into. After about twenty minutes of romping about I whistle for them and after two attempts they come running.

"Good boys," I tell them and tug on their collars to get them to sit.

I walk in front and as they lope behind me I've never felt so safe in all my life. Another dream has come true, I have my babies and my new home... all that's missing is Pax or a reasonable facsimile of the man.

10

Getting ready for bed Sunday evening I check off the items I must accomplish before the long Fourth of July weekend coming up. Monday I have three meetings I must attend, pick up Star's copies of the articles she will proof, email them to her vacation home in the Hamptons. Thankfully she didn't insist I join her for a 'working holiday' which is an oxymoron if ever there was one. Lately I resent the time I spend away from my home and the boys, who are growing inches a day and filling out too. There's nothing like pulling into the garage and hearing their deep resonating woofs when they recognize my scent. I let them run free for the first twenty minutes and lately the Hutchins kids are watching for me and racing out the door to join us in our play. The boys are very good with the dogs and they quickly tire the behemoth pups out which means I get a half hour to an hour to myself to unwind.

Listening to them stretch and moan on their bed in the corner of my room I remember our first night together, they howled and carried on something fierce when I left them in the garage kennel. The minute I joined them they'd settle down and be good as gold. I asked Marc to install two large doggie doors to give them entry to the garage and the back of the house which has worked out tremendously. No more whining to go outside, they simply do their business and walk back indoors. They're already house broken so I leave the one doggy door open that leads out to the garage. Marc and his nephews moved the chain link kennel around to the other side between the house and the garage giving the pups grass to play in and a place to relieve themselves. They're secure during the day and free to wander outside. Looking over at my babies I smile as they get comfortable and settle down for the night. I click off the TV and turn off the bedside lamp when my cell phone rings. The boys raise their massive heads then return to their slumber when I tell them it's all right. Looking at the unknown number flashing on the screen I answer the phone.

"Hello?"

"Harper its Pax, how are you?" he asks and just the sound of his voice sends my heart into arrhythmia. "Are you there?"

"Yes, I'm here, what do you want?" I ask trying to keep my voice on an even note.

"Just to hear your voice," He says and I can hear him smiling.

"Okay, well thanks for calling and goodbye," I reply but he cuts me off.

"Please baby, don't hang up," he says in such an urgent tone I can tell something's not right.

"Where are you Paxton?" I ask knowing I'll regret speaking to him later but right now I can tell he needs something.

"In the hospital, waiting on somebody to get me I think… What day is it?" he asks scaring me now.

"Paxton, tell me this instant where you're at, look around the room and tell me what you see," I tell him praying he's not drunk but he's chuckling at me. "You have exactly three seconds before I'm hanging up… one, two …"

"Melanie and I were in some charity race. She was driving and missed the turn, now she's in surgery and I'm waiting for somebody to come get me… wait I already told you that. Pay attention Harpo…" he says then starts laughing again.

"Oh Pax, what have you done?" I ask wishing I could pick him up and bring him back here…no that's not what I want. I want a man that can take care of himself. I shake my head to clear it and play hardball.

"Well, you chose to be with the dragon lady," I tell him hating how cold my voice sounds. "What do you expect me to do? Where are you again? Are you in Ottawa?"

"Nope, I'm in Essex England, Great Britain, the UK, across the pond…and boy did I ever make the wrong choice," he says sounding like he's sobering up. "Harper I called to tell you I'm sorry for walking out on you, for running away actually. I thought I wanted to be free but I found out what some people think of as 'freedom' feels like loneliness to me."

The tears pool in the corners of my eyes and I reach for a tissue.

"Please talk to me, even if all you do is yell at me, at least I'll be listening to a familiar voice," he whispers sounding tired and distraught as I shift the bed pillow behind me at sit up.

"Tell me about the wreck, is Melanie going to be alright?" I ask hoping to keep him talking whether for his sake or my own...I've missed the sound of his voice.

"She's in surgery right now, but I don't know anything. She had a lot of blood on her face and down the side of her white coveralls," he tells me.

"Pax, are you hurt?" I ask praying he's just in shock.

"Nope, I mean I hurt but no cuts or broken bones," he says. "Actually, I walked away from the accident and pulled Mel out of the car before it burst into flames."

"Thank God," I sigh but he jumps on my relief.

"You still care," he murmurs as if he's shocked I feel anything towards him but anger and I'm shocked too. "I still love you, you know that, right?"

"No Pax I don't know that," I tell him not letting myself get suckered back into his charming web. "You broke my heart; left me at the altar, cheated on me probably the entire time we were together... that doesn't sound like love to me."

"I'm sorry," is all he says.

"Well, I'm sorry too," I reply then must end to the call before I say or do something stupid. "I hope Melanie is okay, oh and call your mother in case she hears about the wreck and assumes the worst."

"Yeah, I better call her," he says and I can hear the weariness in his voice.

"Pax I hope you find whatever it is you're looking for," I begin. "But please don't call me again; my heart can't take another hit from you. Take care of yourself, goodbye."

"I love you Harper..." is all I hear before I end the call and then cry myself to sleep.

11

Wednesday morning I look around my office and try hard to focus on clearing off my desk. Monday was the hardest day to get through thanks to my lack of sleep, the increase in my workload now that the chain of command has shifted due to Melanie Swann's mishap. The woman was lucky, per the office gossip reel. She was driving an older model Porsche in a cross country race for charity. The magazine was one of the sponsors of the event so Melanie was out front and center. The only trouble is she's apparently a horrible driver. Ms. Swann had a ruptured spleen, a broken collar bone, fractured wrist, and minor neck and facial lacerations. Pax had a concussion, bruising on his right arm and shoulder but nothing else. He called Monday evening but I was out walking the dogs, his voice mail just said he'd call back later due to the time difference.

Tuesday all anyone could talk about was who would fill in for Ms. Swann, and just now I've had my worst fears realized, Star Bridges will be moved up to acting CEO with all the headaches that will require. Someone from the parent company in Ontario will be filling in for Star while Melanie is incapacitated. The change will go into effect July

10, when Star's vacation is over which gives me a reprieve I intend to utilize by shutting off my phones, computers, and locking my doors.

"Ms. Mead, call for you on line two," my secretary pops her head in the doorway. "Says its overseas, should I patch it through, maybe it's Ms. Swann wishing you good luck."

"Not likely but go ahead and transfer the call," I tell the new girl.

Tara Compton is a great assistant but she appears a tad too cheerful. Picking up the receiver I take the call.

"Harper Mead speaking," I say into the phone and know it's not Melanie calling but her co-pilot. Pax has called twice this morning filling me in on his plans to return to the States.

"Hey sweetheart," he begins like we're still a couple. "Can you meet me at the airport? I emailed you my flight schedule. Afterwards we can grab a bite to eat and catch up, how does that sound?"

"Like you're still suffering from a concussion," I tell him amazed he thinks he can pick back up where he left off in our previous relationship. "I sent word to Melanie's driver and he'll be waiting on you at gate 8. He'll drop you off at your place or who knows, maybe the two of you can get a bite to eat... either way, I have nothing to do with your return. Now, was there anything else, I've got a ton of work to do before I can leave tonight."

"Harper come on, don't you want to see and hear me grovel?" he teases knowing that's something he'd never do. "Let me make it up to you, I've missed you so much, I need you Harper."

Closing my eyes and taking a deep breath I let him have it with both barrels.

"First off, I don't need to see or hear your poor excuse of an apology for leaving me at the altar. Second, buying me supper doesn't come close to making amends you idiot," I snap at him chuckling on the other end of the line. "Finally, I don't need you. I may still want you, the women of Albany can't be all wrong. But I don't need you nor do I have any intention of discussing our past, present, or your make-believe future. I turned my key in to Wiley two months past and moved on with my life. You wanted your freedom, you got it. Have a safe flight and I'll see you in the boardroom next Wednesday, along with the rest of the sales staff. Goodbye."

"You still love me Harper, I know you do and I'll take great pleasure in proving it. See you soon baby, I love you," he says in a manner that sounds like a warning, no wait more like a challenge...

"You're too late Paxton," I tell him knowing he will freak out when I tell him I've got new roommates. "I'm currently living with two brothers and they're very protective of me, so watch yourself."

"Two brothers... What the hell are you talking about?" He is practically screaming in the phone. "You moved two guys into our apartment? Are you fucking crazy?"

I can't help it but laugh and say, "We don't have an apartment together anymore," I sneer. "Didn't you hear me? I turned in my set of keys to that frat house. Didn't Wiley mention that to you in the last two and a half months? Oh well, I needed my freedom too and have moved out and moved on…you should do the same. Don't call me again Paxton… goodbye."

"Harper! God dammit… Harper? Don't hang up the phone," he shouts. "You better be waiting at the apartment when I get back. I'm going to take great pleasure in evicting your ménage a trois."

"Good luck on that score," I laugh and end the call to his ranting and raving.

That should keep him occupied as he flies across the Atlantic. After hanging up the phone I press the intercom button and Tara picks up.

"Yes, MS Mead?" she asks and I can hear her typing away on her laptop.

"Tara, don't put anymore of Mr. Barrett's calls through to me," I tell her. "He's so abusive on the phone and I just don't care for his tone of voice."

"I agree," she giggles, "but he's defiantly a treasure to look at."

Apparently, she is unaware of my former relationship to the man and I prefer to leave it at that.

"Looks can be deceiving," I tell her. "Has Star called back yet?"

My new assistant and I talk about our new job duties and time schedule for a couple minutes then I hang up and finish the pile of paperwork in front of me. Later I glance at the wall and see it's almost four o'clock. Shuffling the articles Star had me research I power down my laptop and lock up my desk intent on leaving early. Reaching for my purse I slip the laptop's shoulder strap over my arm and make a run for the elevators. No one stops me and soon I'm flying down the highway in my roaring black beast, wind in my hair and feeling like a million bucks. As I head towards Lake Sinclaire I keep going over the food list Poppy emailed me for tomorrow's bar-b-que. I pull into Lake Sinclaire's one and only grocery store across the street from the pet shop and smile at Mr. Bolton as he waves goodbye to a small little girl following her daddy and the small aquarium kit he is carrying. She has a small clear plastic bag of fish and talking to them.

"How's the boys?" he shouts across the street when he sees me, pushing his worn-out broom over the brick sidewalk.

"Getting bigger as we speak," I tell him making him laugh and nod his head.

"I love the photos you emailed me," he says tipping the visor on his baseball cap at several of the town's ladies walking past him. "Take care Harper, and have a safe Fourth of July."

"You too," I reply and grab a shopping cart at the front of Jack's Mercantile and mark off items on the list. An hour later I pull into the driveway and see Silas Hutchins run across the side yard and stop before his foot touches the pavement of my driveway.

"Hi Miss Harper," the little Hutchins says. "Can I play with York and Kirby?"

Getting out of the car I walk around to the passenger side of the 'Vette' and grab the over-flowing canvas totes I love to carry my groceries in.

"How about helping me get my groceries inside first," I counter his request. "Can you open the door with this key?"

He takes my keychain from my hand and nods his head.

"I'm big enough to help carry that bag of chips inside," he says making me laugh at the hopeful look he's giving me.

"That would be great," I tell him pulling out the family size yellow bag of potato chips and offering them to him. Looking around for his siblings I ask, "Where are the brothers?"

"Mom has Trav and Trev scrubbing the deck chairs because they smarted off to her and Dad is watching Joey but he fell asleep on the couch," he says as he unlocks the side door and pushes the heavy door open with all his body weight. "I'm supposed to be in my room picking up toys but I reckon I'll just get them back out in a couple of hours so they might as well stay on the floor where I left them."

Laughing at his reasoning I carefully set the bags down on the island and reach for the large bag of chips he's reluctant to release.

"Would you like a snack before I let the boys out?" I offer. "I have those fruity drinks in boxes you like and I think you earned a small bowl of chips, how about that?"

"Great!" he says and pulls out one of the saddle barstools I found at the local thrift shop and stained four green and the other four blue. "Miss Harper, can you call Fabian and see if he'd like to spend the night with you?"

Laughing at the small boy I quickly put my purchases away and ask him why he wants Fabian to stay at my place.

"Don't you want him to sleep over at your house?" I ask helping myself to a salty chip I poured into the small dish.

"Well, Mom says there are too many boys under her feet but if it was alright with you I could spend the night here when Fabian is staying with you," he explains.

"You my young friend are in luck," I tell him wiping my

greasy fingers on a paper towel. "Fabe is going to be here tomorrow for a couple of days while his Mother is out of town. You, kind sir, are most welcome to spend the night."

Silas pumps his small fist in the air and laughs making me join in until I hear a knock on the side door. Looking around the boy I notice his father is motioning for his precocious son to get outside. I walk over to the door and open it for my neighbor.

"Hi Darrell," I greet the harried looking man, "I was just inviting your son to spend the evening tomorrow night since my God son Fabian will be spending the weekend with me, that is if you're okay with the plan."

"Sounds like you and Silas' new friend are going to have a roommate," he laughs and keeps staring at the small bowl of chips on the island. "Those sure look good and salty…"

"Help yourself," I tell him and scoot the bowl towards him.

Looking over his shoulder towards his house he quickly grins and devours the snack with Silas. I walk over to the fridge and pull out two fruit punch drinks and offer the guys a drink.

"Slow down fellas," I advise them finding it unusual they're acting like they've never had a chip before.

"You don't understand," Darrell whispers again looking over his shoulder. "Pam is on some stupid diet or something life changing as she calls it but she won't allow salt into the house…Salt? I mean really, who lives without salt?" He mumbles licking the greasy ends of his fingertips.

"Yeah, and she won't let us eat hot dogs or hamburgers anymore, only chicken and fish, right Daddy?" Silas bemoans his new diet as he leans over the counter for another chip before his father eats it. "Everybody eats hamburgers and hotdogs, because that's what kids like."

"That's right," Darrell says continuing with his gripes leaning around me and reaching for the bag of chips to refill the bowl. "The other day I took the boys into town and bought them each a frozen sorbet in a waffle cone from Nob's Snack Shack. It wasn't even ice cream for crying out loud but she acted like I bought them beer and cigarettes. She went on and on for hours... by the way, do you smoke?"

Laughing at the funny man with the hopeful look on his face I shake my head and glance out the windows and snatch the drink boxes and bowl of chips out of their hands when I see Mrs. Hutchins on her way over.

"Diet guru at three o'clock," I tell him turning my back towards the door and dumping the snack evidence in the trash can under the sink.

"Silas, wipe your mouth son, you've got crumbs on your chin," Darrell says wiping his own lips on the sleeve of his shirt. "Pick up a banana and don't say a word about our cheating, okay?"

His son grins and nods his head making me laugh at the father and son bonding moment. In the meantime, I walk over to the door and hold it open for Pam and Joey riding on his mama's hip.

"Hi Pam, come on in and join my grocery delivery team," I tell the nosy woman quickly glancing about my kitchen, looking for signs of ... I'm not sure.

"Thanks, but I just came over to tell my husband that my parent's will be arriving for the weekend in about an hour, so we need to get going," she says in a sing song tone I know is masking her true irritation.

Silas slips off the stool and tells his mother, "Fabian is spending the weekend and Miss Harper invited me to spend the night, is that alright?"

Smiling at her son she nods her head and looks up at me for confirmation.

"Fabian's mother is dropping him off tomorrow morning so if it's alright with you, Silas and the rest of the boys are welcome to hang out as well." She appears delighted at the chance of unloading her brood onto someone else. "Plus, my family is coming over for a big cookout and we're going to watch the fireworks on the lake."

"Oh, you'll love that display," she tells me shifting her son onto her other hip. "The first year we saw them I was pregnant with the twins, remember hon," she says quietly reliving some fun times.

"The town council tries to outdo last year's show by coming around and collecting money donations right before the event," Darrell grumbles crossing his arms over his chest and leaning back on the barstool. "Nothing's free anymore."

"Hush Darrell you love the display and always give quite generously," his wife reminds him waving her free hand in front of him in dismissal but Darrell is on a roll.

"They time the collection committee's arrival when you're good and loaded," he says taking his son from his wife. "Remember last year, you gave a donation and then they hit me up for one without saying they already pocketed your check."

"I'm sure that was an oversight on their part," she says reaching for Silas' hand. "No matter the boys look forward to the event and so do you."

The Hutchins walk outside when Silas runs back in,

looks up at me with those sparkling blue eyes and says, "I didn't get a chance to play with the boys, but I'll be over tomorrow after cartoons, okay?"

Ruffling his sun-bleached hair I hug his slight shoulders and say, "Fabian will be here around ten so why don't you wait until you see his Mama's SUV before you come over."

"Okay, but I hope she's not late," the young neighbor says over his shoulder before he ducks under his mother's arm as she nods at me in farewell and closes the door.

I smile at the crazy family and walk outside to let the pups run for a while before I start supper.

12

The phone ringing in the middle of the night wakes me out of a deep sleep. The pups bark and run around in circles as I turn on the bedside lamp and pick up my cell. Not taking the time to read the identity screen I answer the call.

"Hello?"

"Where the hell are you?" Paxton's voice practically shouts in my ear and I can tell he's been drinking.

"At home in bed not that it's any of your business," I snap back. "What do you want?"

I glance over at the digital clock and note the time then drop back down on my pillow.

"My God Paxton it's three o'clock in the morning, why are you calling me?" I angrily ask the inconsiderate oaf. "Where are you?"

"Sitting in the middle of our bed wondering where the hell you're at," he replies slurring his words. "Why'd you move out? And where's the stove and refrigerator?"

Laughing at the absurdity of his question I reply, "I moved out because there wasn't enough room for York and Kirby, we needed a bigger place and I bought and paid for the appliances on my own when you said we didn't need to upgrade the kitchen remember?"

That sets him off on a tirade that even the pups can hear.

"I can't believe you moved out without telling me," he snaps letting his temper fly. "The least you could have done was wait until I returned and go through the apartment together."

"You're either drunk or crazy," I tell him. "You walked out on me, then left the country with your tail between your legs and with another woman but you're upset because I didn't stick around? Honey you need a CAT scan because I think you hit your head harder than they said."

"Very funny," he sneers. "Tell me where you're at."

"I'm at home silly," I tease knowing this small payback is probably all I will get from him. "You're at your bachelor pad and I'm in my new place. I'll keep talking slow like this so you can keep up."

"You're awful brave while you're hiding out," he laughs, "but I'll find you. I'd bet my next commission check you're staying with Ginger Simmons, am I right?"

"Nope, not even close. She said the boys and I were too rowdy so she only lets us visit, but then we have to leave…" I can't stop the giggle from escaping my mouth when he practically roars in frustration.

"Dammit Harper stop this nonsense and come back here," he growls but I interrupt his tirade.

"You broke it off with me, we're over." I remind him. "I've moved on so for the last time Paxton leave me alone. You didn't want to be together, so we're not. You made me a laughing stock to my family, friends, and co-workers. Do you have any idea how hard it was to return to the office knowing everybody there is aware you walked out on our wedding?" I shout the last part causing the pups to become anxious so I take a couple deep breaths and end the conversation.

"You got what you wanted, now leave me alone and go enjoy your single life, goodbye," I tell the still shouting man and end the call. Just to be safe I turn off the ringer.

The boys amble over to the bed resting their muzzles on the mattress while I scratch behind their ears.

"I'm sorry that bad man called and woke you up," I coo to them. "Go lie down," I point to their large doggy pillow and they walk back to their bed and curl up together, whiff a couple times and as I turn out the light York does a funny sounding yawn and soon we're all three-fast asleep.

13

The dogs and I are running up and down the shore line first thing the next morning enjoying the cool morning air before the fourth of July heats up. Their tongues are lolling outside of their mouths as we chase each other across the pebbled beach. I can see the Hutchins and their company are enjoying breakfast out on their covered patio and wave back at them before my troop climb up the notched earthen steps towards the back of our house. My neighbors will head into town in a little bit to watch the parade and so will my family. Lake Sinclaire goes all out for the holidays and I look forward to participating in several events the merchants are sponsoring.

Last weekend I ran into Pauline Naples at the hardware store and she informed me about all the festivities the residents of Lake Sinclaire enjoy over the Fourth. At ten o'clock today there will be a beauty contest for the crowning of 'Little Miss and Mister Sparkler' and Lake Sinclaire's crowning of 'Miss Firecracker'. The VFW, American Legion, and several church groups are sponsoring food stands that will serve at eleven selling everything from fried elephant ears, roasted ears of corn on the cob, homemade pies and full pork chop and fried chicken dinners with all the trimmings. The contests for best yard and mailbox patriotism themed decorations will be announced with some civic awards handed out, one her husband is vying for; 'Most Civic Minded Merchant.' He owns the only hardware store in town and his entire building looks a patriotic bomb exploded leaving red, white, and blue Mylar shrapnel all over the place. Even the man himself will be decked out in his famous 'Uncle Sam' costume he wears each year. His wife was so proud of him. I couldn't help but wish him the best of luck in the contests. A parade will begin its route through town at twelve thirty showcasing entries as grand as the Lakeside Marching High School Band, the local sportsman club, the VFW and American Legion and the Lady's Auxiliary plus several dance teams, a dog obedience training class and rare and collectible antique vehicles. Fabian is looking forward to seeing the parade with the Hutchins brothers. Trevor and Travis told me the candy thrown at this parade is of the highest quality. This year they must sneak the treats while their mother isn't looking. Silas told me they will ask Fabian to collect their share, for an extra part of their loot.

While York and Kirby quench their thirst from the massive water bowl setting outside the back door I refill my coffee cup and check my messages. I noticed I have two from Paxton, one from my dad, and another one from Ginger. My father and best friend were just checking to see if I needed anything before they left the city and to remind me Fabian's dad would pick him up on Saturday instead of Sunday. Paxton's messages were simply a repeat of last night except he was hung over and even grouchier than when he was drunk.

"Did you take my WWII DVD collection? I'm missing my FDNY navy T-shirt… you know the one you always used to sleep in? Where is it Harper? I'm also missing some CDs as well."

His second message is easier to listen to.

"Pick up the phone and talk to me Harpo," he says using his silly nickname he always called me when he was in a playful mood. "Let's go to Lombardo's, you know you love that place, my treat." He sighs in the phone then says, "I'll call you later, I love you."

The misery I hear in his voice sounds real, but I know he's just lonely and will quickly have a couple different women to fill in for me. Now that's a depressing thought. I shake myself out of my gloomy mood and bake the roll out cookies I promised Fabian. He goes wild over them, same as Cassie. Once the last batch is removed from the oven I hear a vehicle pull into the drive. Glancing at the large clock on the living room wall I see it's a quarter to ten, my first guests have arrived. I walk out onto the screened in porch and wait for my hugs from the Simmons family and Marc Keenan who looks especially handsome in his white pin cord shorts, faded red chambray shirt and worn boat shoes. He kisses my cheek and hands me a wicker tray filled with fresh fruit.

"I love this place," Ginger says opening the side door and walking into the kitchen after we hug hello. "You've done so much since I was here last. Ooh, I love the barstools." She says rubbing her hand over the saddle seat before plopping her denim covered bottom on the one closest to the coffee pot. She looks wonderful in her cut off blue jeans, blue and white striped T-shirt and deck shoes. Her red pony tail bobs as she takes in the finished rooms. "You've become a bit more countrified since you moved." She lightly touches the potted red geraniums I have on the center of the island and winks at me.

"Your dream home," she smiles and her eyes mist over. "You've found your niche, sweetie."

"Hi Fabe," I greet my God son wiping the tears from the corner of my eyes at his mother's compliment. "Silas and his brothers will be here any minute. They've been watching for you from their driveway so I'm going to give them to the count of ten before they are knocking on the door. One, two, three…"

I'm interrupted by the sounds of dogs barking, little boys laughing, shouting, and banging on the door. Walking over to let them inside I introduce my eager neighbors to Marc. After checking the counters for snacks the boys scurry outside and let York and Kirby out to play in the back yard. Keeping the dogs in the fenced in area is practical plus safer. They get rambunctious when there are so many people around, at least until they get to know the visitors. They love the boys and follow them everywhere when they come over so I know they'll be safe.

"Are you decorating these cookies or are they ready to eat?" Marc asks picking up one of the cooled star shaped cookies.

"Sure, help yourself…" I tell him snatching the treat out of his hand, "Just as soon as you bring the folding chairs out of the garage, please."

He grins and bends over Ginger's shoulder for a kiss then takes the unfrosted cookie from me and runs outside hollering for the boys to come help him. Ginger stares after the man with such longing I know things are getting serious between them. Actually, this holiday weekend is the first time they're going away together. I cup the sides of her head and kiss the top of her hair.

"Somebody is getting in deep," I tease her making her blush. "So, tell me about you two."

She grins and the dimples pop out in her cheeks, a soft look washes over her face and she speaks in such a dreamy voice I can't help but feel envious. We whip up the red, white, and blue frosting and together as she tells me about her new relationship we decorate the stars and clean up the mess before the guys make it back inside. The pups are lagging, already looking tuckered out from the rowdy play.

"Can we have a cookie?" Fabian asks wrapping his sweaty arm around my waist, "please?"

I smile and scoot the small plate of cookies I set aside for the boys keeping most of the batch well out of sight and reach. Marc opens the fridge to put the fruit tray inside and then looks over his shoulder towards Fabian.

"Fabe, take the guys with you and carry in the small blue cooler and your horseshoe set," he says tossing his keys to the boy. "I'll help you fellas set up the stakes."

Marc and Fabian have a good friendship developing with no animosity on the younger Simmons part since his father has remarried and started a second family. The six-year-old is as easy going as his mother is volatile. The kids and dogs traipse through the living room and out the side door, letting the screen door slam shut behind them.

"So, where exactly are you two going?" I ask knowing Marc is keeping their destination a secret even from his date.

"That way," he points towards the front yard. "Then maybe this way," he says crossing his arm over his other one making us laugh at his silliness. "It's a surprise, and if you know… she'll know."

We tease and banter with each other as we set up the tables on the screened in porch. The ceiling fans are creating a soft gentle breeze that will feel wonderful as the day heats up. An hour later my folks arrive bringing most of the food since my father is a control freak for preparing a meal. By the time Vic, Shawna, and Cassie arrive we're ready to head into town for the big parade. Looking over head I see some clouds in the distance and pray the rain will hold off until after the fireworks, but it's looking risky. Pauline said the Mayor had a contingency plan just in case the weathermen were correct about the possibility of severe thunderstorms later in the evening.

Riding in Mom's SUV I look over at my folks and smile to myself. Dad's arm is wrapped around Mom's shoulder while she rests her hand on his khaki covered leg. Pax and I always drove our vehicles touching each other… a sigh escapes me making my dad look in the rearview mirror at me.

"Don't worry Princess," he grins, "we'll get them next year for the 'most patriotic' themed mailbox award," he says making Mom notice all the red, white, and blue bunting draping the mailboxes along the road.

"Well, I think your flower pots of red and white petunias at the edge of the driveway are subtle and the American flags in the center is just the right touch," she says as we reach the city limits and traffic is slower. "Oh, my God," she laughs placing her hand on her blue and white gingham covered chest. "Look at that horrible display."

She is pointing at a lovely couple named Beechum's mailbox; I met them in town at the post office when I first moved in. The white metal letter holder is covered entirely with yards of looped tri-colored ribbons and streamers, large bundles of bottle rockets, roman candles, and what appear to be small missiles pointing in all directions. Mylar ting-ting adds a reflective element but the real kicker is the empty red, white, and blue aluminum beer cans randomly placed in the arrangement like flowers in a bouquet. Three large flags are protruding out of the monstrosity and on the end of one flag hangs a blue grand champion ribbon awarded for best show. The Beechum family is gathered on their front porch and wave at us when Poppy honks his horn in congratulations. The four kids are jumping up and down congratulating themselves as we drive past. That entry will be near impossible to top next year…it reminds me of the Naples's hardware store.

Pam Hutchins waves us over to their picnic table once we make it to the food area and introduces her parents as we purchase pork chop dinners for the adults, hotdogs and soda pop for the kids. The town's people are having a blast and the parade line-up instructions are being blasted from the bull horn Mayor Fields is carrying on his well-cinched belted red and white striped slacks as he gets into his element of directing anybody and everybody. The parade is almost an hour long but well worth the sweat as we watch the final entry pass by. We're all hot and sticky by the time we make it back to my house and ready for a dip in the lake with the dogs and all the kids. A couple hours later the dark gray clouds roll in blocking the sun and bringing in a cool breeze. By five o'clock, Poppy has the meat on the grill, the beer bottles are open, and my mother's secret recipe sangria has been poured. The boys are in the side yard playing horse shoes, the pups are stretched out in the grass under my Adirondack chair resting in the shade when Vic walks over to stand beside me. Looking up at him I'm shocked to see the look of anger that greets me.

"What's wrong?" I ask while he squats down beside me, using the wide armrest to support his forearm.

"See that sailboat in the center of the lake?" he asks pointing to a nice size vessel dead center in the water. "Here, use these," he says offering me the set of binoculars hanging around his neck he must have taken from the watch tower.

Focusing in on the lone man I can see he looks familiar then I notice he's looking at me with his own binoculars and waves. Oh no, it's Pax. He's found out where I live and I can't help the tingle of excitement that races down my spine. Letting out a sigh I lower the glasses and look up into my brother's concerned eyes.

"Tell me you didn't invite him over," Vic hisses at me. "Poppy and Mom will both blow a gasket if they even hear Barrett's name. You're not seeing him, are you?"

"No, for God's sake Victor," I snap at him trying to hide the thrill I'm experiencing knowing Pax is so close and he's watching me. "The man broke my heart, okay? Remember me, the one dressed in white left at the altar?"

"Shhh," he replies, "keep your voice down or Dad will hear you. I just wanted to be sure you weren't falling back into his lying, cheating arms."

"Thanks for worrying big brother but I've learned my

lesson thank you very much." I raise the glasses once more and wonder aloud, "How did he find me so quickly..."

"Ten to one he either bribed somebody at your office or threatened them," Vic laughs. "He's a real stand up kind of guy, huh?"

I smile and nod my head feeling conflicted. Part of me never wants to see him again. The logical side I guess. But the tender side, my emotional side wants to run into his arms and let him convince me he's changed, that he's sorry for what he did...

"... then we're all set," my father is saying.

I was so deep in thought I failed to notice him walk up carrying a tray laden down with his famous chicken pesto and cherry tomato kabobs and wonderful medium rare steaks.

"Sorry Poppy, I must have been day dreaming," I tell him. "What are we waiting on?"

"The burgers for the boys," he smiles and walks away with his contribution to the meal.

"Snap out of it," Vic says jabbing my shoulder with his finger. "Do you want me to have a talk with the man?"

"No, heavens no don't do that," I plead smiling at the wicked grin appearing on my brother's face as I rub the sting out of spot he poked. "Stop it Vic," I warn him. "Get the kids and I'll set out the rest of the sides Mom and Dad brought. Make sure they wash their hands at the outdoor sink."

He raises his arm as confirmation he heard me and walks away to gather the children. A strong-arm drapes around my shoulders and I know it's Poppy.

"Just tell me you didn't invite him," he whispers in my ear before kissing my temple.

"No sir, I didn't know he knew where I lived," I reply in all honesty not bothering to act surprised my father knows that's Paxton on the lake.

"Good enough for me," he says and steers me over to the porch where we set up one long table to easily seat twenty but last head count is at fourteen with the Hutchins boys sitting at the end of the table laughing and joking with each other and gobbling down mounds of potato salad, burgers, chips, and soft drinks. I know it goes against their mother's wishes, but I can't say no to a hungry kid. The food is delicious, the drinks are flowing, and the conversation is fast paced and full of good nature ribbing and lots of laughter.

After dinner, the dogs are asleep under the table having begged for enough food to feed an army; the kids are involved in a rowdy game of tag munching on the festive cookies while the lovely fruit tray is slowly being picked over. Marc and Ginger are sitting under the large Maple trees nearly at the property line watching the water skiers on the lake, Dad and Mom are playing a modified game of croquet with Cassie while Vic is asleep in the porch swing, and his head is resting on Shawna's lap as she slowly pushes the swing back and forth.

While no one is looking, I grab my glass of sangria and head up to the watch tower to use my powerful telescope trying to catch a glimpse of Paxton. Moving the view finder, I get a clear shot of him on the bow of the boat. He's shirtless, wearing only a colorful pair of yellow, red, and blue blocked swimming trunks and sunning himself through the small break in the thick clouds. The sunglasses reflect the sun bouncing off the lenses. Part of me wishes he was here enjoying the holiday with my family and another part of me is terrified he'll crash the party. I love the way his muscles move as he turns to look over my way. He lifts the powerful binoculars to his eyes. He waves again then smiles when he catches me spying on him. I laugh at the situation. Within seconds my cell phone in my back-pocket rings.

"Hello there you little voyeur," he says when I answer the call.

"Is this Peeping Pax?" I laugh suddenly feeling lighter; he hears the happy note in my voice and chuckles.

"Looks like you're having a good time," he says with a touch on sadness.

"I am," I reply refusing to fall victim to his emotional blackmail. "You know I always love the Fourth of July. I'm a sucker for fireworks."

He laughs and says, "I remember last year when we made love on the roof of our building while the sky kept lighting up... that was the best fourth I can remember."

That was a special time for both of us. We went off like two roman candles.

"That was a special night," I agree loving the way the colorful bombs put his sexy body in shadow while he made wild, passionate love ...now that was a grand finale.

"So, York and Kirby are dogs," he laughs with a touch of piqué in his voice. "You really had me going with the thought of you living with somebody else. I'll have to think of a good payback for the misery you put me through."

"I didn't lie," I remind him. "They do need room and I love living with them...they're so trustworthy, offering unconditional love… and so far, they've never had a bad day, a bad mood, or even thought about running away."

He smirks at my dig, "I get it, you're coming across loud and clear," he says. "But even though they might be good company, they can't possibly love you as much as I do…"

Before I can respond he urgently says, "I think you better get back to the party," and I see he's pointing over towards the edge of my property. Quickly I move the telescope to my back yard and see a frightened Joey running towards my mother, screaming in pain and holding his arm.

"Thanks, I gotta go," I tell him, "talk to you later, love you, bye."

As I pocket the phone I realize I professed my love to him like I always did when we ended a phone call. Oh well, it was a slip of the tongue and right now I have issues bigger than him hearing I still love him. Racing down the steps I almost collide with Ginger running over to my baking cabinet for the baking soda.

"Joey fell on a nest of yellow jackets," she says running back outside with a water bottle and the baking agent in the gold box.

Running after her I holler for the boys, "Trevor, Travis go home and get your parents, tell them what happened, hurry up."

They take off like a shot while I join my mother and Ginger making a paste to apply to the multiple stings I see swelling up on his small arm. Victor is holding a crying Cassie who feels bad for her friend while my father and Marc are comforting Fabian and Silas.

"He's going to be fine," my father says holding a trembling Silas. "Where did this happen?"

122

Silas wipes his eyes smearing dirt across his cheek and points over towards the tree line between my property and his parents.

"Joey and Cassie were picking those flowers and she screamed when a bee landed on her. Joey shooed it away but tripped on a rock and fell down," Silas says between sniffles.

"His arm was covered with the bees," Fabian whispers to Marc. "Is he going to have to go to the doctor? Will they give him a shot?"

"We'll see Fabe," Marc says hugging him closely. "Hey Silas, do you know if Joey is allergic to bee stings?"

He shrugs his shoulders and then drops his head on my dad's shoulder. I can hear Pam and Darrell's raised voices as they reach the side porch with the boy's grandparents.

"Where's my baby?" the frantic mother asks searching for her crying son. "Oh, Joey, Mommy's here, let Daddy look at your arm, okay?"

The small boy's bottom lip is quivering from the pain and the tears continue to fall from his big blue eyes breaking my heart at his misery.

"Is he allergic?" I whisper to Darrell who is shaking his head gently holding his child's injured arm.

"Those boys are virtually indestructible," he teases making Silas run over to his father and be lifted in his secure arms. "He's going to be alright Si, I promise, right Mommy?"

Pam smiles up at her son and says, "It only hurts for a little while, then he'll be good as new. Let's take this drama home and let you folks enjoy the rest of your evening."

"No Pam, let the boys stay all night, that way you can take care of Joey and the kids will be out of your hair for a while," I tell her and she still is unsure but Travis hugs his mother and says, "We'll go home with you, help with Joey, then maybe we can come back and watch the fireworks?"

"Yeah Mom, please let us come back," Trevor begs. "You know how much noise we make, Joey won't be able to rest at all."

The Hutchins laughs at the truth in that statement and agree to let the kids come back once Joey is taken care of. They single file return to their house next door. Once the crying and drama is over I notice Marc checking his watch and tilting his head towards Ginger signaling they should take off.

"Well, thanks for a wonderful day," Ginger says hugging me and then my parents. "Chip will be by to pick up Fabian on Saturday morning. His father is taking him up to their cabin, right?"

Fabian grins and says, "Their Lake is much smaller than yours, but I get to go fishing with Dad so it's fun. Bye Mom, bye Marc, I'll see you Monday… Love you."

Ginger hugs her son again then the two lovebirds leave to go on their mystery trip. Walking back towards the gang I notice Cassie is sound asleep on Vic's shoulder wiped out from the recent drama. My mother is clearing off the table and Dad is cleaning up the new grill I bought last week.

"I'd say her maiden voyage was a huge success," I tease him as he takes the grids over to the backyard spigot and washes off the residue.

"It was a perfect day until Joey got hurt." He admits then looks up at the sky. "That storm is quickly coming in, I hope it holds off until the fireworks, otherwise you're not going to get the bang for your buck."

Looking over at the water line I no longer see Pax's boat and tell myself it's a good thing. By the time the table and chairs are returned to the garage, the grill installed on the back porch with its new cover on top, the first raindrops fall. We walk back inside and then a deluge of water befalls us making a fireworks display seem unlikely. The sky becomes dark and it appears the rain has set in for a spell. The pups are asleep on their downstairs bed in the corner of the living room, oblivious to the thunder and lightning booming and flashing around them. I make a pot of coffee and we have a second round on the cookies when a pair of headlights pulls into the drive. Fabian runs to the side door and opens the screen door to the three Hutchins brothers and their Dad.

"Come on in guys," my dad holds the door open when the wind tries to take it out of Fabian's hand. "Harper go gets some towels for these young men, and their dad."

"Don't bother on my account," Darrell says eyeing the platter still piled high with cookies. "But I'd love a couple cookies for the road."

Mom holds the platter towards him and Darrell takes six cookies, then a couple more.

"I'll take a couple to Joey," he says then picks up a couple more before he drops a dozen of cookies in the plastic bag Shawna is holding out for him. "Thanks, I appreciate that," he says taking two more treats before he hugs the boy's goodnight. "Be good, or I'll tell your mom you're over here eating chocolate chip cookies, fudge, and French fries... ooh that sounds good, doesn't it?"

We laugh as he intended and he takes his leave after assuring us Joey is fine and they counted only two bee stings, the other whelps were from the wild rose bush he rolled into trying to get away from the stinging insects. I feel so much better knowing the little guy will be all right.

The Meads soon leave when it's apparent the rain is not letting up. I round up two umbrellas and after everyone is loaded up Dad hugs me to him and says, "It's okay if you want to talk to the man, I know you love him but just be careful, alright? I'd hate to have to go after the guy for hurting you again. I like Pax, just not as husband material for you."

I don't even bother denying he read my thoughts but tell him, "I'm not the same person I was two months ago, trust me… I see his faults, but you're right I still love him, can't seem to help myself."

"Just take it slow, who knows, maybe he realizes what a good thing he had going with you," Poppy says kissing my forehead, "time will tell. I love you princess, and I'd go check on the boys if I was you, they're way too quiet."

Laughing and then worrying I close the door on him, turn off the porch light and make my way upstairs where I hear them playing in the watch tower room. Their backpacks are wide open revealing hundreds if not thousands of army men, cartoon characters, and all the accoutrement that goes with the latest 'got to have' action figure. Walking back down stairs I walk over to the new sectional I bought locally at Whidbey's Furniture Emporium, turn on the miss-matched lamps on the whitewashed end tables and drop down on the soft pastel teal blue sofa. I laugh when the pups try to fit underneath the low coffee table, just to be near me. I must have dozed off because the soft knocking on the screened in porch door startles the dogs and wakes me out of my slumped position on the sofa.

Trying to calm the Mastiffs I stand up and walk over to turn on the porch light and see the former love of my life standing in front of me, drenched to the bone and looking like a million bucks. A crooked smile appears on his handsome face as I unlock the door and my protectors and I step outside onto the porch and wait for him to make the first move.

14

Paxton bends down and pets the excited dogs making them lick and paw him as they introduce themselves. His laughter is a two-edged sword making me anxious and relieved all simultaneously. But the second he focuses his dark gaze on me I know I'm a goner.

"Hi," he softly says stepping over the pups and slowly wrapping his arms around my shoulders, giving me plenty of time to step back but my body will not pass up his touch and I embrace his waist not even noticing his dampness soaking my T-shirt.

A sob escapes me as he enfolds me tightly to his body and I feel his lips in my hair.

"Shhh, don't cry just let me hold you," he whispers as all my senses wake up and take stock in the man I can't help but love.

He smells of the outdoors, a heady mix of sandalwood, rain, heat, and man. I hear his sharp intake of breath when I wrap my arms tighter around his waist, burrowing my face in his neck. Even if I tried I couldn't have stopped the flow of tears seeping under my tightly closed eyes.

"Baby, don't cry," he softly pleads. "I'm so sorry I hurt you, but I'm here now, stop crying please."

He pushes me away far enough he can bend down and reach my mouth with his lips and the second we touch sparks fly. The taste of him is a drug to my heart, body, and soul and like an addict getting reacquainted with its drug of choice I lose myself in the kiss, clawing at his back, and then pulling on his hair trying to get closer to him. His hot breath washes over me as we battle with our mouths, pulling, tugging, licking, and sucking on one another until I feel the evidence of his arousal pressing me in the belly. How far we would have gone is debatable but just then the pups bark as the kids race down the stairs, laughing and shouting at each other to see who will reach the kitchen first. I push out of Paxton's arms feeling his reluctance in letting me go but he does and I look past him at the boys unaware of my unexpected caller.

"Aunt Harper we're hungry," Fabian says then stops short causing the other boys to run into his back, then sending him to his knees. "Hey, look out," Fabian laughs with the Hutchins.

"Sorry Miss Harper," Travis says, "We didn't know you had company."

"Yeah, sorry for interrupting," Trevor apologizes. "Can we have something to eat?"

"There's chip and dip left isn't there Miss Harper?" Silas asks looking around the strange man who refuses to step away from me.

"Hi Uncle Pax," Fabian laughs when he recognizes Paxton. "I didn't know you were back, are you staying here now?" the innocent question is asked and before Paxton can speak I smile at my honorary nephew and explain the situation, at least enough so he's not confused.

"No, Uncle Pax happened to be in the area and stopped in to see us, right Pax?" I finally look up at the man wreaking havoc on my senses and pray he doesn't argue the point.

"I'm just visiting," he smiles at the youngster then softly, so I barely hear him he utters under his breath, "for now."

Quickly glancing up at him he smiles but it never reaches his eyes which are black as night and sparkling like diamonds then he reaches out and picks up Fabian, flipping him over his broad shoulder like he used to do when ever they'd see each other.

"Introduce me to your buds," he says to the boy hanging upside down his back before he playfully swats his behind making the Hutchins laugh and York and Kirby dance around barking at the playful new game.

"This is Trevor, Travis, and Silas," he says between giggles, "they're brothers and live next door. You already know Aunt Harper," he teases so Pax pretends to drop him, making all the boys squeal in delight.

Smiling at the crew I walk into the kitchen, flip on the light and check out the leftover situation in the fridge.

"There are some chicken kabobs, pasta salad, and a couple pieces of steak, or you can each have a burger...your call," I offer them their choices.

"No potato salad left?" Travis asks trying to see past my shoulder while Silas scoops in low and nudges me back so he can check out the contents of the refrigerator himself.

"I'll have a burger and chips" Fabian informs me and the three brothers echo his request.

Turning to step away from the youngsters I smile and

say, "May I have a burger and chips please," causing the Hutchins to question me with a look when Fabian smiles.

"Sorry Aunt Harper, May I have a burger and chips?" he asks using his manners.

"Yes, you may," I reply and watch as Pax carefully sets Fabian down on the island counter top and reaches around me for a bottle of beer.

"May I have a beer?" he politely asks making me smile and the boys ask the same question.

Laughing I tickle Silas and say, "Yes you may in fourteen years."

Paxton laughs and twists the top off his drink then hands the boys a couple juice boxes from the door of the icebox.

"Here, you guys can catch a sugar buzz instead," he tells them and one by one he tosses the containers at each child making the drink box appear to shoot upward out of his hands making it easy for them to catch. "Go play for a while and I'll help Aunt Harper get your snack together, okay?"

"Sure, I want pickles and ketchup, but no mustard on mine," Fabian places his order and the brothers counter their requests each getting more particular as the go.

"I don't want any pickles on mine, just ketchup oh, and some cheese please," Travis tells me.

"Can I have cheese, pickles, onions, tomatoes, ketchup and mustard on mine?" Trevor asks reaching for the open bag of chips on the counter.

"Hey, gimme some," Silas whines as his older brothers and Fabian help themselves to the chips.

"Boys," Paxton says in a firm tone of voice. "Put the

chips down, wash your hands in the bathroom and we'll call you when your food is ready."

But the kids just stand there digging their hands into the bag and making a mess on the floor. He puts his hands on his hips and says "Harper, forget about the snacks, they don't seem to want to mind, do they?"

Trevor and Travis snatch the bag from Fabian and together profess they'll listen.

"Sorry Uncle Pax, we'll do what you said," Trevor replies while Travis and Silas bend over and clean up the crumbs they let fall on the floor.

Fabian walks over to the adult, pats Pax's bulging bicep and says, "I've missed you, welcome back."

He and the Hutchins walk out of the room and take turns at the sink in the half bath then run up the stairs to the watch tower, yelling and shouting at who gets to be the hero and who gets to be the villain. I can't hold the laughter back and slide down the front of the cabinet holding my sides at the look of accomplishment on Pax's face. But soon the pups run over to investigate why I'm down on their level so I'm bombarded with wet tongues and cold noses. Holding out his hands he helps me to my feet but instead of stepping back he leans forward trapping me between his hard body and the cabinets pressing into my back. Like magic our mouths find one another and start the mating ritual dance again only this time I feel my own desire rise to the surface, making me climb up his leg to press my center into his burgeoning front.

"I want you so badly," he murmurs against my lips urging our lower bodies to mesh like our chests and arms. "I could come right here just holding you," he whispers resting his forehead on mine.

"This is such a bad idea," I reply kissing his neck and jaw. "You're too dangerous to my peace of mind but I want you too. I've missed you, your touch… I just need to taste you a little more."

My words send him into frenzy as he cups my full aching breasts in both his hands, kneading them until I'm ready to scream. Surging my hand down the front of his relaxed jeans I stroke the long length of him loving the growl that escapes his lips then he's surging into my hand as I cup his crotch and gently squeeze until he forces me backward and turns away, bracing his hands on the marble counter top and dropping his chin on his chest as he tries to get himself back under control.

"You're the only woman in the world that can make me lose control like this," he says grinning at me over his shoulder. "If we were alone I'd have you flat on your back, lying across this cold hard marble, screaming out your release."

Staring at the intense fire smoldering behind his black eyes I swallow hard, pushing my own desire back down to the core of my body.

"I'd let you too," I tell him in a soft, hushed voice. "I went through Paxton withdrawal for the first two months, then my libido went dormant, but it only takes a couple kisses from you and all I can think about is screwing your brains out."

He barks out a laugh at my honest and direct response nodding his head in understanding. But before he can walk over to me the boys shout from upstairs.

"Is our food ready yet?" Fabian asks.

Smiling at the look of chagrin on the man's face we forgot what we were supposed to be doing. He helps me re-heat the left-over burgers in the microwave and set out the makeshift buffet. Fifteen minutes later the kids are digging into their meal, sitting around the island and chattering a mile a minute.

"What was your favorite thing in the parade?"

"How did that man walk on sticks?"

"Who cleans up after the horses?"

"When will they shoot off the fireworks? Or do they have to wait until next year?"

"I hope it stops raining soon, I don't like the thunder."

"Are you scared?"

They argue over who fears storms for a couple minutes before Fabian turns to Pax and asks, "What are you afraid of?"

Paxton sets down his beer after taking a sip and clears his throat before he looks over at me and says, "Losing the one person I love most in the world."

"Who's that?" Fabian asks finishing his burger. "I love my mom, but I can't lose her. But sometimes she says she's losing her mind, are you afraid of losing your mind?"

Chuckling at the way the boy's mind works Pax swipes a chip off Fabian's plate and says, "I've already lost mine, but no, I love your Aunt Harper."

I bite my lower lip at his heartfelt response and feel myself slipping back under his spell until Fabian asks his next question.

"How come you and Aunt Harper didn't get married?"

Paxton looks over at the small boy and says, "Because I lost my mind."

"Are you going to marry her when you find your mind?" Trevor asks making his brothers laugh and talk about where Paxton might have misplaced his mind, creating a reprieve from the tension I feel filling up the space between me and my former fiancé.

"Can we have, I mean may we have a couple cookies?" Silas asks jumping down from his stool and walking over to the spot on the counter top where he sees the plastic container of the star shaped treats.

Pax stands up and reaches over the top of the blonde-haired boy, removes the lid off the container, and holds it out to the hungry quartet letting each child grab two cookies all without taking his eyes off me.

"Don't make a mess but take your dessert up to the watch tower and we'll join you in a little while," he tells the children.

I know he wants to be alone, talk about what happened between us three months ago, and an hour ago but I'm scared to be alone with him. He still has a powerful hold over me no matter how much I want to believe differently. Standing up I leave the room with the boys when his arm snakes out capturing me and holding me still while he whispers in my ear.

"Please don't run away," he says gently biting my earlobe. "I need to speak with you, clear the air between us because I'm not going away Harper. Give me a second chance; let me show you I've grown up in the last couple of months... please."

I hear the boys reach the top of the stairs and accepting

defeat I nod my head and walk around his rock-hard body, reaching for the opened bottle of merlot and pouring myself a glass while he snaps the lid back on the cookie bin before placing it back on the counter and opens the fridge for another beer.

"Let's go in the living room," he says allowing me to go ahead of him.

I walk over to sit in one of the matching high back wicker chairs I bought as a set for the porch but put up the swing instead of using all six. I put the other two chairs in each bedroom with different colored cushions. He walks into the room and smiles when I sit so far away from him.

"Really Harper, am I that intimidating to you?" he taunts me trying to get me to sit on the sectional with him but I'd rather be safe than sorry.

"I'm not intimidated exactly," I smile up at him as he turns around and sits on the light blue sofa. "I'm vulnerable where you're concerned," I resent the smirk he is wearing so I finish with, "at least sexually. It's been a while for me, how about you?"

His face loses the mirth and he stares down at his feet, unable or unwilling to meet my gaze giving me the answer to my question. My jealous tongue flicks inside my mouth.

"Well, I hope you used birth control," I tell him shocked at the flinch I see on his face.

"I deserved that, and more but it's not what you're thinking, I swear," he says taking a pull on the brown glass bottle. "I know you're going to hate what I have to say as much as I'm going to hate having to explain," he confesses but continues after taking a deep breath and looking over at me. "I cheated on you because I was afraid of losing you."

Blinking several times trying to make sense of that statement I set the wine glass down on the small white painted table between the chairs and lean forward, resting my forearms on my thighs.

"Come again," I tell him licking my suddenly dry lips. "You slept with someone else, while we were engaged to be married, while I was pregnant all because you were afraid of losing me?" I laugh at him when he nods his head and looks over at me. "That's the lamest excuse I've ever heard and I must say it lacks a certain ring of truth to it, don't you think?"

"I'm not proud of what I did Harper, but I'm not lying, I promise," he says making me angry at the way he keeps throwing around that phrase 'I promise'.

"Your promises mean squat Paxton," I tell him taking a large drink of my wine. "You promised to love me, marry me... be there for me...remember those promises? I believed you then, but how can I believe you now?"

He scoots forward nearly off the sofa cushion and says, "Baby, I fucked up, okay? I know I hurt you, embarrassed you, caused you a great deal of grief, but it's only because I was so scared..."

Before I can respond the boys race down the stairs, interrupting what would be a shouting match between me and the man.

"Can we watch a movie?" Fabian asks bending over to scratch Yorke behind his ears.

"I brought my best Spiderman movie to show Fabian," Silas tells me kneeling in front of the TV stand getting ready to put his DVD in the player but stops and looks back at me over his shoulder, waiting on me to say he could.

I feel Pax staring a hole into my head, wanting to continue our discussion but I decide now is not the best time to get into his cheating on me… too many little ears to pick up on the adult conversation so I smile and nod my head for the little sprite to play his movie before glancing over at my angry former lover and shrug my shoulders. He doesn't return my smile but sits in the corner of the sectional, not pouting, more like plotting his next move. Twenty minutes into the loud, fast paced movie I hand the kids a large bowl of popcorn and a smaller bowl for Pax then excuse myself and bid them all goodnight. I lean over and kiss Pax on the lips and whisper, "it's still storming, you can sleep in the guest room since the boys will be in the watch tower. We'll talk later."

He smiles and nods his head and I can feel his eyes on my retreating back as the dogs and I head upstairs. The fierceness of the storm, with the lightning and thunder raging outside makes me glad I'm not alone. Getting ready for bed I notice the dogs circling the room, eager to be downstairs but wanting to stay with me as well so I holler down the stairs for Fabian to call for dogs. Once he does they race down the steps to join their new playmates leaving me to sleep alone. My head touches the pillow and I'm out like a light until I feel the mattress give. Rolling over I see Pax slipping between the sheets and shushing the pups and telling them to go lie down.

"They're not used to sharing their space," I whisper smiling thinking about him having to fight his way to my bed.

"They'll get used to me," he whispers and snuggles me to his side.

My heart flutters at the old feeling of sleeping in his arms again but my head is over-riding my hormones for a change.

"Paxton, this isn't a good idea," I tell him glancing over his broad chest to the red numbers on my digital clock. "It's two in the morning, you're lonely, and I'm available…"

He snorts and says, "I know what time it is. I was almost asleep after getting the boys into their bed rolls, getting glasses of water, listening to their excited talk about the storm. Barely ten minutes later, I heard Fabian whispering in my ear they were afraid and wanted to sleep in my bed because the watch tower was too close to the lightning or something like that."

Looking up at his face I can make out his smile even in the dark shadows before he continues, "the next thing I know, they're sleeping four across and I'm sitting in the wicker rocking chair. I came to your room hoping I could share your soft comfy bed, save myself a trip to the chiropractor."

Chuckling at his reason for joining me I kiss his naked shoulder and wrap my arm around his waist, getting comfortable before I tell him, "You could have slept in the watch tower, or on the sectional."

Tightening his arm around my back he softly laughs and says before kissing my forehead, "and pass up a chance to sleep with you again, not on your life. Go to sleep, we'll talk about us tomorrow."

He yawns and lets out a contented sigh matching the one York makes and then I hear only the soft thump of his heart beating in my ear as I slip into a dreamless sleep.

15

Burrowing into the sweetest smelling pillow I slowly feel myself being shifted over onto my side as a warm arm slips around my waist and another hand grips my naked hip. I press my bottom backwards and feel the slide of a thick shaft slip between my legs, nudging my folds apart and crowding its way into my narrow chasm, filling me to capacity then backing out before slaking forward again. The continuous motion works the inner muscles of my body and wakes me from my peaceful slumber, slowly making my body respond to the silent demands of Paxton Barrett.

"You feel unbelievably good," Pax whispers in my ear as he presses his morning erection into me again. "I've missed you so much, missed how you make me feel, how you make me come unwound inside of you… feel how much I need you baby," he groans moving deeper and lower as he picks up momentum as my dormant body comes alive.

I arch my back and push against him while I reach behind my head, compelling him to move forward and kiss me. Melding our tongues together he drives faster. Pax pushes me over on my belly, spreads my legs and with both his hands lifts me up on my knees giving him greater access as he pummels me from behind. Biting my pillow, I let go of the emotions he brings to the front of my heart, ignoring the slight discomfort his marauding flesh is inflicting on me until I'm no longer resisting. Panting with him I scream out my release after he slips his long fingers between my damp legs, exposing my delicate nerve center and thrusts me into my first climax in over three months.

"Let go baby," he gasps as I spiral out of control. "Feel how much our bodies missed each other, how right we are together..." he blows his hot breath on my neck sending goose bumps down my spine and another orgasm slips out of me as he finds his release, groaning between my shoulder blades as he spews his seed deep inside my womb.

"I...love...you...Harper" he wheezes before he slams into me one last time letting me feel the shiver that courses through his system before he collapses on top of me.

My heart continues to race as my mind fires synapses again. What the hell have I done? I've fallen back under his spell, knowing how hard it will be when he leaves and I know he'll leave again. I turn my head on the pillow and let the tears flow freely from my eyes, not even bothering to hide the sobs escaping from my mouth. He pulls out of me and slides over to his side before turning me over settling me on top of his body. The soft gentle caress his hand gives me down my spine calms my inner turmoil.

"Harper I didn't mean to upset you," he whispers lightly drawing circles on my arm and shoulder. "Tell me what's wrong; I need to know why you're crying."

I sniff twice then say, "Because I love you and nothing has changed."

He laughs at my response which puts the wind back in

my sail. I elbow him in the gut as I struggle to get out of his grasp.

"Oh baby, you have no idea what you're talking about," he whispers capturing my wrists in one of his hands and holding my arms above his head. "You're crazy if you think this," he uses his free hand to point down at our bodies, "doesn't change things. We still have a hell of a lot of things to work on but one thing has changed," he continues pulling on my arms until my heaving breasts are in his face. "I'm not going to leave willingly, ever again. That is one promise I intend to keep."

He takes first one nipple then the other into his mouth and draws deeply making me squirm against his chest. Our combined juices make me slippery and when I straddle his chest he releases my breasts and slides me down and over his quickly inflating staff.

"Ride me," he whispers making me tingle at how much I always loved being on top. "Take me deep inside and ride me, hard."

With his dark encouragement, I send us both into another realm as we find our release one more time before falling asleep, still connected to one another. The next time I wake it's morning and I'm alone in my bed, the dogs are gone and a steaming cup of coffee is setting on the antique black bedside table with a red foil wrapped dollop of chocolate candy setting next to the mug. Smiling at the sweet gesture, I unwrap the candy and pop it in my mouth savoring the creamy milk chocolate on my tongue before I take a sip of coffee. The rain is still falling but only as a drizzle now that the storm has passed. Stepping into the connecting bath I slip off my nightgown and turn on the shower. Ten minutes later, dressed in a pair of short blue jean cut offs embroidered with flowers on the front pockets, my favorite brown braided leather belt, and a white tank top I'm ready to face the day. My hair is still wet as I braid it in a single rope and walk barefooted down the stairs and straight for the coffee pot. I can hear laughter and dogs barking but it's from a distance.

After I refill my cup I head towards the back-French doors where I watch the kids chasing the dogs on the pebbled beach while Pax keeps watch over them all. He looks amazing in his gray t-shirt that shows off his strong, tanned arms and the low riding jeans he had on last night. Just the sight of him standing barefoot in the pebbles, drinking his coffee makes me needy for his lovemaking once again. Sipping my coffee I argue with myself over last night and this morning. On one hand, he knows I'm not willing to go back to our old relationship, well, all but the sex… there was never anything wrong in that department. But after having him back in my bed, and in my body, I know he will assume we're back together. I'm not ready for that. There's still too much we must hash over.

I step away from the distraction of his physique and put slices of bacon on a wire rack inside a baking sheet to cook in the oven while I whip up the eggs. A dozen eggs should take care of this hungry crowd and I make a mental note to replace a few staples from the grocery store today. Once I can smell the bacon I put the eggs on the burner in my favorite sauté pan and make toast. I love the feel of preparing a meal for my make-shift family. There is something so soothing about setting the dining room table, filling juice and milk glasses and dishing up different flavors of jams and jellies into my antique dessert dishes. Removing the bacon from the hot oven I hear the crowd of early risers stomping on the deck then the back door opens and the pups enter the house first followed closely by the four chatter boxes and bringing up the rear, the best babysitter in the whole world…my Pax. He grins at me over the boys' heads and nods his approval at my outfit and then the table setting.

"Good morning," he whispers as he leans over and softly kisses my lips. "I love you," he tells me making the kids gag and fall down. "Very funny boys," he tells them handing me a couple daisy he picked from the property line. "If you're feeling sick I'll put you all back to bed and eat your share of the grub."

The smart alecks are instantly contrite and assure the man they meant no harm.

"We were just joking Uncle Pax," Trevor tells him smiling over at me and says, "Good morning Aunt Harper."

The rest greet me in the same fashion making me smile at the honorary title they've bestowed upon us as their aunt and uncle. Carrying the platter of bacon over I watch as each boy waits his turn at the sink and washes his face and hands before returning to the table and plopping down in one of the eight chairs. Paxton walks over and picks up the heavy skillet and sets it on the hot pad in the center of the table while I refill our cups of coffee from the fresh pot I put on to brew.

"Let's eat while it's hot," I tell the kids and fill the large serving spoon with the soft, fluffy eggs and three strips of bacon for each kid, then accept the plate Pax hands me for himself and we clean up the rest of the skillet. The boys fill me in on their treasures they found that washed up on the beach last night after the storm. Travis found a small beach ball, Fabian discovered a blue glass bottle, and Trevor found a deck shoe and a special shell.

"We found several really great pieces of drift wood, right Uncle Pax?" Silas asks before shoveling a heaping fork full of eggs into his mouth.

"Slow down Si," he tells the boy. "You can show Aunt Harper after we clean up the dishes."

I look down the table at him with raised eyebrows shocked he's offered to clean up after the meal. He winks at me and nods his head before reaching for a couple strips of bacon. The conversation revolves around last night's storm and all the tree branches down in the neighborhood. Each boy tells a bigger and more unrealistic story about how close the lightning must have been to our house. As we enjoy our toast and jelly a knock sounds on the door making the dogs bark and race over to the French doors on the side porch.

"I'll get it," Fabian offers wiping his greasy lips on the natural linen napkin before he runs over and let's Darrell Hutchins inside. "Guys… it's your dad."

Darrell walks in the room smiling at the scene of his children sitting down and enjoying a meal without spilling, fighting, or yelling with one another, as Silas told us that's normal at their house.

"Good morning," he says noticing Pax sitting at the head of the table. "Hi, I'm Darrell Hutchins, these munchkins' father."

"Paxton Barrett," the man says shaking my neighbor's hand. "I must say you have a lively bunch of boys."

"Thanks, I'm going to take that as a compliment since I see you made it through the storm last night. How'd you do boys?" The older Hutchins inquires then he sees the bacon left on the platter with a couple pieces of buttered toast.

"Can I offer you some coffee or maybe a bacon sandwich?" I ask smiling at the look of sheer pleasure on Darrell's face as he pulls out one empty chair and makes himself at home.

Before I can stand up and get him a cup of coffee Pax walks over with an empty cup and fills it to the rim before refilling our two mugs. Pax sets the empty pot down on the burner and returns to the table, picking up Fabian from his chair to the right of me and sets the boy on his lap then leans over and kisses me.

"That was delicious," he says licking his lips. "And the meal was terrific too."

Darrell and I both laugh as the boys roll their eyes and look over towards Pax.

"May we be excused?" Trevor asks while Travis, Silas, and Fabian wait for his response.

"Sure, go wash your hands. Aunt Harper and I will clean the dishes but you guys are on lunch detail, got it?" he asks smiling at the relieved look on the kids' faces.

"Thanks,"

"Got it, Uncle Pax,"

"Come on guys, before he changes his mind."

"Come outside when you're done, okay?"

Soon the room is peaceful again as the pups followed the boys outside. Darrell is finishing his sandwich and looks over at the two of us.

"What did you do with my kids, and how long can they stay here?" he teases making us both laugh at his quick wit.

"How's Joey's arm?" I ask scraping up the mess of crumbs from the placemat on my left.

"He's fine," the relieved father says. "He was in a lot of pain so we gave him an antihistamine and some children's pain reliever and he settled down after that. Pam's folks took her and Joey with them into town so they could see the shops on Main Street. I said I'd come over and rescue you but everything seems to be fine. How'd you sleep?"

Pax and I both look at each other and smile before he tells my neighbor, "We watched a couple movies and one by one they dropped like flies. Then the boys were too scared to sleep in the tower so they slept four across in the guest bedroom.

"Did you get caught in the storm last night?" Darrell asks fishing for Pax and my story but neither of us wants to discuss our tentative truce.

"No, I arrived shortly before the storm and ended up sleeping on the sectional after I got the kids settled." He smiles at me and says, "Harper's family left shortly after you dropped off the munchkins so I stayed and helped her with the boys, who are really great kids."

Pax carries on a conversation with Darrell discussing the twins and how difficult that must have been. Darrell shares funny details on each of his four children making me laugh out loud twice. After a half hour Darrell checks on the kids leaving Pax and me alone for the first time since I woke up.

"Are you alright?" he asks wrapping his arms around my waist as I load the dishwasher. "I hope I wasn't too rough with you. But the second I felt your body wrap around me I knew I was home."

Smiling at his description I turn to face him and lean up to kiss his lips.

"You were magnificent, as always," I tell him knowing it's the truth.

"Why thank you my dear," he says making me laugh at the bow he takes for his performance but then he becomes serious and reaches for my hands. "I just remembered we didn't use any protection… I'm sorry. Are we in danger again?" he teases making me feel good about his not losing it over the possibility of getting pregnant.

"No worries," I tell him picking up the empty glasses and placing them in the top wrack. "I went on the pill shortly after the miscarriage so we're golden."

The look on his face almost appears crestfallen but that makes no sense since he has no intention of becoming a father. He kisses the top of my head and finishes clearing off the table.

"I need to make a couple phone calls," he says pulling out his cell from his back pocket. "I'll join you and the others outside in a couple of minutes, okay?"

I smile at him and his considerate behavior. He remembered my comments on his secret calls and texts so he's being upfront and honest with me again making me see small, subtle changes in his attitude. The Hutchins and Fabian are trying to teach the dogs to play fetch but the pups are refusing to return the balls they've got clenched between their teeth. Sitting down on the deck I enjoy the warm but overcast weather and must say this has been one of the best Fourth of July parties I can remember.

16

Darrell takes the boys back to his place for the afternoon leaving Pax and me to our own devices. My first thought was to go back to bed; make up for lost time but the man had other plans. We cleared up the backyard of debris, straightened up the porch and swept all the leaves and branches that fell last night from the driveway. The entire time we're working together the pups are playing underfoot. He explains where he's been for the last three months.

"After I left Mom and Stan's I went back to our place, picked up my flight bag and left for Ottawa. Melanie insisted I take a couple of days off so I got drunk and spent the next four days in a stupor at an apartment the magazine owns," he says pushing the garage broom a bit harder than necessary.

"Was she there?" I ask making him smile but shake his head.

"I never slept with her Harper," he tells me. "Sleeping with the boss is never a good idea."

Bending over to pick up a large stick I look at him and say, "Who was it then."

He bows his head for a couple seconds and when he looks up at me I see remorse.

"Candace Whitaker, but it's not what you're thinking," he says dropping the broom handle and walking over to stand in front of me.

"You slept with Candace? She's married and has two kids…" I remind him stunned that the woman I saw, talked with, shared a coffee in the break room several times since my non-wedding was the woman he cheated on me with.

"Calm down Harper," he begins when he sees the anger on my face. "Let me explain."

"Oh, please do," I snap at him feeling more embarrassed and hurt than before knowing the woman's identity. "She and I are working on several projects together. How am I supposed to finish them now? No, wait, I know… when we break for coffee or lunch we can compare notes, study your moves, and maybe improve on your technique."

I brush past him intent on going back into the house and locking him outside but he has other plans. He scoops me up in his arms and carries me into the house with me kicking and screaming at him to put me down and leave, all of which he ignores. He drops me on the sectional and covers me with his body, preventing me from getting up.

"Harper God dammit stop it," he hisses at me as I push on his chest. "Listen to me, I only slept with her one time, after that all we did was talk, I swear to you."

"You swear to me? Like you promise me?" I sneer at him and notice the split second he loses his patience. He grabs my chin between his fingers and holds me still before kissing me hard, I mean punishingly hard. I continue to fight him but with my hands in his hair, pushing our mouths closer together. Instead of a sensual kiss it's an all-out assault. Digging my hands in his scalp I grab a handful of his thick brown hair and pull back making him release my lips from his. Panting and gasping for air I glare up at him as he angrily stares down at me.

"I don't think I'm ready to hear about your sexual escapades just yet," I whisper hating the break in my voice and the tears that start to well up in my eyes. He let's go of my chin and sits up on the sofa leaving me cold and on the verge of an emotional breakdown.

"Harper I never cheated on you the entire time we were together, except after I found out you were pregnant. Candace and I were at the main office on one of my trips and we ended up in the bar, commiserating on our troubles. Her divorce was being drawn out by her husband and she was feeling as badly abused as I imagined myself to be," he says not even looking at me but down at his feet.

"You were that angry at me over the baby?" I ask shocked he felt that way.

"Yes," he replies then looks over at me and I see the shame in his eyes but also the flash of determination. "Neither one of us remembers much about that night but when we woke up the next morning she was as mortified as I was. We spent the morning talking about what happened with our perfect lives and we became each other's confidant."

Pushing up off the sofa I angrily turn on him hurt he could talk to a virtual stranger, well a one night stand instead of me.

"Why didn't you come to me? Do you have any idea how much hearing you'd rather talk to a one night stand turned buddy hurts me?" I shout through my tears as he just sits there letting me rant at him.

"I thought you were insensitive before but now you're just unbelievable," I rail at him venting my hurt, my anger, and a crushing desire to punish him for his infidelity. "You went on several trips to Ottawa, when did you start sleeping around on me?"

He leans back on the sofa and shakes his head at me, refusing to tell me details.

"What's wrong? Can't you remember? Or where there others besides Candace?" I shout at him but again he refuses to divulge more information. "If you're not going to tell me I think we're done talking. You better leave before I say something we'll both regret later."

Pax smiles up at me then crosses his arms over his chest and says, "You mean there are more insults you want to throw at me? Go ahead, get it out of your system that way we can clear the air and start over."

Amazed he's making fun of my feelings I walk out of the room and slam the bathroom door shut, turning the lock so he'll leave me alone. Staring at my reflection in the mirror I'm surprised I still look normal. My hair should be singed, my eyes bleeding, and my jaws swollen from gnashing my teeth together. But all I see are tear stained cheeks, a pinched, pale complexion and red rimmed eyes. What I can't see but can feel is my aching heart. Splashing water on my face I sit down on the closed lid of the commode and rest my head in my hands, dreading going back out there and hearing more of his new 'friendship' with a woman that offered me a sympathetic hug on the first day I returned to the office. My God how she must have laughed her head off telling him how gullible I was during one of their many pow wows. I feel the anger rush through my system like the first hit of caffeine in the morning. Drying my eyes, I unlock the door and walk back into the living room but he's no longer sitting there. A movement out on the side porch catches my eye as I see Pax talking on his cell phone. It takes no genius to figure out who he's calling so I turn and head out the back door and walk down towards the lake needing to clear my head.

The clouds are clearing revealing the soft pale blue sky above which helps me feel somewhat better. The pups run after me making a smile appear on my face at their still awkward gait but they're the best company right now. We walk with no destination in mind, stopping sometimes to investigate some new object they've never seen before. I wave at several residents either on their decks cleaning up the debris or in their yards assessing any damage they might have received from the tempest of last night.

Half way around the lake I turn around and head back home before the pups tire out completely and I must carry them, which would be a sight since they already reach my mid-thigh. Picking up a stick I toss it in front of me where they chase after it and playfully fight over the piece of wood until I tug it out of their mouths and start the game all over again. After the third throw I notice we're back home on our share of the beach and I see Paxton is still on the phone but he's now sitting on the back deck, ankle crossed over his knee as he lounges back in one of the Adirondack chairs. Just as I walk past him his hand snakes out, catching me in a vise-like grip that makes me stare down into his espresso colored eyes.

"Hey thanks brother," he says into his cell phone, "Yeah, I'll see you then, bye."

He sets his phone on the wide arm of the chair and continues to stare up at me.

"Feel better?" he asks smiling as Kirby puts both his front paws on the man's lap forcing him to release my arm so he can protect himself against the affectionate hound. I continue inside the house and hear him talking to the pups before he opens the door and the dogs walk inside, him included.

"Harper come on, let's finish this discussion and then we never have to speak about it again," he tells me walking over to stand in front of me.

"Until you speak with your girlfriend," I tell him making him bristle at my tone. "Tell me Pax," I continue needling him, "what did she say when you spoke to her while ago?"

His silence speaks volumes letting me know she was who he was on the phone with when I stepped out of the bathroom. I brush past him and open the fridge, pulling out a jug of orange juice and fill a small glass before putting it back.

"I called her to say we were talking again, okay? Is that a crime to talk to my friend?" he says starting to let go of his own frustration.

"It is when that 'friend' is the woman you screwed while we were together," I snap at him taking another sip of the refreshing drink. "She actually hugged me in sympathy over our non-wedding the first day I returned to work, can you believe it? I'll bet she called you and the two of you had a good laugh over that, didn't you?"

I toss back the rest of the juice and set the glass in the

sink, but when I turn around Pax pins me to the sink, caging me between his strong arms. Looking up into his angry face I feel the first touch of fear I've pushed him to his limit and I did.

"Cut the crap," he snarls down at me leaning mere inches from my face. "I told you about Candy, but if you choose to believe otherwise I can't stop you. But I won't have her thrown up in my face anymore. It was one time Harper. One stupid, purely physical release only, uneventful time and we both regretted it believe me."

I stare up at him and know he lied once again.

"I thought neither of you remembered what happened?" I hiss at him and he snaps.

Grabbing my upper arms, he pulls me roughly to his body where his mouth punishes mine in a brutal kiss. My temper finds the perfect outlet and I come unwound on him. He lifts me up and I wrap my legs around his waist, clawing at his shirt needing to touch his hot skin. I feel his teeth nipping on my bottom lip as I pull his hair, forcing him closer. Together we maul one another until our shirts are off, my bra is pushed up under my arms and he's attached himself to my breast, clenching his hands on my buttocks.

He is rough with me but it's what I need, raking my fingers down his back and across his powerful shoulders. When he picks me up and sets me down on the cold marble counter top of the island I barely notice so engrossed in his turbulent lovemaking. Only when he unbuckles my belt do I come to my senses.

"Not here," I tell him afraid the boys might come back and interrupt us.

"Right," is all he says then tugs me off the counter and

races upstairs pulling me forcefully behind him. "Hurry up," he says over his shoulder still in a brutal temper.

"Move it then," I reply in a harsh tone, "You're in the lead."

He frowns at me but picks up his pace and once we're in the bedroom he slams the door behind him and locks it. Kicking off his shoes he unsnaps his jeans when he notices I'm not getting undressed.

"Harper, if I have to strip you down I will," he makes me grin at that image but it works and I'm naked under the sheets in mere seconds with him lying between my legs. The anger is dissipating but not the need. He scoots down until his shoulders and head are positioned at the apex of my thighs. His hot breath is blowing across my sensitive flesh as he lowers his mouth to my core.

"Just so you know," he begins and presses a kiss in the crease of my thigh and torso, "I never kissed her like this."

I press my legs together when I realize he will talk about his making love to Candace but he stops me with his hands on my thighs.

"No, you started this, you'll hear me out," he tells me and opens my folds with his long blunt tipped fingers and kisses me in my most secret spot. "I never touched her like this; it never crossed my mind to be intimate with her… not like we are with each other."

His words cut me like a knife but he refuses to stop.

"She never cried out from her soul like you do when we make love. There was no touching, caressing, or even deep, wet kisses as I recall, not like when we touch," he says sliding one finger inside my passage, making me start to squirm from his ministrations. "She never whispered how much she liked it the way you do, especially when you want me to move deeper or harder inside you…"

My body goes up in flames as he suckles my nubbin, bringing forth one soulful cry he was talking about. I grab his head with both my hands and force him harder between my legs, rising off the bed as I strive to reach that special place he always takes me to. Repeatedly he laps his tongue across my flesh, making me twist and turn for more until he rises and swiftly enters me in one long stroke, seating his shaft to the base.

"God I can't get enough of you," he growls, "Hold on baby, I'm not going to last but a few strokes" and he pumps his life force inside me after the second drag of his rod. Pax loses himself in me until he's spent then drops down on my chest, refusing to pull out of me but needing a moment to catch his breath. When he raises his head, he stares at me without speaking then kisses me softly, with love not passion. Once again, he brings me to tears with his gentleness.

"I never made love to any woman but you," he whispers. "There's a difference between a mercy fuck and what we share, remember that next time."

"There won't be a next time," I tell him raising my chin in defiance. "If I catch you with someone else, you won't have anything left to fuck with."

He stares at me for two seconds then cracks up laughing, making me giggle. We kiss one final time before he separates our bodies and rolls over on his back staring up at the ceiling.

"Forgive me?" he asks making me turn my head towards him and smile.

"You have to ask me that after what we just experienced?" I tease him making him turn his head towards me and grin.

"We always burnt up the sheets didn't we," he replies with a hint of pride in his voice.

"No complaints there," I tell him and let out a sigh of satisfaction.

We doze off for a little bit only to be woken from a knock on the bedroom door.

"Aunt Harper? Are you in there?" Fabian asks a touch of worry in his voice.

"Yes Fabe," I tell him nudging Pax's sleeping form next to me. "I'll be right down."

"Wait until you see what I got at the store," he says then I hear his footsteps thumping down the stairs to speak to my unseen neighbor. "She's hear Mr. Hutchins, I'll see you later, guys." Then he runs past my door and I hear him stomping up the stairs to the watch tower room.

"Tell the boy mommy and daddy is sleeping," Pax yawns rolling over on his side.

"Get up Pops," I tell him swatting his backside on my way to the bathroom and picking up my clothes as I go. "Or should I send the pups in?"

"Geesh," he groans. "A man needs his sleep especially after that last round. I'll be down in a little bit, okay?"

"Okay, but you're on your own for lunch mister," I warn him and he chuckles underneath the sheet as I close the bathroom door.

As I step into the hall a couple minutes later I hear Fabian in the tower room. Quietly walking up the stairs I'm shocked at the loot the boy has strewn about the room.

"Fabian? Where did all these fireworks come from?" I

ask picking up cartons of low grade explosives and making a place on the cushioned bench underneath the window for me to sit down.

"Mr. Naples said he was letting these items go at cut rate prices," he quotes the hardware store owner. "'The rain put a damper on the festivities,' he said so Mr. Hutchins bought the lot and then said me and the boys could split the items he didn't want."

"Fabe, you've got enough stuff to host your own fireworks display," I warn him. "Where are you going to shoot these guys off?"

"Well, Mr. Hutchins said the town was going to have the firework display tonight at ten o'clock, so he's going to have a warm up show," he tells me. "We're invited to watch, but he said we couldn't help him. Mr. Samuels is going to help him. He bought a lot of stuff too."

The Hutchins boys' grandfather, Nick is a pistol and I can imagine the blast those two men will have detonating their glitter bombs over the lake. I hug the boy and ask if he's hungry to which he replies, "Yes, all I had to each since breakfast was a granola bar. Mrs. Hutchins doesn't cook normal food. Can I have a sandwich or something like that?"

"You sure can, how about some loaded nachos instead?" I offer wanting something hot and spicy myself.

"Yeah that sounds great," he laughs and hugs me back. He looks up at me and says, "Mrs. Hutchins asked me if you and Uncle Pax were getting married. Are you going to marry Uncle Pax?"

Smiling down at his innocent face I tap the end of his nose and say, "not anytime soon buddy."

"We haven't really discussed a time frame yet pal," Pax says from his leaning position in the door frame, he's dressed in his low riding jeans and nothing else. "But when we do set a date, you'll be one of the first to know, deal?"

"Deal," he says nodding his head and reaching for Pax's hand. "Look at all the cool stuff I got from Mr. Hutchins."

Pax lets the boy pull him towards the window seat where the stash is piled up. He looks at me as he passes and says, "I meant what I said, and we will get married, soon."

"Let's discuss this topic later," I hedge and step out of his reach making him chuckle before he turns his attention back to Fabian. "Hey Harpo, I'd like some loaded nachos too."

Shaking my head at his silly grin I walk downstairs and pet the pups waking from their nap. It dawns on me my house feels like a home and I fix my crazy family the best nacho supreme dinner they've ever eaten.

17

Sitting in the Adirondack chair next to Pax I smile as he links our fingers together and brings them towards his lips. His kiss, no matter what part of my body he touches makes me tingle all over. We're watching the pre-fireworks show courtesy of the Hutchins-Samuels family. The boys are getting bored due to the long lapse of action. The amateurs are giving it their all but it doesn't appear to be enough to keep the kids entertained.

"I'm going to see if I can help speed this show along," he leans over and kisses my lips. "I don't want you to fall asleep before I put you asleep."

I laugh at his turn of the phrase but get his meaning as he walks around the side of the house. We've spent the afternoon playing with the kids and their small-scale fire crackers, smoke bombs, and bottle rockets. The pups no longer jump at the shrill or pop of the devices having gotten used to the noise by now. York is lying under my chair, at least his front shoulders, head and paws. Kirby follows Pax but stops when he shoos the dog back towards me. Kirby listens and meanders back towards me and drops down in the grass beside his brother with a doggy harrumph...

"This is boring," Fabian whines as he walks over and sits down in the vacant chair beside me. "How much longer before the real show begins?"

I look at my wristwatch in the small light left in the sky and see there's only a half hour to go. The pathway lamps are on, the fireflies are out and I can hear the frogs and the cicadas singing their nightly serenade.

"Soon," I tell him and ruffle his soft brown hair. "Are you getting excited about fishing with your dad?"

He grins and replays the long list of things he will be doing with his father. It amazes me how good Ginger and Chip get along since their divorce. I've known both since college and have to admit they're better apart. Even after her ex-husband announced he was getting married, the former couple remained great friends. There is such a thing as a mutually satisfying divorce. The Hutchins brothers' race over towards us and lean against both the chairs, out of breath and excited about something. Little Joey runs over to me and holds out his arms wanting me to pick him up on my lap.

"Hey there little Joe," I snuggle with him as he wiggles on my lap. "I haven't seen you in so long, how's your Ouchy?"

He holds his arm mere inches from my face to show me two dinosaur plastic bandages and he points to each one.

"This one really hurts," he says intently staring at the green and brown cartoon character on his arm. "But this one really, really hurts."

I smile at the little guy as he turns around to face the lake like he's getting ready to watch a movie. He leans back onto my chest and plays with my fingers holding him steady.

"Aunt Harper, guess what?" Silas asks me. "Uncle Pax is helping Daddy and Grandpa make a big 'Splosion!'"

"He is? Oh man, this is going to be great," I reply with a touch more enthusiasm than I'm actually feeling. "Are they getting ready?"

"Yeah," Trevor says sitting on the arm of Fabian's chair while his brother Trevor is on the other side. "They told us to find a seat and sit back for a wild and crazy show."

Silas runs around to the other side of my chair and climbs up on the arm, leaning into my shoulder for support. We wait for a couple more minutes before a dozen bottle rockets shoot up in the air, one after the other. The boys laugh and point at each one, seeing if it went further than the last. Another barrage of pinpoint light shoots up and over towards the lake making several neighbors clap at the mini show of lights. Next hundreds of screaming, twirling, and colorful tails are streaking across the sky making me laugh with the kids. Soon an answering volley from across the far side of the lake makes our guys amp up their showmanship with roman candles exploding into the stygian night sky. For the next twenty minutes the sky is lit up with microbursts of glittering bombs while good natured ribbing is exchanged between the opposing camps. As a grand finale on the Hutchins side another battalion of mini torpedoes streak across the water some barely clearing the surface, but the reflection on the water doubles the impact. The show was a complete success, the crowd was impressed according to the oohs, aahs, and applause they garnered.

When the men come around the house we all applaud their magnificent display of fire power. Carrying a small cooler Darrell hugs his kids and accepts their generous praise. Their grandfather is laughing and tipping his bottle towards Pax as he walks over and picks up Fabian then sets the sleeping boy back on his lap. Leaning over, careful not to wake a sleeping Joey I kiss him and whisper, "This comes close to the excitement of last year's display…"

He laughs out loud and says, "that's just the appetizer sweetie," and winks making me giggle like a school girl. Soon Pam joins us and spreads a blanket on the ground for the boys while they set up their lawn chairs in a row. She walks over and takes her sleeping child from my arms and whispers, "Thanks but I know your arms must be getting tired. Your man did a marvelous job of setting up the fireworks, didn't he?"

Looking over at his grinning face I pick up his hand and say, "that's one of the reasons I keep him around, he lights up my life."

She laughs at the double entendre and then walks over to her kids stretched out on the blanket as the first of the professional fireworks begins. I can feel Pax's eyes on me, watching my reaction and thinking about where we were at last year. Licking my upper lip I whisper, "Watch the sky not me."

"They're just bursts of gunpowder and magnesium, you're what's amazing," he teases and refills my wine glass from the half empty bottle lying between our chairs. "If we were alone, do you know what I'd be doing right now?" he whispers sending a shiver of pleasure down my spine.

"Yes, you'd be coming inside my mouth as I pleasure you with oral sex," I reply making him spew the sip of beer he just took. I laugh as he mops up his chin with his shirt tail.

"Damn, you read my mind," he laughs and reaches for my hand, linking our fingers together as we watch the thirty-minute show. He leans over and kisses me long and deeply as the grand finale explodes across the sky, but my interest lie in the bright flashes going off behind my closed eyes as he begins the prelude to our lovemaking.

Fabian and Silas come running over waking up the dogs as they relive the excitement of watching the display. Not wanting Pax to feel slighted Fabian says, "But yours were better because I know you and you didn't know what you were doing but it turned out great."

Poking my Godson in the belly he replies, "Thanks a lot Fabian that makes me feel a lot better."

"You're welcome," he says then turns towards me. "Can Silas sleep over again tonight?"

Silas whispers something in his friend's ear and Fabian nods his head before he says, "May Silas sleep over again tonight?"

Pax and I both laugh when he says, "Sure, the guest room or the watch tower?"

"Watchtower!" they shout in unison then laugh and walk back to share the good news to Silas' parents.

"Way to go Pax," I tell him. "Now we have to keep it down to a roar."

"I'm going to sex you up so much you'll lose the ability to speak," he promises and nuzzles my neck until the boys return.

"Hey Uncle Pax would you like to play with our army men?" Fabian asks all excited about having another sleep over.

My sweetheart turns and says, "Don't worry; I'll be back as soon as I kick the enemies butt."

The boys burst out in giggles and tug on the grown up's wrists helping him get out of the chair. He lifts each boy under his arms and carries them up to the deck before he turns and hollers for me.

"Come on woman, don't you want to send your man off to war with a smile?" he asks making the neighbors within hearing range whistle and clap with offers to take my place.

Reaching for the wine bottle and empty beer bottles I catch up to the silly trio and open the door for them and wait on the pups to come inside. Pouring the last of the wine in my glass I notice the time, quarter to eleven.

"By the time it takes me to finish my wine, you boys must go to bed, including you Paxton," I tell him making him wink at me. "I'm taking a bath so don't forget to wash up and brush your teeth before you go to sleep, okay?"

"I'll take the fold up bed into the watch tower room, get them situated and then I'll be down," he says rubbing the pups behind their ears. "Just don't fall asleep in there."

"Or in the bed, right?" I counter making him wag his finger at me.

"I'll have to punish you if you do," he whispers and grins at the image that popped into his head. "On second thought…"

"I'll wait up for you," I interrupt his deviant thought making him frown and snap his fingers in disappointment. "Goodnight guys," I tell the boys and head upstairs alone since the dogs will stay with Pax until he comes upstairs.

Setting the glass on the vanity I fill the tub and light the candles for the ambience I want to create. Soft music is playing from the stereo in the bedroom as I undress and slip into the hot oil scented water. The smell alone is enough to put me in a sensual mood. The earthy fragrance of sandalwood always relaxes me yet stimulates my senses. Next to Pax it's my favorite scent…

18

By Saturday evening I'm exhausted and ready for bed by nine. Chip picked up Fabian around eleven this morning and even though I hated to see him go, he was ready to spend some time away from the Hutchins brothers. Chip assured me Fabian would have a blast at their cabin and he congratulated me on my new place making Pax stare at me for a couple seconds before hugging Fabian goodbye. After they left we took his boat out for the afternoon, had a picnic lunch, made love in the small cabin below deck and each of us received a great deal of sun. Over a light supper of grilled chicken breasts, salad, and raspberry sorbet we talked about his new position in Ottawa and how even though it's only temporary, he likes the people he works with. We spend a quiet couple of hours watching TV before he says he's beat. Once we're in bed however he gets a second wind. After a rousing hour of fireworks, he hugs me to his side.

"You're not renting this place, are you?" he asks making me laugh as I turn my head on the pillow to face him.

"No, I bought it, at least the bank and I did, why?" I ask drawing lazy circles in his chest hair.

"So… you're not planning on returning to the city, except

to work," he states showing me where this conversation is heading. I lean up on my elbow and look at him through the moonlight streaming in through the French doors leading out to the balcony.

"No Paxton, I live here, this is where I call home," I softly reply. "You thought I was going to move back to your apartment, didn't you?"

"Yeah, I did," he says in an exasperated tone. "What the hell Harper, you're stuck out here and don't get me wrong, it's a great place and I love the small town of Lake Sinclaire, but we work in the city, we travel because of our jobs… so you're telling me you're going to commute both ways, every day from here to Albany. That's going to get old real fast, babe."

"Paxton I've changed. I don't want the fast-paced city life any longer," I tell him making him snort in derision. "It's true. I felt an instant pull the second you and I drove past this place back in March. I love it here, with the boys, the lake, the pups…and besides, Star doesn't travel all that much and she'll travel even less when she takes over Melanie's job. I'm content, for now."

He's quiet for a spell then asks, "What about us?"

"What about us? It shouldn't matter where either of us lives; it's not like we're getting married silly. You have your place, I have mine," I tell him. "I thought you'd like that aspect of our getting back together."

He shifts his position in bed, scooting up to rest his shoulder blades on the oil finished metal headboard.

"No, I don't like that idea at all," he says in his old petulant tone. "We'll be forever driving back and forth.

That's at least ninety minutes out of the day spent in our cars."

"Oh, boo hoo," I tease him making him glare at my response. "Traffic at rush hour is every bit of that time and possibly more. What's really pissed you off is I'm not moving back to your place, and I haven't asked you to move in with me, right?"

He finally grins at me and admits I'm right.

"I want to be together on a permanent basis Harper," he explains drawing me over to kiss my lips. "Don't you want to live together again?"

I press my lips to his and soon we're lost in a deeply satisfying kiss. Pressing back so he can see my face I reply, "No, I don't want to live with you in that apartment, with Wiley and his minions coming and going below us. I want to put down roots, live in my own house; I've grown up and won't revert to your college-like atmosphere again. I'm sorry if you assumed I'd move back in with you, but I like living out here in the middle of nowhere."

"Don't you love me? Don't you want to share my life?" he asks totally confused at my lack of enthusiasm over us getting back together.

"Honey I love you, with all my heart. But I'm not going to repeat the same mistakes we made. I told you I'm not the same woman." I kiss him over his heart before I whisper, "and I certainly hope you're not the same man."

"What's that supposed to mean?" he demands tugging on my hair so I must look up at him.

"You nearly broke me three months ago," I remind him. "All I said is I hope you're not the same man that would do that to me again. Didn't you learn anything from our non-wedding?"

"Stop calling it that," he hisses getting upset with me. "And yes, I learned plenty," he snaps at me tossing off the sheet and getting out of bed. "I thought you'd be happy I wanted to get back together again, and I really thought we were going to do just that, especially after spending the last three days together, but I guess I was wrong."

"Yep, you were wrong," I tell him leaning my head in my hand as he paces the width of the room in agitation. "Pax, stop this nonsense and come back to bed."

He twirls around and says, "Nonsense? What the hell are you calling nonsense? The fact I want to get back together, move in with each other again, and see each other exclusively... is that what you're calling nonsense?"

"No, I called your behavior nonsense," I remind him. "You think because you came back to the states, spent the holiday with me and my family that I want to jump back into the same old scene with you, right?"

He nods his head in reply and I can't help the laugh that escapes my lips.

"Paxton Joseph Barrett," I sigh making him cross his arms over his chest and fume. "Baby, you're sure good looking but apparently not all that bright."

He storms off into the bathroom so I get up and wander downstairs, the pups following me as I head into the kitchen for a glass of wine. I know in this mood he will argue all night long. Uncorking a bottle of Merlot I fill a glass from the cabinet and walk into the living room, turning on a lamp on the end table.

"What are you doing down there?" he shouts from the landing. "Come back to bed and let's discuss this."

That usually means he wants to make love and convince me he's right so I pick up my glass and take a sip before setting it down and scratching Kirby's belly.

"Nope, I no longer solve problems by 'sleeping' on it," I holler back and can't help but grin when I hear him tromp down the stairs.

"What the hell is that supposed to mean?" he demands again, reaching for my glass off the table.

"I didn't stutter Pax, you know exactly what I meant," I take the glass from his hand and hold it in mine looking up at his angry face. "You're not going to bully, intimidate, coerce, or convince me you're right, so knock it off. Now we can spend the rest of the night fighting or we can go back to bed, make love, and then have bacon and pancakes like we used to do on Sundays, your call."

He continues to stare at me then lifts his arms out to the side and drops his chin on his chest in defeat. I guess he'll never outgrow that maneuver.

"Let's go to bed," he says holding out his hand. "You certainly have changed, I'll give you that."

"I have you to thank for the changes," I tease him making him wrap his arm around my neck and tilt my head back he plants a rough kiss on my lips.

"You're welcome," he whispers and then softens his next kiss as he takes the glass of wine out of my hand, offers me a sip before he finishes it and leaves the stemware on the kitchen island as we walk past and head back upstairs.

Later he rolls us over on our sides and he buries his face in my damp hair before he says, "I love you even though you've become a bit more assertive, almost belligerent at times."

Looking over my shoulder I smile and say, "Thanks, I love you too even when you think you can manipulate me. Get used to it Pax, I've grown up and I won't be pushed around, walked on, or lied to. Remember that and you and I will have the best relationship imaginable."

"Shut up and go to sleep," he chuckles and I do just that.

19

Sunday we spend together knowing he must leave so he can get back to his place in the city. After the promised breakfast of pancakes, maple syrup from Vermont, and bacon we take the dogs out for a romp on the beach. Pax returned his rented sailboat yesterday so we spent the day in the lake, swimming, playing with the dogs, and acting like kids with one another. We even spent several hours in bed. I'll ache for a week but it was well worth it. By six o'clock he got moody and I knew it's because he had to drive back to the city alone since I refused once again over breakfast to move back in with him.

"Paxton, for the last time no," I snapped at his constant barrage of jabs over breakfast. "You're behaving worse than the Hutchins brothers when they didn't get their way yesterday morning. They're four, six, and seven years old... knock it off or leave for the city now." I told him making him remain silent for a whole three minutes.

"Sorry," he apologized, "it's just I'm afraid of losing you, again."

"You threw me away the last time, remember? If you want to leave again, I can't stop you, but know this... I won't take the high road with you again," I told him and even though he didn't like what I said, he believed me and that's all that mattered.

Now stretched out on the sectional, spooning my back to his front he falls asleep. Just as I'm about to nod off my cell phone rings waking him enough to tell me, "your phone is ringing," before he rolls over and nearly pushes me off the sofa.

"Hi Mom," I say into the phone after checking the screen for the caller's name. "What's up?"

"Hi honey, just calling to see how your weekend was, did Fabian enjoy himself?" she asks giving me the lead in to describe the holiday weekend I spent except for Pax, I fill her in and we talk about the upcoming week and that she was sorry we didn't have our normal Sunday brunch but with the holiday and having closed the restaurant my father is super busy. We talk for about a half hour and she tells me to have a great week and she'd see me next weekend. Ending the call I walk back into the living room and see Pax is awake. I sit at the end of the sofa and wait for him to speak.

"You didn't mention to your mom I spent the weekend here," he says almost in an accusatory tone, "Why not?"

"Honey you know why I didn't," I tell him. "But don't worry, Dad, Mom, and Vic know you spent the fourth on the sailboat watching me."

"What? They know and yet you didn't mention we made up? Why not?" he demands and I'm starting to feel he's picking a fight with me for some reason.

"First off, we're not fourteen years old, and we didn't get back together, at least not like you're implying. I'm too old to go steady with you." I tease him but he sees no humor

175

so I continue. "Second, I said they know you were in the vicinity, I didn't say they'd not come unglued if they knew you spent the weekend with me. Besides, it's really nobody's business what we do. Plus," I rally in my argument, "I'm not sure where we're going with this revised you and me thing, it's too new, too personal that I don't want to jinx things if you can't accept the changes in me."

"What the hell are you talking about?" he asks sitting up and running his fingers through his hair. "We're back together. I'd shout it from the roof tops but only three families would hear it out here. And don't think I give a damn what your family thinks, because I don't. I love you dammit... we belong together."

Crawling over to sit on his lap I cuddle with him until he wraps his arm around my shoulders and tugs me backward. Kissing me in such a soft, gentle manner I moan in delight until he lifts his head and smiles down at me.

"You're going to miss me when I'm gone," he whispers making me grin up at him.

"Ditto, so instead of arguing, let's make love, right here, right now," I offer and he removes my black tank top and unsnapping my khaki shorts when his cell phone rings. "Don't answer it," I warn him having a sick premonition that call will cut short our time together.

"Give me a second," he says after he looks at the screen and sees the caller's name. He scoots me off his lap, stands up and walks out of my hearing.

Whoever is on the other end must be important so I straighten my clothes and stand up to let the dogs outside for a late afternoon romp. We're outside maybe ten minutes when Pax joins us pulling his overnight bag over his shoulder.

"Sorry hon," he says leaning down to pet the dog's heads. "I got to go, but I'll call you later."

"What happened?" I ask knowing he's going to either clam up or become vague, and he chooses vague.

"Wiley needs me, and trust me you don't want to know why," he laughs but the amusement never reaches his eyes. He's lying.

"Okay, drive safely back to the city," I tell him standing on tip toe to kiss him goodbye.

He stares at me as if he wants to explain but then changes his mind and reaches for my hand as we walk towards the drive where he's parked his jag all weekend.

"I'm sorry," he begins but instead of listening to his lame excuse I force his head down towards me and kiss him with all the love and passion I feel for him.

"Just say goodbye, don't lie to me, please." I tell him and he nods his head in understanding.

"You're the only woman I want Harper Mead, remember that," he opens his car door slinging his bag across the seat. "Will I see you tomorrow?"

"No, I don't return until Wednesday, but I'll talk to you before then," I assure him and already I miss having him around.

"Take care sweetie, bye York and Kirby," he bends down and ruffles their fur. "Take care of mommy until I get back." Then he stands up and pulls me roughly in his arms and says against my lips, "You and I are back together, whether you admit it or not," he kisses me hard and quick before he leans back and says, "I'll be back here real soon."

"I look forward to that," I reply and mean it too. "Drive

safely and I'll see you Wednesday at the sales meeting, don't be late."

"Nag… nag… nag…" he laughs when I stick out my tongue then the powerful engine roars to life and he's pulling out of my drive and onto the old highway heading back towards the city.

"Come on boys," I sink my fingers in to their coats, "let's go get me a drink and you a treat and rethink this whole Paxton situation, okay?"

They follow me indoors and together we spend a boring, uneventful and lonely evening wishing Pax was still with us.

20

Walking to the executive conference room Wednesday morning I can't wait to see Pax. We've spoken every evening since he returned to the city but just the thought of seeing him today made sleep virtually impossible last night. I was up at the crack of dawn trying to decide what to wear. Finally, I chose a deep salmon colored sheath I belted with a thin brown leather belt, and then paired it with a white blazer and brown leather pumps. I feel empowered, even sexy and can't wait to see the man. Carrying my traveler mug with my electronic tablet I walk into the room and see several people already seated but I don't see Pax. Star walks in and then the meeting proceeds without him. Halfway through the sales meeting Wiley walks in looking ragged, at least by his standards. He nods at Star and apologizes for being delayed then spends the next hour avoiding eye contact with me.

When we break for lunch I wave at him catching his attention but then he turns and quickly leaves the room. Before I can reach him, he's gone, as if he's disappeared. I head back to my new office and eat the lunch I prepared and keep checking my messages but Pax is not returning calls or texts, same goes for Wiley. Ginger joins me in my office and sits down, crosses her long legs and sighs brushing imaginary lint off her black pencil skirt.

"When are you ever going to learn?" she asks staring a hole in me making me aware she is unhappy with my dating arrangement. "Tell me my son has a wild imagination, or that he's delusional…anything but that his Uncle Pax spent the weekend with you two and you're getting married, this time for real."

"I take it Chip dropped off Fabian last night," I tell her and from the smirk on her face, she got an earful. "Everything except for the marriage is true. We're seeing each other again, but before you come unhinged know that I'm not repeating the same mistakes I made last time."

She reaches over and takes half of my turkey and Swiss sandwich without being offered and says, "No, you're making all new ones, aren't you?" She takes a large bite of my sandwich and I watch as a large dollop of salad dressing oozes out of the tightly gripped entrée. "Dammit, I dropped mayo on my new blouse," She cringes as she tries to wipe off the oily condiment from her white silk blouse but is only making it worse.

"Don't start," I warn her. "He's supposed to be in this meeting, he even said 'see you tomorrow,' when I spoke to him last night on the phone; but where is he?"

"God, it's starting already," she snarls at me then changes her tone to an irritating squeaky little girl's voice. "Oh Ginger, where is he? Who's he with? Is he cheating on me again?"

I snatch the uneaten sandwich out of her hand and say, "Bite me."

"I'd rather hit you," she replies and leans forward. "Girl he's not to be trusted, what's it going to take to make you see he's a snake?"

"Leave my office Ginger before you say something I won't be able to forget," I warn her before she stands up and heads for the door.

"Don't say I didn't warn you," she snaps then races back over to my desk and takes back the unguarded half of my sandwich before she runs out the door.

Forty-five minutes later the meeting resumes but still Pax is a no show. Now Wiley is missing. I lean over towards Star and look at the notes she's notorious for taking.

'Applegate doctor apt'

'Hughes at funeral'

'Whitaker family emergency'

'Wiley at doctor appointment -r blood work'

'Barrett jury duty'

There is no way in hell those last three excuses are valid. I slip my phone under the table and text Pax.

"Where the hell are you?"

"Don't ask" he replies immediately.

"Too late and don't lie"

"Can't tell you"

"Kiss my ass"

"Would love too"

"Fat chance"

"You're just the right size"

"You're an idiot but I love you anyway"

"Thank God"

"Harper! I asked if you have the updated figures for last quarter." Star asks me interrupting my texting and bringing me back to the meeting at hand. Focusing on the moment I hand her the documents she's asking for and somehow make it through the rest of the meeting without another incident. I feel like the afternoon drags on for hours when it's only three o'clock. Star walks out of her office and says, "I'm heading out, have those figures for me first thing tomorrow morning. You look a bit worn out, go ahead and leave when you've finished that report, okay?"

I smile not telling her I finished the report ten minutes ago. I quickly grab my purse, briefcase, and travel mug and leave the building deciding on surprising Pax at his place. Pulling over to the curb I notice Wiley's vehicle is parked out front in its usual spot behind Pax's Jag. That means he's home and about to get into trouble for playing hooky.

Walking up the steps I open the front door, which is always unlocked and slip upstairs unnoticed by Wiley. Pax always left a spare key hanging on a small nail behind the newel post so I take the key and let myself inside our old apartment. Little has changed, the living room is mussed up, shoes and socks strewn about the floor, dirty dishes and empty beer bottles cover the coffee table. I walk through the other rooms and see they're in need of a good cleaning as well but Pax is not home. I drop my bags on the sofa and start to tidy up the place. By the time I reach the bedroom I'm shocked at the women's clothing draped over the club chair and at the foot of the bed. Make up, hair products, and perfume are scattered across the vanity in the bathroom proof the man has not been living alone. I pick up one of the perfume bottles and accidently drop the lid into the sink making a lot of noise. I bend down to retrieve the cap and hear Wiley in the living room.

"Pax, I'm glad you're back. You should have seen Harper today," he begins thinking he's unloading on his best friend. "She was shooting daggers at me. You have to come clean man, before she finds out about Candace and the girls…"

He stops short when he sees me standing in the doorway. The man has been home long enough to change out of his business suit and looks comfortable in khaki cargo shorts, black t-shirt, and athletic socks.

"What the hell are you doing here?" he demands then holds his hands up in front of his chest as if to keep me from running out of the room. "It's not what you think," he begins but it's exactly what I think and he knows it. I walk up to him and stomp on his sock feet making him jump out of the way. I race out of the bedroom, grab my purse and bag and run down the stairs to the front door. Taking the front steps two at a time I make it to my car before I hyperventilate. Taking two calming breaths I rest my head on the steering wheel. When I feel under control again I look up just in time to see a taxi cab pull up to the curb and Pax gets out of the vehicle then turns to assist Candace out and he wraps his arm around her waist. She leans heavily on him and he practically smothers her in his arms as they walk up the steps and enter the building. I turn the key in the ignition and burn rubber pulling out of my parking space. There are no tears, no words of recrimination, nothing. I drive home as fast as I can, put the car in the garage and run inside to the bathroom before I throw up. York and Kirby come running into the house to greet me but stay outside of the small bathroom as I continue to vomit until nothing is left, not even dry heaves. When I can stand, I clean myself up, walk over to the kitchen and take out my phone from the handbag I threw across the counter and turn it off completely.

I know Wiley told Pax what he saw but I don't want to talk to anyone, least of all Paxton Barrett, the pig. I change clothes and take the dogs with me down to the beach where I sit and gaze out across the smooth surface of the lake until it's too dark to see. Walking back indoors I pull the cork out of the opened bottle of merlot and drink straight from the bottle. Once the boys are fed I walk upstairs to the watch tower and sit on the green and blue cushions, looking out towards the water and imagine sailing away…

The dogs are barking something fierce when I roll up into a sitting position having dozed off after finishing the wine. Somebody is pounding on the screen door but unwilling to come any further. I lean over to look down the porch roof line and see Wiley talking on his cell phone. I slowly open a window and eavesdrop on his side of the conversation. He can't see me at the window, with the lights off,.

"What the hell kind of dogs are they?" he asks continuing to look over his shoulder in fear one big sounding beast rips through the porch screen.

"She's not answering her phone either Pax," he says opening his door and getting inside the car. "No, I'm not going to break into her house you idiot…because whatever relationship you might have with those dogs, I do not. I'm sorry but she's just going to have to wait for you to explain your double life."

Is Pax seeing Candace and me simultaneously? My heart splinters a little more but I continue to listen to the one-sided conversation.

"Yeah, well one of us has to draw the line and I just did.

If she forgave you the last time, she'll forgive you this time too. Some women are just that gullible," he says then laughs before he replies, "Still using the old fireworks parable? Oh, don't even joke about that. I wouldn't stick my neck or any other part of my anatomy out this far for any woman, no matter how wonderful you think she is... okay I'll try her phone again but if she doesn't answer... I'm heading back to the apartment. Please have Candy out of there before I get back. You two make a lot of noise when..."

He closes the car door on the last sentence but I can imagine the ending of that sentence. I wish I could throw this empty wine bottle through his windshield but he'd only send me the bill. I hate Wiley and Paxton Barrett. Eventually the dogs run up the stairs signaling the strange vehicle has left. I slide to the floor and let the boys lick my face as I bury my head in their fur, and soon the tears come and I cry myself to sleep on the floor of the watch tower room surrounded by my trustworthy dogs, cursing myself for being the gullible woman Wiley accused me of being.

21

Concentrating on the computer screen this morning is proving to be the greatest challenge I've been expected to overcome since the last time Paxton Barrett broke my heart. But I trudge along; I told Tara I wasn't taking any phone calls today. I get the correspondence ready for my assistant when I receive another email from Paxton Barrett. I refuse to open it like all the others he sent and I hit delete. Another email pops up from an unfamiliar name, Cody Whitaker. I open the missive and feel like someone just kicked me in the teeth. Three photos appear on my screen and they're all of Paxton and Candace, Cody's wife.

"Thought you should know the sort of man you're sleeping with. Candace has taken my children from me, kicked me out of our house, and now is posting these pictures on her media page... She doesn't deserve to be called wife or mother. I'll take care of her; you take care of him... CW."

His unsettling email is worth showing to the authorities but I can't take my eyes off the pictures of the man I love making love to another woman, someone's wife and mother. The first photo is of the two on a beach, her riding on his shoulders and they're both laughing like children. The next photo had to be taken with a high-powered lens because it shows her touching his naked shoulder as he sits in front of a window in what appears to be a hotel room. He's wearing the black and red jockey shorts I bought him for Valentine's Day and she's wearing a lovely lavender and black lace bra and panty set. The last one shows the couple hugging one another in a passionate embrace. Her hand is touching the front of his dress slacks and he's grinning down at her. The background is familiar…wait a second, it's Melanie's old office, or Star's new office. The artwork hanging on the wall belongs to Star, this photo was taken two days ago, when the movers finished bringing in my boss's new office décor…

I forward the email and photos to Paxton's address with a short note.

'Close the window blinds before you fuck another man's wife, Harper Meade'.

He sends a reply but I hit delete instead of reading his lame excuse. Star is in meetings today and tomorrow so I can work from home. Walking out of the office with my bags and traveler I hear Tara on the phone.

"I'm sorry sir but she's tied up now," she tells Pax then flips the mute button on her headset and says, "you might want to take a long lunch, Mr. Barrett said he knew you weren't in a meeting. He is determined to speak with you."

"Thanks for the warning," I tell her and say, "I'm going to be out of the office for the rest of today and all day tomorrow. Tell Mr. Barrett I'm working with MS Bridges and can't be bothered."

She smiles at me and says, "I've got your back."

Tara will work out just fine. I exit the office just as the

elevator door chimes its arrival. I quickly open the door to the stairwell and just have enough time to see Pax storm past the doorway and barge into my outer office. I can hear his raised voice but can't make out what he's saying. Jogging down the three flights of stairs I make it to the parking lot next door, unlock my car and stow my bags on the floor board just as Paxton reaches the lot. He's waving his arms at me to stop but I gun the engine past him and flip him off as I drive by. Knowing he's in one hell of a mood I decide not to go home just yet. I swing past Poppy's restaurant and see both Mom and Dad are there. I pull into the alleyway and slip inside via the service entrance. The restaurant always seems busy, no matter what time of day it is. Leaving my purse and bags on one long table being set for the lunch crowd I wrap my arms around Poppy's waist and hug him to my chest. He sets down the tray of glasses and laughs at the pleasant surprise.

"Well if it isn't my Princess," he says turning around and hugging me back. "Deidre leave the books and come say hi to Harper. Is everything alright?"

"You bet," I tell him. "Star is out of the office today and tomorrow and I'm going to play hooky and work from home. But I wanted to stop by and see you."

"Hi honey," my mother says walking out of the small cubicle my parents call an office and she hugs me to her. "Why aren't you at work young lady?"

"She's playing hooky. Finally, you're acting like my daughter," my father says making us laugh. "Can you stay for an early lunch?"

Suddenly I feel the need to spend as much time with my folks as I can. I nod my head and the three of us spend a lovely hour eating some of the best lobster mac and cheese imaginable. But Poppy gets called away to the kitchen and mom must take a call so I kiss her on the cheek and whisper for her to hug Poppy for me and I head on back home. With the wind in my hair, the stereo blasting away on an oldies rock station I make the forty-five-minute trip with time to spare. Pulling into the garage I'm shocked Paxton isn't waiting on me. I open the side door and put my bags on the island when I notice the dogs aren't coming out to welcome me home. Looking out the back yard I see them running after Pax. I knew it was too good to be true. Locking the doors and throwing the deadbolts I race upstairs and change into a pair of cutoff jeans shorts and a gray V-necked T-shirt. Braiding my hair into a long rope I walk up to the watch tower room and see him looking at his watch as he makes his way up the notched earthen steps that lead to the back door. He's going to know I'm home when he can't get back inside the house. He didn't squeeze through the doggie doors so I'm not sure how he unlocked the door in the first place but I'll change every lock by tomorrow. I hear him trying to open the back door and then he's cupping his hands to the glass trying to see if I'm inside the house. Finally, he yells my name.

"Harper I know you're in there, open the door and let me in so we can talk, please," he says then waits for me to comply.

He pulls out his cell phone apparently calling me but since it's downstairs and the ringer is off he can't hear it ring. The dogs must sense I'm home because I hear them running up the stairs looking for me. They make the final flight of stairs and run right into me as I crouch below the window sill.

"Hi babies," I cuddle with them until they've had enough and run back downstairs in search of Pax. "Traitors," I mumble to myself as I hear him hollering for me again.

"Harper, open the God damn door or I'll kick in the glass and unlock it myself," he threatens.

Believing he'd do just that I walk down stairs and pull my cell phone out of the bag and call Darrell next door. He answers the phone on the second ring.

"Hi Harper, what's going on?" he asks sounding so normal and I hear the kids in the background.

"I have a problem and I need your help," I tell him. "Without going into detail Pax and I are no longer seeing each other due to he seems to have a wandering eye, and several other body parts. The favor is this," I tell him. "Pax is threatening to kick the door in if I don't let him inside. I'm scared. Can you come over and talk with him, please?"

"I'll be right there, and keep the doors and windows locked," my neighbor directs me. "One question," he says. "He's not drunk or armed, is he?"

"No, unfortunately he's stone sober and still acting like a jerk," I tell him.

"I'm on my way," he says and hangs up the phone.

The entire time I'm talking to Darrell I could hear Paxton trying every set of French doors and each window to see if he could get inside. I walk back up to the tower room and wait for Darrell to come to my rescue. A couple minutes later I see Darrell and the boys walk across the drive toward the front of the house.

"Hey Paxton," I hear him shout in greeting. "Look boys Paxton's here for a visit."

Talk about passive aggressive behavior at its finest. Hutchins brought his kids so Pax wouldn't make a scene or threaten me. He's a clever and manipulative man, who knew? Trevor and Travis with Silas start asking the angry man many questions while Joey holds up his arms to be picked up by his honorary uncle which he does and even hugs the boy. I can barely hear what Darrell is saying but Paxton's voice rings loud and clear.

"I know your Aunt Harper would love to invite you kids inside but she isn't answering her phone or the door." He looks directly at Darrell and turns the table on the man. "Do you boys think she's alright? I hope she didn't trip over the pups or fall down the stairs."

Darrell nods his head in silent appreciation of being manipulated by the man he was manipulating.

"Call for your Aunt Harper boys," Pax urges the youngsters knowing I'd never want to worry them like this.

"Aunt Harper? Can you hear us?"

"Aunt Harper pick up your phone!"

"Daddy maybe you should call 911 like they told us to do in school."

God, he's won this round. I pick up my phone and call Darrell's cell.

"Hey Harper let me put you on speaker phone, the boys and Pax were worried something might have happened to you, are you alright?" Darrell plays along.

"Oh, thank you guys but I'm sick, the flu. I can't let you in or you'll catch it too and have to go to the doctor and get a shot in the bottom, like I had to do," I tell them and hear them start talking about shots, doctor's offices, and the last time all the boys were sick at the same time.

"Thanks for checking on me but the doctor said I needed to rest and not be bothered, so go back home and I'll see you all this weekend," I tell them then say to Paxton, "Sorry you made the trip out here for nothing Pax, but I thought you saw me give you the signal not to bother me. Thanks anyway, talk to you next week at the office."

"Come on over to our house Uncle Pax," Silas tells him. "We can play with the dogs over there too."

"I'd love to guys but I guess since Aunt Harper isn't feeling well I should take the pups back to the city with me..."

"Don't you dare take my dogs Paxton Barrett," I scream at him without thinking the kids can still hear me. "Shit," I utter under my breath but he heard me anyway.

"Open up Harpo or I'm rescuing the dogs," he tells me.

"Darrell, please take me off speaker," I ask my neighbor.

"You bet, there, you wanted to tell me something?" he asks.

"Hand the phone to that two-timing son of a bitch," I tell him and within seconds I hear the despicable voice of Paxton Barrett.

"Don't even think about taking my dogs off this property," I hiss at him. "I'll call the sheriff if I have too. Just go back to the city and your girlfriend and leave me the hell alone."

He speaks loud enough for the others to hear him, "I wouldn't dream of going off to the city and leaving you here, sick as a dog yourself with no one to look after the boys."

"I hate you," I tell him.

"Good, right now I feel the same way about you," he replies. "Open the door."

"Put Darrell back on the phone," I instruct him.

"No, Darrell and the boys are going back home so they don't catch the bug, say goodbye to him and I'll be waiting at the side door. I mean it Harper, let me inside." The last sentence was whispered but I could hear the steel in his tone.

"Bye Harper, I'll call you later to check up on you, sorry I couldn't help you out," Darrell says.

"Get better Aunt Harper"

"Eat some chicken soup"

"Can the dogs get people germs?"

"We'll make you a get well soon card"

Then there is only silence, telling me my rescue team failed. Walking down the stairs I see Paxton, dressed in his navy suit, white shirt, and sky blue tie leaning against the white painted brick of the fireplace on the porch. The dogs are sitting at his feet. He straightens his body and the second I unlock the door he gains access to my stronghold and reaches out for me but I evade his grasp by running into the kitchen, keeping the island between us.

"So, you want to play," he taunts me slowly walking towards me, making me back up.

"I want you to leave," I tell him making him shake his head.

"Not going to happen," he replies, "at least not until you've listened to what I have to say."

"Fine, talk fast then leave and never come back," I tell him as I continue to step backward for each step he takes forward.

"Baby, that's not how this is going to play out," he

whispers then tosses the barstools behind him making an obstacle course.

If the pups would have stayed back, I'd have made it to the stairs but with the crazy game Pax is playing they get excited and I trip over Kirby and fall over backwards. That's all the advantage Pax needed and he's on top of me in a second.

"You lose," he whispers as he straddles my hips and lowers his torso on top of me. "Now you have to listen."

The dogs run over and see us on the floor and romp around, walking over my legs, bumping into Pax's back and finally pushing the man off me. I crab walk backwards as Pax tries to scramble to his feet but I'm already up and running. He swears under his breath and must be careful not to step on the boys so I have a head start and make it up to the watch tower room but just as I close the door he presses with all his might and sends me flying backwards. He slams the door shut on the playful pups then panting and wheezing he holds up his arms to prevent me from escaping. But I'm shot. I shake my head since I can't make a sound and sit down on the green and blue cushions ready to hear his tall tale.

22

Paxton walks over to stand in front of me. All I can do is look up at his strained face and heaving chest. We're both exhausted, angry, and dreading this next confrontation.

"Go ahead, explain away you missing yesterday's meeting, or Candace's personal items in your bathroom and her clothes strung across the bedroom, I dare you. But don't for a minute think you can explain those photos," I snarl at him.

He stares at me for a couple seconds then quick as the snake he is, pins me underneath his strong body, forcing me in the soft cushioned seat. He holds my face in his hands and kisses me. Not angrily, or passionately, but so softly and sweetly so I have the hardest time not responding.

"You have no reason to be jealous baby," he whispers across my cheek while his hands roam over my body. "I told you the truth, why won't you believe me?"

Kissing him back he quickly deepens the kiss until I take advantage of the distraction, wrap my arms around his neck and roll us both off the window seat and onto the floor where I push away from his hold.

"For God's sake Harper," he growls grabbing a hold of

my ankle, "will you stop acting like this and listen to what I have to say?"

"You lied, multiple times as it turns out, so anything you have to tell me is meaningless. Just another version of 'your truth'," I hiss at him kicking out with my free foot and hitting his shoulder hard enough to make him loosen his hold.

"I didn't lie to you," he shouts rubbing the sore spot, "I told you about Candace, remember? Why bring it up now?"

"Why? Because yesterday you skipped a sales meeting to be with her," I glare at him. "I stopped by your apartment to surprise you but I'm the one that got the surprise. Her underwear was on the unmade bed dammit."

He drops his head to his chest and says, "she's been staying there but not with me."

"Her children moved in with you too?" I snidely ask watching him bristle at my tone.

"Nobody moved in with me, they were with their father over the holiday, but when he brought them home he started threatening her, so she and the girls stayed at her parent's place... listen, it's complicated. I was with you over the weekend, remember the two of us, surrounded with other peoples' children?" he asks in a derogatory fashion. "So how could I have been with her when I was with you?"

"Pax, you left my place Sunday after you received a phone call," I say staring at his face. "Was it her?"

Without flinching he tells me, "No, it was Wiley calling to say she was going to spend a couple days at my apartment but that she was taking the girls to her sister's place in Buffalo. When she got back late Tuesday evening that crazy Whitaker was waiting on her." He runs his fingers through his hair and says, "She called at two in the morning from the ER. They patched her up and I brought her back to my place but I slept on the sofa. I was just helping her out; you'd do the same if a friend asked for your help."

Sighing at him parts of his story are feasible but I saw him tenderly holding Candace yesterday and she looked as lovely as ever.

"I was parked out front of your apartment when a taxi brought you two back to your place," I relay to him. "You and she were in quite a clench brother."

He snaps back, "For the love of God Harper I was helping her out of the cab! That son of a bitch cracked two of her ribs when he kicked her. You should have seen the bruises on her arms and back. If he'd been anywhere near me I'd have returned every punch and kick he dealt her."

Feeling awful for the woman and for raising such a ruckus I draw my knees up in front of me, rest my head on my arms. He scoots across the space between us and wraps his arms around my shoulders enveloping in a hug.

"Harper I love you, please don't be angry at me over this situation," he whispers.

Turning my head to face him I hold out a while longer.

"Explain the photos," I reply seeing the look of hope in his eyes die a sudden death.

He removes his arm and falls backward, lying on the brightly colored area rug and blows out his breath.

"You're impossible," he sighs then covers his face with his arm. "Which one bothers you the most?" he asks losing his temper again, "The one where I took her and the girls to the water park... You knew about the two of us meeting at a hotel room for a sympathy screw... So it must be the one in Star Bridges office, where she and I were clowning around waiting on Star to arrive for our proposal, right?"

"Her hand was on your crotch Paxton," I grind my teeth at his tone. "I don't know how things are done in your department, but in my office and all other offices I'd suppose, cupping a co-worker's genitals is considered bad form."

He laughs at my droll comment but he sits up and tugs on my braid.

"She did not cup me," he says. "The photo looks like she did but actually she was bringing her arm up to hug me… which wouldn't have looked any better to you I suppose."

His unconcerned voice sets me off and I push him over and stand up ready to leave the tower room when he reaches out and grabs my ankle, halting my progress.

"Let go of me," I shout out him. "If you don't see anything wrong with the way you've behaved then I guess there's nothing left to say."

"You're wrong," he tells me sliding his hand further up my leg until he is kneeling in front of me. "You just have to trust me Harper, please."

Feeling a meltdown coming I shake my head and try to escape him again.

"Please Pax, let me go," I whisper but it's too late; I can't stop the flood gate of tears as they fall down my cheeks. "Why'd you have to sleep with her?" I cry.

He stands up and gathers me in his arms, gently swaying us back and forth while I continue to fall apart. A white linen handkerchief appears in front of me and I press the sweet-smelling fabric to my face, inhaling his scent as I do.

Pax releases a deep sigh and says, "I love you Harper,

with all my heart but if you can't trust me…we're through. I won't bother you again."

His softly spoken words finish the job of breaking my heart in two. Bending down he kisses my lips and I taste the sorrow of both of us but I know if we continue the lack of trust will only grow until we end up hating one another.

"Make love to me," I tell him. "One last time…"

He smiles and shakes his head, "Another sympathy fuck? No thanks Harper. I only want to make love with you, anything less won't do."

Angry he's making me feel guilty I push out of his arms and tilt my chin up. Handing him the linen square, I press my lips together and nod in agreement.

"Fine, then I guess this is truly the end of you and me," I tell him noticing the slight flaring of his nostrils and narrowing of his eyes at my statement.

"Yep, too bad we're not the type of people to become friends with benefits as they call it," he jokes but doesn't laugh.

"Never saw the payoff on that kind of relationship," I murmur. "Take care of yourself and I'll see you around."

"Probably not since I'm leaving for Ottawa looks like sooner than I was expecting," he explains. "I was planning on coming back to Albany, but now there doesn't appear to be a reason to stay."

Swallowing deeply at the hurt I can't let go of I cross my arms under my breast and glare up at him.

"Why are you acting like this is my fault? Would you be so quick to forgive and forget if it was Wiley and me in your place? Or even Jai and me?" I ask mentioning first his best friend then a co-worker neither of us are close to.

"We'll never know," he replies and pulls out the key he used to get inside my house. "Here, you might as well take this back since you never really gave it to me."

"Where did you get this?" I ask knowing he had to have snooped in my kitchen drawer to have found it.

"I saw it lying in one of the drawers when I was looking for a cork screw and I took it," he says smiling down at his wingtips. "Of course, that was when I thought you wanted me back, but now... knowing how you feel you'd probably have the locks changed tomorrow anyway, am I right?"

"You're not stupid," I laugh when he rolls his eyes but he leans forward and hugs me to his chest.

"Harper I'll go to my grave loving you, I swear," he whispers then kisses me softly on the cheek before stepping back. "You don't have to walk me down; I'll say goodbye and good luck."

And with that he turns, opens the door, and walks out of my life...

23

Walking out of Star's office I'm checking out a text message from Ginger on my phone when I accidently run into the one woman in the world I'd just have soon forgotten existed, Candace Whitaker. The fact she looks like a supermodel, movie star, and a top-notch executive only makes me want to snatch her coiffed blonde hair in my hands and wrestle her to the floor. Serve her right if she must attend the dinner tonight sporting a black eye, a split lip, and maybe some emergency dental work.

"Excuse me," I mumble and walk around her not bothering to check if she's all right. My mind slips back to our last confrontation almost six weeks ago. She stopped by my office the following Monday after Pax and I split up. To say she was angry would be an understatement.

"What the hell is wrong with you?" she hissed at me barging into my office and slamming the door behind her. "You've got to be the thickest headed woman out there. Tell me Paxton didn't accept that VP of Sales position because of the fight you two had?"

"Not that it's any of your business," I told her standing up and walking around to the front of my desk I leaned against its surface and watched the lovely woman lose her temper.

"We slept together one time!" she shouted pacing the floor in front of me. "For God's sake neither of us even enjoyed it."

"Yeah right," I told her sneering at that ridiculous statement. "I've been on the receiving end of that man's ticket and I know what kind of a ride he offers. Just say what you came here for and then I never want to see, speak, or hear from you again."

The woman laughed in my face before she jeered at me.

"Honey, that man is only hot for you," she said. "And you just sent him packing to Canada all because you got jealous. Let me tell you about jealousy..." she started to say but I interrupted her, not wanting to spend another second in her presence.

"Candace, it doesn't matter anymore," I began. "He lied, cheated, and then continued to lie to me. I forgave him for leaving me at the damn altar, I forgave him for his supposed 'sympathy fuck' as he referred to your hotel hop, but I saw the photos your charming husband sent me... they don't lie. He was with you last Monday, and Tuesday, and for all I know he spent the weekend with you. I DON'T CARE!"

"Shouting you 'don't care' speaks volumes doesn't it," she told me turning on her expensive heel and walked over to open the door. "You don't deserve him," she said glaring back at me. "He changed, grew up after he ruined your wedding day, now I think it's your time to grow up. But since you 'don't care' maybe I'll take him up on his offer of becoming his personal assistant... the girls might like Ottawa."

She laughed as she quietly closed the door behind her and I snapped the ink pen I was holding in two. That was the one and only time she and I spoke until now, six weeks later.

"Hello Harper, happy to see me?" she sneers as she looks down at my phone. "Making plans for the long weekend?"

Hoping she's only here for Melanie Swann's reception and not returning to this office I refuse to chit chat with her.

"Hello to you, and no I'm not particularly happy to see you, and my weekend plans are none of your business," I say in a sickeningly sweet tone of voice.

"Aren't you precious?" she laughs and walks backwards. "We'll see you at Melanie's reception tonight. Dress in something... nice." She laughs again and walks down the hall to the Sales Department looking like she stepped out of a glossy fashion advertisement with her tailored red suit... she is one stunning lady.

Looking down at my own outfit I guess I have been slacking in my wardrobe, but I lost about twenty pounds over the last seven weeks and nothing fits me anymore. The skirts hang off my too slender hips; my blouses look like they're still hanging on a hanger... Today my weight loss is noticeable but I never cared before until now... that blonde haired witch has made me self-conscious. Calling Ginger I pray she picks up. She does on the third ring and I can hear how busy she is now.

"Make it quick sweetie," she says in lieu of her usual greeting.

"Do you have time to shop over lunch?" I ask her.

"Not today, why?" she asks as she's typing on her keyboard.

"Candace Whitaker made fun of how I look and suggested I wear something 'nice' to this evening's reception," I tell her knowing Ginger will commiserate with me.

"That bitch is nothing but trouble," she murmurs into the phone. "How much time do you need?"

"Hell, I don't know," I begin suddenly not wanting to go tonight but Ginger set me up with Jai Carlson of all people and in a weak moment I agreed to go but now I just want to hold up in my house, walk on the beach with the boys and ignore everyone around me.

"Go on line and check out that new dress boutique on Lark Street, oh what's the name of it… wait it's called 'Unexpected Turn of Events'… they have some great items, new and retro. See what they have and you can stop by and pick up what you like."

"Thanks, I'll do that," I tell her feeling better I at least have an option for this evening. "Anything I can help you with?"

"I wish," she replies. "But since you can't draw a stick person or tell the difference between Cadmium yellow and ochre… thanks but no thanks."

"Thanks a lot," I laugh knowing she is speaking only the unvarnished truth I end the call with a promise I'll meet her and the guys at the fountain in the Civic Center at seven o'clock.

I spend the rest of the morning browsing on-line between finishing up Star's speech she's to give tonight and the production meeting scheduled for next Tuesday. At four o'clock Star sends us home so I drive over to Unexpected on Lark Street and pick up the dress I fell in love with on their website. With an hour set aside for dressing I make it home in time to take a long soak and get dressed in my new finery. As I take stock in my improved look I can't help but smile at the reflection I see staring back at me. The woman in the black sequined sleeveless dress looks strong, sexy, and playful. The low dipped V in the front of the dress was patterned after the 1920's silhouette later mimicked in the 1970's fashion houses. Even though I'm not that flat chested I've lost some of my curves, hopefully I'll appear svelte and not gaunt. Either way I feel good and for the first time in weeks feel like going out.

I leave my longer hair unbound but I straightened it and the silky strands slide across my exposed shoulder blades when I walk. Since the shoes are new too I look down and like the thin strappy sandals that make my precocious pink toenails look sexy. With the additional three inch heels, I'm feeling like a giant. Jai Carlson is not a tall man but at least I won't tower over him either. Grabbing my silver clutch I walk down stairs to the living room where the boys are sacked out in the corner.

"You two behave," I tell them loving the way they barely raise up their heads when I speak to them. At five months, the boys are as large as most large breed dogs. Smiling at the pups, which seems funny to call them that but they're not even halfway grown yet. "Mommy will be back later."

They both lie back down and go to sleep. Well so much for anyone worrying about me tonight. Collecting my car keys, I lock up the house and step into my sexy black ride. The air is soft with a hint of a storm kicking up. I look forward to watching Star be relieved of her pro temp duties which means my job description reverts to executive assistant to chief editor. I can't wait to get back to normal. Handing my keys to the parking attendant I smile and accept the ticket before walking inside the spectacular atrium to the Civic Center. Melanie Swann returning to Viva La Femme is a big deal and I can't wait to see the woman. She is so lucky not to have been more injured. I wonder if Pax will be here; that thought both makes me dread and look forward to seeing him. I spy Ginger and Marc standing over by the large water fountain speaking with several men in dark suits. Jai separates himself from the group and walks over towards me smiling in appreciation of the effort I put forth this evening. He is so good looking in his formal attire, more approachable than the last man that wore a tuxedo for me...

"You look smoking hot," he says whistling under his breath as he takes my hand and kisses my cheek. "Damn, I hardly recognized you. Come with me and I'll get you a drink at the bar."

I look around and notice several people from my office, but this is mostly about Melanie and much of the people here are from the corporate level so it doesn't surprise I recognize few in the group. Marc and Ginger join us at the bar refilling their champagne glasses before hugging me.

"My goodness Miss Harper," Ginger nearly swoons as she slips into a bad southern belle impersonation. "You surely are looking mighty fine missy."

"I agree," Marc says touching his glass to mine. "You had us worried there for a little bit, but I guess you're back on track now, right?"

"You guessed it old man," I tease him making him frown at my calling him old. "Should I amend that and say sexy old man?"

"Better, but watch that saucy tongue young lady," he warns.

"Where are we sitting?" Jai asks sliding his hand from my waist and over my bottom.

"If you don't move that hand back up to my waist you'll be sitting on the floor holding your future children in your hand," I playfully threaten him but he does as he's told and everybody laughs at the look of chagrin on his face.

"It never hurts to try," he slyly smiles at me and kisses my temple.

"You're wrong," I tell him. "It just might hurt you, Jai Carlson."

"I'd listen to the lady if I were you Jai," a deep, sexy, and unfortunately familiar voice says standing directly behind me. Briefly closing my eyes, I paste on a plastic smile and turn to face the man that once again turned my world upside down. He is standing next to Star Bridges and her husband Drake. I hold out my hand and he quickly envelops it into his larger one.

"Good to see you again Harper," he says leaning in to kiss my cheek.

His warm breath on my skin makes my heart skip a beat but as he steps back I notice Candace Whitaker walking over and placing her arm around his shoulder.

"Sorry that took so long but I wanted to check on the girls," she tells him ignoring the rest of us until Ginger breaks the ice…over the sultry blonde's head.

"I love your dress," my best friend says making the woman smile at the compliment until Ginger turns and asks, "didn't you wear that same dress two years ago, at the Farley – Jacobs wedding?"

Candace's smile becomes a sneer at the put down but only the ladies and Pax hear the slam. He quickly takes a sip of his champagne but Star doesn't hide her mirth.

"Good one Ginger Snap," the old woman says. "No need to be so snooty Candy, we all work together, shouldn't be any surprises amongst us, right?"

"I don't particularly share your point of view," Candace says looking over at Ginger with a touch of malice in her eyes.

"No but you do share other things that don't belong to you," I mumble under my breath making Pax cough and spew his wine on his date.

The entire group laughs but Candace glares at Pax before turning on her designer shod heel and walking over to the ladies room.

"You won't be getting any of that tonight," Jai says without thinking. He turns to look down at me his smile disappears and he whispers in my ear, "I'm sorry, I wasn't thinking. I didn't mean to remind you of those two…God, I think you need to cover my mouth with your hand."

"More like duct tape," I laugh making the others ask what we're talking about.

"Just sweet nothings," Jai says making everyone but Pax laugh at his joke.

I can feel my ex-lover's eyes on me, burning a hole in my forehead but I refuse to meet his gaze. Two Advertising Executives join the group so I press my hand on Jai's arm and nod my head towards the opposite direction.

"If you'll excuse us, we're going to mingle," Jai says to no one and we slowly make our way around the room. Jai is also in sales with Pax and Wiley. He introduces me to several of his clients that are witty and charming and ready to talk about their home state of Texas. Ten minutes later a director picks up the microphone from the dais and asks everyone to return to their seats so the meal can begin.

We wander over to table number twelve and feel such relief that Pax and Candace won't be sitting across the table from me. However, Wiley and his date, a lovely brunette I've never seen before sit four chairs down and I can feel his eyes scanning me and Jai. Like Paxton Wiley isn't crazy about their co-worker dating me, but Jai is funny, charming, and not looking to score he assured me as we worked the crowd earlier. We enjoy our meal and our table mates. Soon the wait staff serve cake and coffee while Melanie Swann appears on the dais looking wonderful in a full length evening gown of deep chocolate brown that clings to her shapely body even though she appears to walk with a slower than usual gait. Her hair is shorter and darker making her appear younger, more natural than her earlier look.

"Good evening ladies and gentlemen," she says looking around the room and smiling. "Thank you all for joining me in my return to the helm. I want to thank so many people for stepping up and filling in for me. But first let me thank each of you for your thoughts and prayers, they certainly speeded up the process of my healing. Next I want to thank a special man in the audience this evening," she pauses for a second to collect herself before she goes on. "Stand up Paxton," she says motioning with her arm for the reluctant Ad Exec to stand up. "Friends, without this man, I wouldn't be here tonight."

The room erupts in applause as Paxton's cheeks become flush with embarrassment. He scans the room and looks over at me then nods his head in my direction. After the applause and accolades are through she turns towards our table and says, "Next, I want to thank Star Bridges for filling in for me Pro Tem," she says and Star stands up and nods her head at her boss and then to the room.

On and on Melanie goes through a list of people she wants to acknowledge from Canada and the UK as well as here in the states. Jai leans over and says, "I hope she isn't going to draw attention to me. Two years ago, at the Christmas party, I ate the last shrimp before she could get it… I was sick for three days afterwards…"

Laughing at his silly stories I can't help but grin when Melanie says, "If I failed to mention anyone tonight, it was not intentional I assure you. Each one of you means a great deal to me and to Viva La Femme. I thank you for working with all of us and for coming to see me return to my old position. But like some good stories, sometimes there isn't a happy ending, well at least the ending you might have been expecting. Star would you please join me on the dais?"

Drake Bridges stands up and scoots his wife's chair out for her. My boss walks over to me and hugs my shoulders.

"I should have told you about my decision earlier but I wasn't ready to speak about my condition. Forgive me for what I'm about to do," she says scaring me as I watch her walk up to the dais. The older woman hugs Melanie and takes the microphone she is handed.

"Ladies and Gentlemen, I've enjoyed my years in the newspaper and magazine medium for over forty-two years. I started working for the parent company of La Femme when I graduated from University and have never looked back, until now." She wipes a tear from her eye and says, "due to health issues besides my advancing years," she jokes making the older folks around me chuckle, "I'm going to be retiring as editor in chief from Viva La Femme. This Femme will enjoy the time I have left doing what I love to do most, spend time with my family in the Hamptons."

A round of applause jars my rattled nerves even further. My boss is retiring, because she's sick? Jai leans over and whispers in my ear, "smile and nod your head as if you knew she was planning this all along. Too many people are staring at you. Be happy for the woman."

Nodding my head in understanding I listen to the woman that mentored me for the last five years. I will have to find a new job...

"... and I've always trusted Melanie's judgment so hopefully my dear friend and the best executive assistant I could ever have wished for will do the same. Ladies, will you stand up please."

Jai and Ginger both hiss at me to stand but I seem to have missed something in the speech. Jai scoots my chair back and as I stand up I notice one other woman standing up as well...Candace Whitaker and she is smiling directly at me, like a shark circling a baby seal.

"Let's give them a round of applause," Star says and then hands the microphone back to Melanie.

"Thank you Star for those kind words, those pearls of wisdom, and we wish you nothing but the best retirement, right everybody?" Melanie asks working the room like a champ.

I tune out the woman and wait for Star to make it back to our table. When she sits back down I nudge Jai to switch seats with me. By the time I'm sitting next to my boss she's looking worn out but also worried.

"Honey, now is not the time for this discussion," she whispers covering my hand I stare at her in amazement.

"Star, I can't work for that woman? Do none of you folks listen to the inner office gossip? She slept with my fiancé for crying out loud." I hiss in her ear. "Please explain who recommended the two of us work together? Does she even know what your job entails?"

"Yes, she does," Star says in that tone she uses when she's tired of being questioned. "You've always trusted me, believed in me… and I've always felt the same about you. But I won't get into this discussion tonight. I'm sorry for dropping this bomb on you, but I've had a lot on my mind lately…" her voice breaks and I see the tears well up in her eyes.

"Forgive me," I rush to tell her. "I had no right to question your decision or Melanie's either. I'll wait for your explanation on Tuesday when you get into the office."

I turn towards Jai and lean over to speak in his ear, "I'm done for, thanks for escorting me tonight but I'm going to head out. Stay and enjoy yourself."

He nods his head and pushes my seat out for me.

"Guys enjoy your weekend and I'll speak to you next week," I tell them hugging each friend before I wave at the rest of the table. Wiley nods his head at me but he's talking on his cell so I turn to face my mentor once again. "I'm sorry for doubting you. Have a nice weekend, both of you. Goodnight."

Jai walks me out and hands my valet ticket to the attendant and smiles down at me.

"You look hot and sexy even though you're sad and confused," he tells me opening the door for me as my Corvette pulls up to the curb. "I enjoyed getting to know you, and I know you're expecting me to go back to your place for a night cap, then maybe a little…"

I kiss him on the lips just to shut him up and it works. But before he can comment he looks up and says, "Hey Barrett, how's it going?"

Great, Pax just saw me kissing his friend goodnight. Could the evening get any worse?

"Sorry to interrupt but I've got an appointment and have to leave," he says. "Don't let me interrupt you two. I'm not in that much of a hurry."

Jai laughs but closes my door before he leans down and says, "I hope you had some fun this evening. I know I did, goodnight sexy lady… see you in the funny papers."

I put the car in gear and drive as quickly as I can to my safe-haven where I can cry myself to sleep over the awful changes about to happen to my world… me working for Candace Whitaker? I don't think so.

24

Half way home the rain starts to fall, just enough drops to make a mess on my windshield. By the time I pull into my drive it's raining cats and dogs. Pulling into my garage I notice a car slowing down and then pulling into the drive behind me. Closing the garage door, I step out of my car and quickly grab an umbrella I always keep hanging on a peg just inside the side door. Opening the musty smelling device, I run over to the car before I notice its Paxton. He smiles and turns off the engine stepping underneath my umbrella and wrapping his arm around my waist he steers us towards the side porch and then removes the umbrella from my hand.

"Thanks for the shelter," he laughs and then kisses me quickly before I can step out of his reach. "I saw you were upset and wanted to make sure you got home alright. Jai should have taken you home."

Dazed at him being here I shake my head and say, "No, I met him there, he didn't drive me."

"Doesn't matter," he replies taking my keys out of my hand and unlocking the door. "Let's go inside before it kicks up any harder."

214

The dogs are so excited to hear Pax's voice they practically jump on top of him in their joy to see their friend.

"Hey guys," he says rubbing their heads and scratching behind their ears, "Geesh you guys have grown," he laughs and looks over at me and smiles. "They must weigh sixty or seventy pounds already."

Bending down to rub York's belly I tell him, "sixty-three and sixty-five pounds, consecutively."

He walks over to the sectional and sits down putting him closer to their level. "God I've missed you guys," he laughs as they vie for his attention. "I've missed you too."

I look over at him and know I will never get over this man.

"Me too," I admit making him smile back at the dogs. "Can I get you something to drink?"

"A beer would be great," he says standing up and brushing the dog hair off his black tuxedo. "How have you been?" he asks joining me in the kitchen where he pulls out a barstool and sits down, twisting the cap off the bottle I place in front of him.

"Good, at least I thought I was doing okay until this evening," I tell him. "Pax how the hell am I supposed to work for Candace? Is this a good karma bad karma thing?"

He laughs and takes a drink of his beer.

"I don't know what to tell you," he begins, "Except she is very good at her job. You could learn a lot from her, if you can get past whom she is, what she's done, and who she's done it with…"

Making a face at his snide comment I reply, "Very funny. But I need this job. What if she's all freakish, you know 'paybacks from hell… my man won't marry me because of you… I need a daddy for my kids."

He sets his bottle down on the counter top and asks, "Are you finished?"

Smiling at him I nod my head and ask, "Are you hungry? I didn't eat much of my dinner." I walk over to the fridge and start pulling out some cold cuts, cheese, lettuce, and mayo when he replies.

"I noticed; was it because of me?" he asks. "You're way too skinny Harper. What happened?"

Bumping the heavy door closed with my hip I set my haul down at the end of the island and stare at the obtuse man in front of me.

"What happened? Are you kidding me?" I snap at him. "You happened, there, are you happy? I admit I lost weight because you and I broke up. Everything in my life went to hell after you left… satisfied?"

I turn to leave the room when he catches up with me, grabs my arm and spins me around to face him.

"No, I'm not happy, and hell no, I'm not satisfied, not by a long shot but I'm coping," he snarls at me. "Unlike you I've apparently bounced back, living the high life as a carefree bachelor again…"

The sarcasm drips off his facetious words making me want to bury my face in his neck.

"I'm sorry," I tell him looking down at his feet. "I know you're not happy, and I'm partially to blame, but it hasn't been easy, you know?"

"Come here," he whispers and I slip into his arms loving the refuge I always thought they were. "Harper, you have to take better care of yourself. Otherwise Candace is going to roll right over you."

Stepping back to look up at him he grins making me realize he's teasing me.

"Thanks a lot Barrett," I grumble and walk back over to the makings of a good sandwich. "Would you care to split a sub with me?"

He joins me at the island and says, "You need to eat a whole one, if not two."

"Don't be mean Pax," I warn him reaching for my chef's knife and the small cutting board leaning up against the side of the fridge. "Slice this tomato while I get the bread."

Together we fix a huge sandwich and share a bowl of chips, sipping beer from the bottle we stick to mundane topics like how his job is going, speculating on Star's health issues, and his new apartment in Ottawa.

"It's small, but comfortable," he says looking around the large open kitchen. "The entire condo would fit in this space," he laughs.

"So... having a pet is out of the question?" I ask loving the salty bite of the chip I placed in my mouth.

He watches me and then shakes his head, "Sorry, what was the question. I got distracted watching you have an orgasm over that chip."

"Hey, I've got to get them somehow," I say without thinking then laugh when he practically chokes on his drink. "Sorry about that, but those particular occurrences are few and far between since you left."

He stares at me for a couple seconds and asks, "How few and how far between?"

Not needing to count I reply, "the last one was six weeks,

two days, twenty-two hours," I look at the large clock on the dining area wall and finish with, "and thirty-eight, no thirty-nine minutes ago."

His laughter heals the nicks and scrapes of my heart. I hadn't realized how much I missed talking to him, laughing at his jokes and facial expressions until now.

"It's good to hear your laughter Pax," I whisper pushing my half-eaten sub towards the center of the island.

"Harper I've missed talking to you almost as much as touching you, smelling your scent, just knowing you're in the same bed, room, house, building… sorry. I know you don't want to hear that but it's true."

"I do want to hear you're as miserable as I am," I confess picking up his empty beer bottle and dumping it in the trash before getting him another one. "Since we're confessing, I bought the same aftershave you wear and after I change the sheets I spray the pillow next to me. It's silly but your scent comforts me as well as drives me crazy."

"That's nothing," he laughs accepting the fresh beer and twisting off the cap. "I buy that dry wine you like even though I hate it. I can't walk past it in the store without buying the stupid thing. Want to guess how many bottles I've got stashed in my tiny new apartment; Seven of them."

We laugh like kids, trying to one up the other with our crazy coping skills. I didn't even notice he pushed my plate of food back in front of me until he picks up our empty plates and carries them to the sink. We take our drinks, his beer and my bitter dry wine as he calls it and sit down on the sectional. He removes his jacket and tie, kicks off his shoes and we sit in silence for a while, listening to the storm continue to rage outside. I slip his arm around my shoulder and snuggle into his side. Soon he's jostling me awake.

"Come on sweetie, let's get you upstairs and into bed." He helps me to my feet and turns me towards the staircase.

"Will you stay the night?" I ask praying he says yes then hoping he says no.

"I'll sleep in the guest room, how's that?" he asks taking the noble route.

"Good, I'd hate for you to have to drive back to the city in this gale," I tell him wrapping my arms around his trim waist as we climb the stairs together.

He flips off the overhead lights and walks me to my bedroom door before he turns to face me.

"Goodnight Harper," he says and kisses me softly on the lips before he turns away and walks down the hall to the guest room.

Part of my brain is relieved he didn't push sleeping with me but the other side of my brain is upset he didn't even try. What's wrong with me? Am I too skinny? Or is his nobility due to someone else being in the picture...namely his date tonight, my new boss Candace Whitaker? Brushing my teeth, I gaze in the mirror and make a monumental decision. Before I lose my nerve, I stomp down the hall and slam open the bedroom door catching him unaware and standing in his black jockey short and nothing else.

"What the hell is wrong with you?" I demand suddenly feeling my wine but I press on. "Six weeks ago, you'd have been all over me; pawing and trying anything to get me in bed... are you seeing someone else?"

He walks over towards me and asks, "Are you drunk?

I'm trying to do what you asked and leave you alone, but you're making it harder and harder to keep my distance."

Reaching out I stroke the front of his full shorts and look up at his tight-lipped face.

"It appears pretty hard to me too," I giggle and feel my feet lift off the floor as he carries me back down the hall to my room and kicks open the door then drops me on the bed.

"Don't tease me unless you're willing to follow through Harper," he growls at me from the side of the bed. "What's it to be, one bed or two?"

His reaction startles me letting me know how close to the edge he's living. My lack of response makes him turn towards the door but before he can reach the knob I whisper, "One bed."

The look of relief on his face as he turns towards me speaks volumes to the need he is feeling.

"Thank God," he sighs and strips off his shorts before climbing under the sheets. "Hurry up Harper before I start without you."

I can't stop the giggle that escapes from between my lips and in less than five seconds I'm sprawled across his naked body, kissing his face and neck while his hands are reacquainting themselves with my body.

"I'm sorry baby but I need to be inside you," he groans as I stroke his heavy scrotum.

"I need the same thing," I tell him opening my thighs for him to settle himself into position. "Just keep in mind you're the last person I've been with, I want you too but don't render me in two."

He chuckles as he holds his hard shaft in his hand, guiding his tool to my waiting channel. The second his body touches mine I feel an inner heat course through me, full of anticipation and eagerness, but he is careful, sliding into me inch by excruciating inch until he is surrounded by my body.

"You feel so good, so hot and tight..." he groans at the exquisite pressure. "Are you alright? Can I move yet?"

"Please Pax, move fast and hard," I gasp as my body is primed for orgasm just knowing the man is buried deeply within me. The small tiny muscles in my chasm are already constricting, grasping his profound girth. "Baby move for me... now!"

He propels his body into mine, hammering me inside and out as I goad him to higher heights.

"Make me yours again Pax," I whisper in his ear feeling him start to sweat. "Pound me baby, give me more Paxton, and give me all you've got..." then my mind ceases functioning and I feel myself plunged into a sensuous stream of euphoria until that stream turns into white rapids... Screaming out his name, he drives me further until I feel like I'm falling off a cliff and again swimming through a river of satiation.

His body quickens and as he prepares to launch a small part of my brain wishes we were trying to create a life, an everlasting piece of each other to have and to hold. But he bucks and thrusts inside me, taking my breath and thought away until he shouts my name depositing his internal essence inside me and then slides back to earth and rolls over on his side and turns his grinning face towards me.

"Are you still on the pill?" he asks minutes later rising onto his elbow.

"Now's a fine time to ask," I tease him making him grin down at me, "but yes, I'm still on the pill."

"Too bad, we would have created a little Harpo or little Barrett with that bout of lovemaking." He jokes making me aware how much he's matured that he can think along those lines.

"If I hadn't miscarried, do you realize that we'd be parents in two months? Does that blow your mind?" I laugh and run my fingers down his spine.

"You'd look cute all big and pregnant," he says making me laugh out loud.

"I seriously doubt if you'd think I was cute when I couldn't tie my own shoes, or went on a crying jag because I burnt the toast…" I tell him only to be interrupted by his hand over my mouth.

"I would have loved you, fat or skinny, happy or weepy no matter what," he says in all seriousness. "Harper I'm so sorry for the all things I screwed up. You're all that's important to me, I realized that tonight when I saw you laughing and joking with Jai. Of course, when you kissed him I wanted to flatten him into the carpet and throw you over my shoulder, but I knew if he made you happy, then I'd have to be happy for you."

I stare up into his black eyes and smile.

"I wasn't as noble as you," I begin, "The second I saw you with Candace I was plotting ways of making you both miserable. Training the dogs to attack, hoping you contracted a genital destroying disease, and my favorite marrying that damn Wiley and having six kids, all named Paxton and have you be the God father."

He starts laughing and tickling me in retaliation until I feel his member twitch. He slides back on top of me and swiftly enters my aching body. Paxton grows inside me until

I feel that blessed pressure and he starts to move back and forth.

"Marry me Harper," he pants as he drives his body deeper into mine. "Be my wife, the mother of my children, and the keeper of my heart. Put your faith and trust in me, I promise not to fail you."

His words along with his body send me into overdrive and I nearly pass out from the deep, hot rush of my climax. The rapture I achieve is echoed in Pax's exultant shout as he too reaches his limit and beyond. Lying next to him the sheer bliss of the moment overwhelms me and I shout, "YES!"

He pulls me on top of him and starts kissing me all over. The pups are whimpering outside the door, the thunder and lightning rage on outside but all is at peace inside this room.

"I will marry you Paxton Joseph Barrett but I don't want to leave my home," I tell him and he nods his head. "I want two maybe three children but not right away. I need time to explain to my family that no matter what, I'm going to be Mrs. Paxton Barrett… oh and no big engagement ring or wedding either. Let's elope."

"Deal," he says and tucks my head under his chin. "What did you do with the other ring I bought you anyway?"

Laughing as I hear the rain gushing down the new gutters I purchased with the money I got from his ring I take great pleasure informing him the ring was put to good use.

25

Working with Candace has turned out to be one of the best career changes I've ever experienced. She has a different production style than Star. My former boss and mentor took an earlier leave than she anticipated. The private woman finally explained about her illness, pancreatic cancer. It is still in the early stages, caught by accident. But the treatments are aggressive and debilitating as well so Star, with little fanfare retired last week. We went out to eat after work on Friday and that was that.

Candace however jumped into her new position as if she'd always been editor in chief. It's refreshing to work with her nimble mind and thought process. We've developed a good working relationship and I've even met her two daughters five-year-old Molly and Millie just turned three. Another big difference between the old and new editors is Star would take work home with her, even on her vacation, staying late into the night, but not Candace. She leaves the office every day at four thirty, picks up her daughters at the sitter and then the evening belongs to her girls.

Today Candace is in court for some custody hearing and I've agreed to pick up the girls at the sitter for her since

I know she won't make it on time. Washington Park is only a couple blocks from the office so I told my boss I'd take them there. I hope she remembers because I've made dinner plans with my folks at Drapers. I answered Pax's last email and can't wait to see him tomorrow. He will be returning to Albany at the first of October taking over for a VP in sales that wanted to swap places with the better territory Pax would leave behind... all for me.

My phone rings and its Candace calling on her cell.

"Hi Candace, how's it going?" I ask then wish I hadn't.

"You are not going to believe what that son of bitch is doing?" she shouts into the phone, so unlike her normal way of handling a difficult situation. "He wants a joint custody hearing, a mental health evaluation, and a home study to be done on me. I'm not the one driving all over God's creation spying on me, stalking me, sending threatening emails and voice mails."

"Turn those items over to the attorney," I tell her hating the way this custody battle is heading. "There's not a judge in the land that would award custody to a man that physically threatened the mother of his children."

"That's the problem, he's unspecific in the threat, too vague my attorney tells me," she says in such a disgusted manner. "But I know what he's capable of, hell I went to the ER a couple months ago, over his 'method of persuasion' as he calls it."

"You had a protective order against him, didn't you?" I ask trying to keep her in the right frame of mind.

"Yes, but he told the cops I instigated the fight," she sighs. "I wish he'd just go away, forever."

"I know, and who knows, maybe he'll get hit over the

head, develop amnesia and forget he was ever married to you and that he has two little girls," I tease her making her laugh.

"Harper, you're a pip," she says then I hear someone in the background calling her name. "I got to go, wish me luck. Oh, and I'll probably be later than I expected, is that a problem?"

Before I can respond she says, "I'll talk to you later," And hangs up the phone.

The rest of the afternoon flies by and at four thirty I power down the computer, flip the phone to automatic voice mail and head over to the babysitter's and pick up the girls. I drive the darlings over to the Washington Street Park where we play on the swings, the slides, and the jungle gym for over an hour. They're getting tired and I'm worn out myself. When inspiration strikes me on how to spend the evening.

"Molly, Millie how does going out for a great meal sound?" I ask loving the way their eyes light up at the mention of going out somewhere. Apparently, Candace has a strict rule about eating their meals at home but since she's the one holding things up I make an executive decision and load the kids up in Jai Carlson's borrowed Jeep and head on over to my parents' restaurant. Jai loves my car and was more than willing to trade vehicles which made me think about getting a different car myself. The dogs are too large to ride in the passenger seat of the 'Vette, and since the Hutchins are no longer next door, at least on a permanent basis I don't have a contingency plan. Even Pax's Jag is too small for both dogs. I leave Candace another voice mail and pull into the alley behind Draper's.

"Girls are you prepared to be treated like Princesses?"

I whisper in awe making them giggle and unfasten their seat belts.

I walk around to help Millie out of her car seat and holding hands the three of us enter the back door of Drapers and let the festivities begin. My entire family is waiting on me at our usual table. Vic and Shawna are now expecting a baby sometime next spring, Cassie is grinning at the girls while my parents both have raised eyebrows at me walking into the joint with two strange girls.

"Mead family, meet Molly and Millie Whitaker, my new friends and my boss's daughters," I introduce the suddenly shy children who are both trying to hide behind me. "Girls, look over there, that lovely little angel is my niece Cassie and she'd love to have you sit by her, right Angel?"

Cassie nods her head and pushes her Poppy over to make room in the booth. My mother gets up and adds a couple more chairs then hugs me hello.

"So, you haven't gotten fired, just demoted to babysitter?" she teases knowing who my boss is and the connection between her and Pax.

"Promoted Mother," I correct her. "Those girls are usually chatter boxes, but suddenly they're shy… just like I was at that age."

Poppy and Vic burst out laughing and soon we're bantering back and forth, the girls are loosening up thanks to Cassie and Shawna. Over a split gourmet burger and cheesy potato au gratin the trio of little girls giggle incessantly making me wish they'd go back to their shy ways. Over coffee and chocolate mousse I fill the adults in on what's been happening at work leaving out the court battle today.

At eight thirty my cell phone rings and its Pax calling me. Excusing myself from the table I answer the call.

"Hey babe, are you calling to tell me you're catching an earlier flight?" I tease.

"No, I'm already in the city be quiet and listen," he says stopping me in my tracks at his urgent tone of voice. "Candace is frantic over the girls; did you pick them up at the regular time?"

"Yes, they're with me right now," I tell him sensing something awful has happened.

"Where are you? I drove home and you weren't there. Didn't you speak to Candy about picking up the girls?" he asks in hard, accusatory tone.

"Of course, I did," I snap at him. "I spoke to her about taking them to the park. She said she'd be late and I tried to tell her I'd take the girls with me to Drapers but she hung up on me. Later I left her several voice mails but she never returned one of them."

"Her purse was stolen right outside the courthouse as she was leaving, can you believe it?" He snarls into the receiver. "How'd you get both girls in your car?"

"I'm driving Jai's jeep," I tell him still upset at the tone of voice he used with me. "I'll trade back with him tomorrow. Tell Candace to come to Drapers and pick up her kids or I can drop them off at her place."

"No, don't do that," he snaps at me.

"Paxton, you need to tone down your voice when speaking with me," I warn him not caring that my family is now listening to my conversation. "Where am I supposed to drop them off?"

"Take them to Wiley's apartment and I'll meet you

there," he says. "I'll fill you in later about what's going on, just hurry up and get the kids to Wiley's."

He ends the call without saying goodbye; he's sorry, or even a 'be careful' warning. Now I must face my curious family. Turning around I walk back to the table and look over at the sisters.

"Sorry ladies but we have to leave," I tell them and hear the whiney little voices that want to play with Cassie a little longer. "I know but your mom's waiting and it is a school night for some of us."

Poppy stands up and inclines his head towards the kitchen. I hug Vic, Shawna, and Cassie goodnight and then whisper in my mother's ear, "I was going to tell you but never got the chance?"

She laughs and says, "Nice try, but bullshit."

I laugh down at her and hug her again. "I'll call you tomorrow, and thanks for the meal and for the entertainment. The girls will be asleep before I can drive across town."

Poppy is waiting for us at the back door and carries little Millie across the rear parking lot and secures her in her car seat while I situate Molly. When he opens the driver's side door he leans down and hugs me tightly.

"Harper Marie Mead if you don't get over that man..." he begins only to be cut off by me.

"Poppy, I love him and have been seeing him again for several weeks," I confess and wait for the bomb to explode.

"Honey, I know you're still seeing the man," he admits making me sharply look up into his smiling face. "Marc mentioned it a couple times and finally I just came right out and asked. Marc said Ginger would kill him if she found out he told, so to spare my favorite contractor and your best friend's significant other, I've held my tongue, but if there's something going on your family should know about, please, tell me."

"Poppy my boss's ex-husband is crazy, causing all kinds of trouble and Pax and I are unfortunately caught in the middle, but don't worry, we're looking out for each other," I tell him praying that's really the case.

"How is Paxton involved?" he asks then looks closely at me and whispers, "son of a bitch."

Laughing I shrug my shoulders and reply, "I know, it's crazy but the woman he cheated on me with is now my boss, and a good friend... who knew?"

He chuckles at the bizarre turn of events and waves at the girls in the back seat, "Drive carefully Princess, and call if you need anything."

Hugging him again I smile and say, "Thanks for trusting me; I gotta go, love you Poppy."

"Bye, call your mother tomorrow..." he says turning and waving his hand over his head as he walks back inside his favorite place on earth.

26

Pulling up to the curb in front of the townhouse I shared with Pax I barely have time to turn off the engine before Pax and Candace run down the steps and collect the girls, rushing them inside the building without even bothering to say a word. I lock the Jeep and grab my bags taking my time walking up the stairs and opening the door to the foyer. I can hear Pax and Wiley talking and Candace asking the girls if they had a good time. When I walk into Wiley's living room the girls race over to hug me making the adults stop talking and nod their heads in greeting.

"Did you tell your mom about meeting Cassie?" I ask them and they turn back to their mother and fill her in on their new friend.

Wiley shakes his head then walks out of the room as the noise level increases dramatically while the excited girls talk over one another. I turn to see Paxton leaning against the fireplace mantle, watching me closely. I shrug my shoulders at him and even though my mind takes in how hot and sexy looking he appears in his dark suit, loosened tie and russet wingtips, I still have enough control over my libido to remain aloof.

"Hello Paxton, have a nice flight?" I ask making him grin at the tone of my voice.

"Yes I did, thanks for asking," he replies then walks over towards me and taking my hand in his he walks me out into the hallway where he presses his lower body to mine, pushing me up against the stair railing and kisses me long and deeply. "Good God I missed you," he murmurs against my bruised lips.

Still feeling miffed I reply, "really, I couldn't tell."

I cross my arms under my breast and unbelievably he laughs at me. I swing my heavy bag at him hitting his chest with enough force to make him stagger in surprise.

"Stop it Harpo," he warns reaching for my purse and tugging it out of my hands. "I always miss you when we're a part, you know that. But tonight, I had a frantic mother on my hands and a missing fiancée, cut me some slack."

"Afraid I can't do that," I tell him reaching for my bag again. "I live by a code, and that code says, 'mean people suck' and you were mean to me… give me my purse, I need to get home and check on the boys." I grab a hold of my leather purse strap and tug.

"The boys are fine unless they're eating you out of house and home," he laughs pulling sharply and making me fall into his arms. "There, now that's where you belong," he whispers and kisses me softly on the lips. My body responds and the two of us ignite. If Wiley hadn't interrupted us Pax and I would have been making love under the staircase.

"Knock it off you two," the former roommate growls. "The girls are coming so put it away."

I laugh at his phrasing but step back and let Pax step

behind me to hide his erection. The girls walk into the hall and hug me goodnight as they walk upstairs.

"I'm so sorry I missed where you said you'd take the girls," Candace says hugging me to her chest. "Thank you so much for caring for them… if they'd have been at Tina's house instead of with you…"

She cannot finish the sentence leading me to believe something bad has happened and I'm still in the dark. I watch an emotionally wrought mother usher her girls upstairs to Pax and my old apartment then turn to face my man.

"Tell me what's going on," I demand and he looks up at the top of the stairs.

"Not here. I'll tell you on the way home, which we're leaving now." He replies and shakes hands with Wiley as he gently pushes me towards the front door and out onto the stoop. "Give me the keys."

"Okay, but I need to stop by the supermarket and pick up a few things," I tell him.

Pulling into our old neighborhood market I spend considerable time restocking the milk, fresh vegetables, and pick up some peaches with a bunch of bananas. Pax is holding the red plastic basket and adds his own items to the pile. By the time we climb back into the jeep we have three grocery bags full and one anxious man dying to get home.

"Would you please tell me what's happening," I ask Pax as he keeps looking in the rear-view mirror to make sure we're not being followed.

"Hold on," he says speeding through the city. "Let me get out of Albany then I can focus on you, okay? What did you have for supper?"

Laughing he needs his concentration to drive but can still talk about food.

"Poppy prepared his famous Moroccan Chicken with couscous and pine nuts," I tell him as if reading it off the menu, "and then he served those honey almond shortbread cookies you love so much with dried fruits and honey."

"Wow, that sounds great," he mumbles to himself and signals at the next exit. "Can you cook like that?"

"No, but Victor can," I admit and smile when he looks over at me with a grin on his face.

"I doubt your brother or your entire family will be thrilled when you bring me to the next brunch," he laughs at the thought, "Your father will stroke out when he hears we're back together again."

"He did not," I tell him making him slow down and look over at me.

"You told them?" he asks amazed I'd admit to seeing him again.

"No, but they all knew and seemed okay with it," I say thinking about how well Mom and Dad have taken the news; neither of them blew a fuse.

"That's good to know," he laughs and then relaxes when we get on the two-lane highway leading to Lake Sinclaire. "Okay, let me tell you what happened, why I was so 'mean' to you."

"You were mean to me," I argue with him. "You really need to work on your communication skills," I say when he reaches across the seat and covers my lips with his index finger.

"Do you want to hear the story or complain about my shortcomings?" he asks making me laugh when he removes his hand.

"Well, short coming has never been an issue with you," I tease him scooting over and placing my hand on his thigh and giving it a squeeze.

"I better drive faster, huh?" he laughs then clears his throat and in a husky voice says, "Seriously I need to tell you about the girl's babysitter."

I stop joking and let him tell his story.

"Candace was at the courthouse all day today as you know," he begins, "but after the last break Cody's attorney requested Cody never returned to the galley. He skipped out and went straight to the babysitter's house. Apparently when he couldn't find the girls, be beat Tina Grossman when she wouldn't say where the girls were at or who was with them."

"No," I breathe at what that poor woman went through. "How badly was she hurt?"

"Not too bad because she knew a form of martial arts and forced him out of her house," he smirks slowing down as we approach a car signaling to turn off onto a dimly lit driveway, "That must have hurt his pride, beat up by the babysitter."

"Did she call the cops?" I ask praying the incident was documented.

"She did, but by the time the cops arrived Cody was long gone. Tina is pressing charges against him so they'll have a warrant out for his arrest but I believe he's not going to leave without attempting to get the girls," he sighs making me feel his frustration.

"Poor Candace, no wonder she freaked out earlier," I tell him as we pull into the drive. I get out and manually open the garage door and flip on the lights while he pulls the jeep into the bay and turns off the motor.

"I like this SUV," he says looking around the illuminated interior after opening his door. "We might need to consider getting one for ourselves," he informs me as he grabs our laptops and his suitcase in the back seat.

Opening the back hatch, I grab two grocery bags and smile at him.

"We're thinking alike," I tell him as he picks up the third bag and closes the back hatch then hits the automatic door opener and the silky glide of chain and gears silently closes the bay door.

"Excellent, but we'll need to add on to the garage," he says unlocking the front door and holding it open for the pups to run out and greet us.

"Actually, I was thinking about selling the 'Vette instead of just buying a second vehicle.

From the look on his face you'd think I wanted to sell our first born child.

"No way! You are not selling the 'Vette." He hisses setting the bags and my purse on the island. "I'll buy it from you before I let you sell that beast to a stranger."

Laughing at his passion for my car I smile and say, "Fine, we'll keep the 'Vette but you have to buy the jeep, I'm currently tapped out of my savings."

He walks over to stand behind me where he wraps his arms around my waist and says, "I want to share everything with you, and that means my name on the mortgage too, that way it's our home, are you okay with that?"

Turning in his arms I reach up and kiss his lips making him growl deep in his throat.

"I'm more than alright with that Mr. Barrett," I say against his neck. "As a matter of fact, let's get married the second you're settled back at Albany, whatever day of the week that falls on."

"Sounds good to me, do you want to go away or meet at City Hall?" he asks putting the perishables in the fridge. "Mom is going to be pissed again… I'm keeping her from having a big wedding in her back yard. What is it with her and weddings?"

"I haven't a clue but that's not the kind of wedding I want anyway," I tell him. "Let's get married at the courthouse, and then leave for that Tahiti trip, sound good to you?"

He laughs and nuzzles my neck with his chin and replies, "I'll even make the reservations, how's that?"

The pups suddenly bark scaring me to death. Pax walks over to the lamps and flips the switch putting us in near darkness. York and Kirby are still barking when Pax opens the front door and walks outside, leaving the excited and baying dogs pacing back and forth inside the living room. I can barely make out Pax's shape as he walks over towards the Hutchins' house. That's when I see Darrell and Silas standing at the edge of the driveway. I can't hear what they're saying but Pax shouts over his shoulder, "Harper, you can let the dogs out."

At the speed of light the Mastiff's race toward the guys; joining the late-night callers I hug Silas then Darrell in greeting.

"It's been so long since I've seen you guys," I tell them placing my hand on York's broad head and scratching behind his ears. "What's going on? Why aren't you back home… wait a second, are you playing hooky young man?"

Silas nods his head making his father and Pax laugh. Wrapping his arm around my waist Pax draws me to his side and explains.

"Darrell accidently left behind some items and came back to get them when he noticed a strange vehicle, a blue four-wheel drive pick-up truck parked in our drive. He started to walk over but the man driving the truck was slamming his hands on the wheel in anger, right?" Pax asks Silas listening to every word.

"Right," he declares and shows us how the man was acting. "He was pounding his hands like this," then says, "I heard him say a couple bad words… which Daddy said he'd wash my mouth out with soap if I said them, right?"

Smiling down at his boy Darrell says, "that's right," then looks up at us and continues, "he was mumbling to himself, seemed all agitated so I grabbed Si's hand and walked back towards our porch getting ready to call you Harper but he peeled out of the driveway and sped away before I could see his tags. Sorry but I was thinking it was you Pax, at least until I heard the swearing."

"Yeah, I never swear, do I honey?" Pax teases nudging me with his hip. "Which direction did he turn?"

"Left, back towards Lake Sinclaire," Darrell says. "I checked your place and it appeared fine, the boys were barking inside but once I called out to them and walked over to the kennel side of the house they were fine. Is everything alright? I mean between you two?"

"You bet," I tell him and share our good news, "we're getting married in a couple months so when I see you guys next I'll be Harper Barrett, can you remember that Si?"

"Sure, but what's your last name now?" he asks making us laugh.

"Come on Si, we got to get going, I told your mom we'd be back an hour ago," the father says to his son, "but we wanted to make sure everything was alright here; I didn't want to worry you so I didn't leave a message on your phone."

"Thanks for the neighborly concern," Pax says squatting down while holding out his arms for Silas to hug him goodbye. The small boy hurls himself into his honorary uncle's arms and hugs him tightly.

"The guys are going to be mad when they find out we were here and got to see you and the boys," he laughs feeling slightly superior to his siblings.

"When will you be back?" I ask running my open palm up and down Silas' back. "Don't you have a fall break?"

"Baby, they've only been in school three weeks," Pax reminds me but he smiles down at me knowing I miss the little Hutchins just like York and Kirby.

"Don't worry, we'll be back towards the end of next month," Darrell says. "Maybe we can have a wiener roast or a bonfire?"

"Yeah! And maybe Fabian can come too?" Silas chimes in grinning from ear-to-ear thinking about seeing his good friend.

"Sounds like I better get started planning a wiener roast, doesn't it?" I tickle the boy who laughs and squirms in Pax's arms. "Okay, we'll let you go and thanks for looking out for our place, I appreciate that."

"No problem," Darrell says taking Silas from Pax and waving as they walk back across their yard and disappear into the house.

"Come on, I'm exhausted, let's go to bed," He calls the dogs and they both come running following us inside the house as we call it a day.

27

"Harper!" Pax growls out my name as he finds his release and drops his sweaty body on top of me. "Oh…my…God," he pants trying to catch his breath and then laughs at my dazed look.

I simply smile and try to nod my head since my body stopped listening to my brain ten minutes ago. Waking up to Pax's lovemaking is the perfect cardio exercise, except my mind is always as exhausted as my body afterward. Rolling over to his side of the bed he gathers me to his damp chest.

"Are you alright?" he asks smiling down into my face. "You look so good, so sexy first thing with your hair sticking to the side of your head…" he teases knowing I'm a mess now.

"Very funny Pax," I softly tug on the hair of his chest making him flinch and cover my fingers with his hand. "But that's what you get for waking me up like that," I tell him. "If you want perfection this early in the day don't attack me when I'm sleeping."

He smirks silently telling me he's never going to stop his early morning sexual jaunts. For the last couple of days, he's woken me by sliding into me as we lay spooning each other. Nothing is like the feel of those first couple of seconds when we join, him slowly going deeper into my relaxed body. This is one of his favorite positions and rapidly becoming my wake-up call.

"What time are we meeting your parents?" he asks stretching to pick up his wristwatch from the bedside table. "It's already nine thirty."

"What?" I jerk into a sitting position, "Oh no, hurry up Pax, we're going to be late as it is…Shit," I hiss under my breath throwing the covers back. "Come on, move it, we're supposed to meet them at Draper's at ten thirty."

Laughing at my frantic exit from our bed he saunters over to the bath and says over his shoulder, "well, it's not like they're expecting me to make a good impression, so don't sweat it and join me in the shower."

"No way," I laugh at his sexy backside, "we'd never live that down, not showing up at all."

"Suit yourself," he says and then turns back to face me, "is the coffee still on?"

Damn, it's an automatic shut off so it's been sitting there cooling off for over an hour and a half. That's what I get for staying up late, making love twice this morning and falling back asleep between each love romp.

"I'll make a fresh pot, just hurry please," I say walking out of the bedroom and down the stairs to find the boys waiting on me. "Sorry guys, no walk this morning."

Ten minutes later with two cups of steaming hot coffee in each hand I follow the dogs upstairs and step inside our bedroom to find Pax sitting on the side of the bed, dressed in a pair of ratty old jeans, a paint stained gray t-shirt and sliding his feet into a pair of grungy boots.

"You are not going to my family's brunch dressed like

that," I insist as he takes his cup from my hand. "What are you doing Pax?"

"Dressing for the part of bad boy meets good girl's parents?" he jokes making me shake my head and set my cup down on the nightstand before walking over to his side of the closet and pulling out a different outfit.

"Sometimes it's like having a thirty year old child…" I mumble but he hears me and laughs out loud.

"You're the only babysitter I want to watch me," he teases coming up behind me and nuzzling my neck. "Come on, no tie today," he groans when he sees the black shirt and gray tie I'm holding up. "Besides, I'll bet Draper wears his navy t-shirt, jeans, and those awful clogs."

Smiling over my shoulder I nod my head at the perfect description of my father's favorite weekend outfit. I relent and put the business casual outfit back into the closet and turn to face the man.

"Pick out something else and please, no holes, stains, or those disgusting boots," I say kissing his lips and pulling out of his arms when he deepens the embrace. "I'm going to grab a quick shower so take the boys out for me okay? I already fed them but they need fresh water outside," I call out as I step into the white and teal colored bathroom.

This weekend has flown by and since he'll be leaving for his place in Ottawa tomorrow afternoon, I doubly hate to see it end. For the next six weeks, he and I will be catching a quick visit when we can. Drying off with a thick fluffy white towel I straighten the wet, bunched up bath sheet he used and left on the tile floor to hang it up next to my own. Pulling on clean underwear I reach for my blue jeans, navy t-shirt, gray sweater, and then slide my bare feet into a pair of raspberry colored suede ballet slippers. Our brunch is always informal but dressing in your best casual clothes is a show of respect. Brushing on some facial powder, a flick of mascara, and a coat of berry colored lip gloss I reach for my blue and white polka dot scarf and head downstairs.

Pax has the dogs outside and I can hear his laughter as the they play double Frisbee. The man looks good in relaxed fitting jeans, black polo shirt, and charcoal gray sports coat. However, he is still wearing those ugly boots, even though it appears he tried to clean them up. This is one battle not worth fighting. Carrying my bag over my shoulder I walk out onto the deck and smile at the boys. One last throw for each and he herds them to the back kennel gate, kisses me as he walks by and looks at his wrist watch.

"We're only going to be a half hour late if traffic is light," he says but I'm not sure if that is to make me feel better or more anxious about showing up with the proverbial bad boy in tow. From the wicked lift of his eyebrows I'd say it was the latter.

"I'll call them once we're on the way," I tell him sliding my hand in his and walking over to the garage.

"What the hell?" he says under his breath and stops dead in his tracks looking at the red paint smeared across the white exterior door to the garage. "Don't touch it," he says releasing my hand and getting a closer look at what appears to be bloody hand prints.

"Is it blood?" I ask looking around to see if there's any more.

"No, it's enamel paint," he says scraping his thumbnail across the surface of the imprinted image, "Looks like somebody is playing a joke or threatening us."

"A threat?" I ask as chills run down my spine, "Whitaker?"

"Who else," he replies pulling out his phone and taking a couple photographs. "Don't worry babe," he says. "Let's go to your folks then we'll figure this out when we get back."

He seems too calm in my estimation. Normally he gets all protective, even territorial so I think he's more worried than he's letting on but I follow his lead and soon we're pulling onto the highway when I call the folks and tell them we're running behind and it will another half hour before we can get there.

"Don't worry Princess," Poppy tells me, "Vic and the girls just got here so everything will be ready in about thirty minutes. Be careful and we'll see you both soon, love you, bye."

I turn to look at Pax and find him staring out the windshield but I'd bet he's driving on auto pilot from the far off look he's wearing on his face. Turning to stare out the window I run through the list of things I must get done this week for Candace. She is meeting with her attorney again Tuesday so I'll be picking up the girls from the sitter, there's a stack of letters to the editor to be sorted, which Tara will help me with, but then there's the dreaded Department Meetings Melanie is so fond of instigating. As I mentally run through mine and Candace's schedule I don't even feel the car stop.

"Are you coming?" Pax asks as he turns off the ignition and smiles over at me. We're sitting at the curb of Draper's Restaurant and from the look on his amused face we've been here several minutes.

"Oh, honey I'm sorry, I got lost in my thoughts," I say

gathering my bag and reaching for the passenger side door handle of his Jaguar. "You seemed deep in thought too."

He links our fingers together as we walk up the front walk to the restaurant now closed due to it being Sunday. Before he opens the heavily ornate high gloss black painted door he turns towards me and says, "I love you, and if this is going to be my last meal, I'm going to order everything on the menu."

Laughing at his silliness I lean into him, press my hand to the back of his head and force him down to my lips. Kissing each other breathless I'm winded when we pull apart.

"Don't worry," I tell him placing my hand on his chest and loving the feel of his elevated heartbeat. "I'll taste everything first, I promise."

Wrapping his arm around my waist he bends me over his arm and kisses me deeply again only this time when we pull apart my family is waiting in the door way. One by one, they clap at our performance making Pax take a bow and I turn beet red. Pushing me in front of him Pax holds out his hand towards my father with his other arm still wrapped around my waist in a possessive manner I love.

"Draper, thanks for feeding me," he says not getting into the past drama.

Taking his hand my father shakes Pax's proffered one and ominously says, "Don't thank me until you've tasted what I prepared, just for you..."

My mother and Shawna laugh but Vic is silent, giving Pax a quick nod as his greeting. Cassie runs over to me and hugs me around the waist.

"Did you bring Molly and Millie?" she asks looking up at me dying to see her new friends again.

"No sweetheart, they're with their mommy, but you'll see them again soon, I promise." I hug her slight shoulders then turn her around and point over at Pax playing chicken with Victor. "But look, I did bring Uncle Pax."

She spins around and runs over to Pax and leaps into his arms. Instinctively he catches her and spins her around making her squeal in delight when he tickles her tummy.

"I'm so glad to see you," she says pressing her plump little cheek to his beard stubble one. "Aunt Harper was so sad you left," she recalls the conversation she and I had the first night she slept over. "I told her you do the best Donald Duck sneeze, do it for me, please?"

He laughs at the angelic little girl with her mop of blonde curls and obliges, making the rest of us laugh when Cassie goes into a fit of giggles before telling him to do it again. Repeatedly Pax pretends to be the beloved cartoon character until Shawna gives him a break.

"Cass, go get the card you made for Aunt Harper," her mother instructs her. "It's in Mamaw's office." I hug my sister-in-law and rub her small little baby bump making her laugh.

"Why don't we go inside," Mom says always playing the hostess. "Draper fixed a large pitcher of Bloody Mary's and I am dying for one."

Walking into the dimly lit vestibule Cassie comes running around the hostess podium towards me with a homemade greeting card made from blue construction paper, glued on felt letters and tons of glitter, which appears behind her like sparkly exhaust. Taking the precious gift,

I gently open the card and smile at the drawings she did of my house, the lake, the dogs, and even a male stick person holding out his branch-like arm towards me, smiling since I know he must be Pax.

"Angel I love it," I tell her and bend down to kiss the top of her curly head. "Look Pax, she even put you in the picture too."

He grins and chucks my niece under the chin but her next woods create a subtle tension in the air.

"No, that's a new boyfriend," she says reaching out for her father's hand looking up at Pax. "You don't live at Aunt Harper's house. Daddy said Aunt Harper would find someone to take your place so I drew him for her... see, he has yellow hair, not black like you Uncle Pax."

I look over at my brother and give him an angry glare but he shrugs his shoulders and bends down to pick up his little girl and walks into the empty dining room to start our meal.

"Sorry about that," Shawna whispers to the both of us. "She repeats everything now and you know Vic, he tends to hold a grudge... unlike his sweet and irresistible younger sister."

She smiles and then laughs when Pax leans over and kisses my temple.

"Thank God she doesn't resemble her brother at all," he grins and walks us into the empty, large open dining area and pulls out my chair, then my mother's too as he takes in his surroundings.

Draper's is a great gathering place with its high tin ceilings, dark stained booths lining the perimeter of the establishment, the black and white penny-round tiles covering the floor resemble area rugs and the lush plants help create the feel of a comfortable sitting room. But the pride of the place is its food...out of this world good thanks to my father's gifts. Vic and I grew up in this place and it will always be a second home to me. Just being here with my family, the easy camaraderie of the Sunday brunch, the man I love sitting next to me...it's as good as it gets and my mood gets even lighter.

"Hey big mouth," I tease my brother sitting at the opposite end of the table from me. "Pour us a couple drinks, please."

"Sure, Shawna here's your straight juice," he says handing his pregnant wife her glass before he looks up at us. "I promise to refrain from gossiping around the little echo machine."

"Appreciate that," Pax says accepting the two glasses from Victor and setting them on the table in front of us. "Something smells delicious Draper, let me help you bring in the food," he says taking a sip of the potent drink. "Damn, I should have had you taste this cocktail first," he whispers in my ear reminding me of my promise to protect him.

"Poppy's drinks always have so much liquor in them, no amount of poison could survive in there," I laugh and touch my tall glass to his before taking a sip of the stout drink then he disappears in the kitchen making the others at the table look over at me in surprise but I shrug my shoulders at them as I watch Cassie play with her silverware.

A couple minutes later my father steps back into the room rolling a server's cart filled with individual plates of Eggs Benedict, baked thick-sliced bacon, curried fruit cups, croissants, and what appear to be his famous streusel coffee bars with Pax carrying another pot of coffee and a grin on his face.

"Take a plate and pass it down," the restaurateur says handing Victor the first plate. "There are strawberry preserves and orange marmalade along with the butter dish already on the table. I'll be back with a second pitcher of drinks in a second." Dad says and wheels the cart back through the swinging door separating the tables from his private domain. I swear the man is whistling as he disappears behind the dark red swinging door.

"I love your father's Eggs Benedict," Pax says sitting down next to me and accepting the plate I hold out towards him. "Oh, hey Shawna, Vic I want to offer my congratulations on the baby," he smiles picking up his drink and raising the glass towards that end of the table.

"Thanks," Victor grudgingly says after Shawna elbows him in the ribs. "We're thrilled," he says rubbing his side as he looks down at his daughter sitting in a tall child's chair. "Tell Aunt Harper what names you picked out for the baby."

Cassie sets her small cup of apple juice down and leans into the table and whispers, "Harley if it's a boy and Dave's son if it's a girl."

Shawna elbows her husband again but it's too late everybody is laughing over her daughter's miss-pronunciation of the motorcycle my brother keeps insisting he needs, it's a running joke with the family.

"Seriously," the expectant mother says, "if we have a boy his name will be Chase Edward and if we have a girl we'll call her Tonya Marie."

Cassie claps her hands over her head and says, "Dave's son Marie."

My father joins the table with a grin on his face, "Harley Davidson again?" he asks his put-upon daughter –in-law making Pax and I laugh all over again.

"Let's eat," Mom says and the conversation flows naturally.

By the time the dishes have been cleared and the streusel coffee bars devoured I'm feeling warm and fuzzy. Resting my head on Pax's shoulder, I can't stop the smile that appears on my face. But Poppy notices it and says, "So, everything seems to be running smoothly with you two."

Before I can say anything, Pax kisses the top of my head and nudges me off his shoulder. Raising my head I look over at him and can't figure out what the smirk on his face is about. He scoots his chair out from behind him and reaches into his gray jacket pocket pulling out a small antique black velvet jeweler's box. Kneeling on one knee he picks up my hand and kisses my knuckles as my mother, Shawna, and I hold our breath.

"Harper Marie Mead," he makes me smile. "We've had a crazy year. I know I've let you down countless times before but I'm begging you, will you please give me another chance…will you marry me?"

He opens the lid of the worn velvet box and removes a vintage solitaire engagement ring set in a yellow gold band. Pax looks up at me and waits for my answer before he slides the ring over my knuckle.

"Yes," I tell him. "Yes, I'll marry you," and tears of joy distort my vision until his image is swimming before me. "I love you so much," I whisper and love the pinch I feel as he pushes the antique ring over my knuckle, sealing my fate since I know the ring must be cut off. It feels like it belongs there, as if I've been missing the weight of this object all my life. A memory of the antique ivory pin flashes in my head and I know this ring will continue to be passed down the line of Barrett's just like the brooch.

He kisses me deeply and then stands up. Poppy is holding a chilled bottle of champagne and six fluted glasses.

"To my bride," Pax says accepting the sparkling wine and lifting his glass towards me, "To a new beginning."

I tilt my glass to his and change his toast, "to our new beginning," and let the sharp tingling bite of the bubbly slide down my throat. The toast is perfect, just like the moment.

After hugs and congratulations are offered I look down at the stunning ring on my third finger and study the honest, simplicity of the item. I love it with its perfect size diamond, and the miss-shaped band from being worn for years on someone else's finger. It is so much dearer than the first one he grudgingly gave me. He leans over and whispers in my ear.

"That was my mother's engagement ring in case you're wondering," he says. "She's praying you'll say yes so we'll call her later with the good news, okay?"

I nod my head shocked at the fact he proposed in front of my family knowing how angry they were at him, but he still professed his love.

"Yes, I'd love to hear from your mother again," I whisper kissing his lips and wishing we were alone, at our house.

"Where might I ask are you going to get married?" my mom asks placing her elbows on the table and resting her chin in her hands. "Keeping in mind my heart can't take another big non-wedding."

Pax grins down at our clasped hands and says, "I can't apologize enough for that dreadful day but we're going to the courthouse here in Albany and then flying off to Tahiti for a couple weeks, right babe?"

Leaning forward I smile at my surprised mother and sister-in-law and laugh.

"I considered Las Vegas, but neither one of us can take the time off right now…" I reply which makes my brother laugh out loud.

"Would Elvis be attending?" he asks and then the rest of the table chimes in creating an outlandish wedding party and reception with past and present stars known for their Vegas acts.

A while later I look at my wristwatch and say, "We need to be heading back to the Lake," Pax nods his head and scoots his chair out. "Mom, Poppy thanks for a wonderful meal and being in on the surprise," I smile over at my father who shrugs his shoulders in what he thinks looks like an innocent gesture.

"Yeah, thanks Draper for keeping my secret," Pax teases making my father deny he knew anything about the proposal until Pax joined him in the kitchen.

"This guy came up with the entire 'pop the question' scenario," my parent tells me hugging me to his chest. "Are you happy?" he asks knowing I'm ecstatic.

"Yes Dad," I whisper and kiss his cheek.

"Well then I guess all Pax has to worry about is you showing up at the courthouse, right brother?" Victor teases but there is still an edge to his voice that makes everyone in the room frown.

"Don't listen to him," my mother says hugging Pax and then me. "He's just being a big brother; you know they never outgrow that title."

"I'll remember that," Pax says and nods his head at the man in question. "See you later."

Cassie runs over to us and leaps into Pax's arms.

"Can I be the flower girl again?" she asks placing both her dimpled hands on either side of his face and holding him still. "I still have the dress and the basket, but the flowers got all wrinkly and Momma threw them away."

Pax's heart melts at the disappointment in my niece's voice. He hugs her tiny body in his strong arms and says, "I'll buy you an even bigger basket this time, okay?"

"Thanks, I love you," she tells him and I swear I see a glistening in his dark eyes before he closes them and hugs the child again.

"I love you too Angel," he whispers and then hands her over to me.

"We're getting married again!" she squeals and hugs me tightly around my neck, wrapping her legs around my waist and laughs. "Can we invite Molly and Millie to the wedding?" she asks getting excited about seeing the girls again.

"Of course," I tell her and set her down on her grandma's lap. "But first we must pick a date so I'll have to check with their mommy and I'll let you know, okay?"

"Okay... Poppy can I have another piece of cake?" she asks already switching conversation at break neck speed as we leave my family behind and head out the door.

We pull into our drive an hour later and suddenly, my world feels different, better somehow simply because I'm wearing a used ring, planning for a civil wedding ceremony, and my fiancé is getting ready to leave for a couple weeks... Yep, my life is perfect.

28

In the next three weeks my life settles down to near perfection. Pax and I are in a good routine even with his living a long distance from me, work is running smoothly, and I feel like I'm finally living the dream. Watching Candace's girls and my niece play with the dogs outside makes me laugh out loud. York and Kirby are getting so tall and filling out more. They each weigh more than Cassie and together they outweigh me by almost thirty pounds. Molly and Millie are staying the night with me and my niece. Pax will be back tomorrow and he's promised to take me and the girls to the newest animated movie after an exciting dinner at the 'Children's Palace' a local pizza and playground restaurant. My cell phone interrupts my entertainment and pulling the device out of the back pocket of my jeans I smile when I see it's Candace, feeling left out no doubt.

"Hi Candace," I answer the phone, "checking up on me?"

"No, checking up on my girls," a deep male voice replies scaring the crap out of me.

"Who is this?" I whisper walking over to see the girls

and the dogs are where I left them ten seconds ago. "Cody?" I ask praying he will not cause trouble.

The police arrested him a couple days after he attacked the baby sitter, but his attorney convinced the judge he was drunk and frustrated because his ex-wife was preventing him from seeing his children. The babysitter, Tina Grossman filed assault charges against him but the charges were pled down to a misdemeanor of drunk and disorderly; he was reprimanded for two days, agreed to attend AA meetings and an anger management class at the local YMCA and let go. No one had heard from him until now.

"It's me Harper," he says like we're old friends. "Why are the girls staying with you? Where's their lying, cheating, whore of a mother? Is she living with Wiley now?"

Unsure how he knows what's going on I motion for the girls to bring the dogs inside without alerting them their father is on the phone. I point up the stairs and cover the mouth piece before I speak to the giggling girls.

"Go on upstairs to the tower room and play," I smile and say, "I'll call you in a little bit and you can help me make tacos for supper, okay?"

The response is loud, affirmative, and said in unison over their shoulders as they run up the stairs, the dogs following close behind. Cody is talking still and I only catch the tail end of what he just said.

"…then she'll know what it feels like to lose everything," he snarls.

"Sorry I missed part of that," I tell him trying to sound sympathetic. "How will she know what that feels like?" I ask walking over to the land line in the kitchen and punching in Pax's number.

"I said she doesn't deserve to raise my daughters," he shouts getting agitated having to repeat himself. "What's wrong with you women? Can't you stay focused for five minutes? God you're alike, just like my father says."

"Back up a second Cody," I tell him trying to keep him lucid long enough for Pax to hear his tirade. "I've never done anything to deserve your condemnation, have I?" I ask and thankfully Pax picks up.

I cover the mouth piece on my cell and whisper into the other phone, "Baby, I've got a problem, listen but don't say anything, okay?"

"What the hell is going on Harper?" he whispers hearing the fear and urgency in my voice.

"Cody is on my cell," I tell him. "The number pulled up Candace's old one so I guess he had something to do with her purse being stolen."

"Let me hear," he says so I remove my hand and put the cell on speaker.

"...why you're willing to continue sleeping with that son of a bitch I'll never know," he is lecturing me. "You deserve a man that would cherish you, want to have babies, and be home every night, not like Barrett. You know he's cheating on you still with my wife, right?"

Wanting to keep him talking, I walk into the living room away from the open stairwell so the kids can't hear him.

"No, he's not cheating on me," I tell him. "We're getting married again... he wouldn't do that, besides he only slept with Candace once."

"You're so fucking gullible," he snarls in to the phone. "I'll bet she's with him right now, up in Ontario screwing each other's brains out while you watch the girls. How are my babies doing? Do they ask about me?" he asks in a one eighty-degree turnabout from his hateful tone to a sad, despondent one.

"Sure Cody," I tell him softly praying Pax remains quiet. "You're their father, they love you. But right now, you're not in a good place to be with them."

That was the wrong thing to say. He comes unglued and threatens Candace, Paxton, Wiley, and even me.

"I'll kill anyone that tries to keep me from my children," he screams into the phone ending a full three-minute tirade then he gets eerily quiet. "Not tonight," he sighs like he's emotionally and physically drained, "but soon I'll be by to pick up the girls, then that heartless bitch will spend the rest of her miserable life wondering where they're at, or if they're even alive…" he laughs in such an evil way goose bumps appear on my arms. "I'll be watching for the right moment, Harper. Who knows, maybe you'll ditch the worthless scum and come along with us. Until then, sleep tight, oh and kiss my girls' goodnight."

He ends the call so I turn my attention back to a deathly silent Pax on the other end.

"Are you still there?" I ask praying he will not freak out on me too.

"I'm here baby," he says. "I've changed my flight to leave tonight, but I won't get in until early morning. Lock the doors, keep the dogs with you at all times and don't go outside for anything, okay?"

"Okay," I sigh in relief he's on his way back. "Be careful he sounds unhinged now."

"He's a fucking nut Harper," he growls in the receiver

and I can hear him rustling papers in the background. "How did he know you had the girls?"

"He probably watched me leave work and saw me pick them up from the sitter I guess. Trust me, I'll be on the lookout for him," I tell him hating the creepy feeling of knowing someone has been following me.

"One good thing, he thinks Candace and I are together," he says typing into his computer. "He doesn't know where she's at. I'm going to call her on the land line and tell her not to call your cell. He may have a tracking device or somehow shadowing her phone. We'll be getting new ones tomorrow." He tells me almost reading my mind on that conclusion.

"I've got to make a couple calls before I leave for the airport," he says hating to end our call. "Do exactly like I said and I'll see you early this morning. Is the garage locked up?"

"Yes, ever since the red paint incident I keep the windows as well as the bay doors locked. The exterior door too but the dogs would be waiting on him," I tell him smiling at the thought of the two beasts attacking him.

"He could shoot them baby," he whispers wiping the grin off my face. "Keep them inside except when nature calls, but don't go with them. They can take care of themselves better than you, believe me."

"Okay, well the girls are awfully quiet so I better go check on them," I tell him walking towards the phone unit hanging on the wall. "I love you Pax, hurry home."

"I'll call you when I'm almost to the house so you won't be startled when I get there, okay? Trust your instincts Harper; I love you. I'll be there soon, bye babe," he says and ends the call.

Cold chills run down my spine thinking about anything happening to those three little girls. Outside the windows is pitch dark making me wonder if Cody is as close as he implied. I turn off the lamps in the living room but turn on the kitchen and dining room lights. I smile when I hear whispers and giggles coming from upstairs. Walking over to the stair well I shout up to the kids, "Who's hungry for tacos?"

"Me!" they shout in unison.

The sounds of a herd of horses can be heard coming down two flights of stairs all excited about helping me cook. Whoever said boys were too loud has never spent the weekend with two three-year-old and a bossy five-year-old little girl. They're louder than all four Hutchins and Fabian combined. But I love the sound of children playing even if the little banshees squeal loud enough to crack the plaster in the ceiling.

Almost an hour later we're all set to eat our masterpieces of tacos when the boys bark, scare the life out of all of us. York and Kirby race to the side porch just as a pair of headlights pull into the drive. My cell phone rings so I grab it off the counter and get a shock when I read Wiley on the screen.

"Wiley?" I answer the phone praying it's him in my driveway.

"Hey there Harper," he replies laughing as he shuts off his car and opens the door. "Bet you'd never be happy to see me huh?"

Laughing out loud I end the call and check on the girls making a mess on the counter but right now I could not care less. Walking over to the door I flip on the porchlight and sure enough Pax's best friend is smiling through the screen door. I unlock it and step back to allow the dogs a whiff of my unexpected visitor.

"Wow those are huge dogs," he says bending down on one knee and letting them get familiar with him and his scent. "Pax said they're still pups?"

"They are," I tell him and the second I close the door he stands up and opens his arms wide surprising me he knows I need a hug.

"Thank you for coming out here," I tell him and feel his strong arms close around me offering comfort and security. "I didn't realize how alone I am."

"Baby Sister, you're only a phone call away," he says kissing my forehead in an un-Wiley like fashion. "Get used to it," he laughs when he sees the confusion on my face. "You're going to be marrying my best friend, and he's already promised to make me Godfather to one of your brood so you're stuck with me. Hey is that tacos?"

He drags me by the hand into the kitchen where the girls are covered in taco sauce, lettuce and cheese is everywhere and there are tomatoes hanging from one white iron chandelier over the island. They're giggling like little imps so when I point to the light fixture they point their fingers at each other and laugh all over again. After tidying up the place Wiley fixes him five massive tacos and accepts the beer I hand him with a nod then turns to the trio whispering behind their dimpled little hands.

"Okay, I need names, ages, and favorite movies… and go," he says snapping his fingers at them making them laugh harder and give him false information until they're through with their meal and ask to be excused.

"Go wash your hands in the downstairs bathroom," I tell them wiping down their stools with enough lettuce, tomato, and cheese to make another couple tacos. "Molly, please help the younger girls, okay?"

She smiles when Wiley winks at her and then takes her sister and Cassie by the hand and leaves the room. The room becomes blessedly silent. Pouring myself a glass of wine I lean my head on my arm and blow out a deep breath.

"I'm so glad you're here," I whisper unable to believe Pax's friend would spend a Friday evening babysitting rather than going out on the town. "Did you get a rain check from her?" I ask and he doesn't even pretend he doesn't understand the question.

"Yeah, she's not real big on kids now," he laughs taking another swig of beer, "but man does she love to mother me."

I snicker at the snake when he fills me in on what he knows.

"Candace is seeing about getting a continuance on the restraining order and will be calling you tomorrow after promising not to show up here and upsetting the girls by ending their sleepover. Pax called the County Sheriff Department and they'll be patrolling the area tonight. I called Ginger and she said you and the girls can stay at her place if you'd like," he says smiling at me. "But you'll wait it out for Pax, won't you?" he grins at me then shakes his head. "I hope when my time comes I meet a woman that believes in me the way you do that boy."

"I'd say there's hope for you yet," I laugh when he throws a stray piece of chopped tomato at me. "No, no, no don't even start with the whole food fight thing," I warn him picking up his empty plate and scooping up the toppings and placing both in the sink. The girls walk back into the room soaked from their arms to their necks.

"I mopped it up," Molly says before I can even ask what happened.

"Thank you dear," I tell her then look over my shoulder at Wiley chuckling at me. "You wait; three little girls, a cartoon movie, and popcorn are on your agenda tonight."

He stands up from the barstool, stretches his long legs and says, "Bring `em on."

Two and a half hours later he is wiped out on the sectional, sock feet propped on the big coffee table, a sleeping girl on each side and one on his lap, sound asleep. Once they decided on which movie to watch they changed into their pajamas, ate some popcorn, chattered, giggled, and danced through the first viewing and then conked out after the first ten minutes of the cartoon as we watched it again. He is almost asleep himself when my cell phone rings from where I left it on the island in the kitchen, its Pax. Quickly answering the phone I smile when I hear his voice.

"Hey sweetie," he says into my ear. "I'm about a half hour away, did Wiley call?"

"No, he showed up at the front door a couple hours ago," I whisper into the phone. "He's the best babysitter," I chuckle when he laughs. "He said you promised he could be Godfather to one of our children. How many are you planning on?" I ask making him get real quiet but when he answers my heart leaps with joy.

"I'd like at least two, maybe three," he says softly but seriously. "Let's plan them a couple years apart, starting next year, how's that sound?"

"Like I'd jump your bones if you were standing in front

of me," I reply making him howl in anticipation. Wiley snaps his fingers in the air from the sofa letting me know he wants to talk to his best friend. "Be careful, drive safely, and the nanny wants to speak with you. I love you and here's Wiley."

I hand him the phone and he sticks out his tongue over my 'nanny' comment but he assures Pax everything is okay here but he'd prefer Godsons...not Goddaughters if he didn't mind. He whispers looking down at the sleeping cherubs in his arms, "Boys have got to be quieter than girls."

He laughs at whatever Pax replies and then says, "She'd have as many as you wanted, trust me. I better go, she's getting that look again," he rolls his eyes at me making me cover my mouth to keep from laughing. "She scares me Pax," he whines and then laughs too loudly making Cassie shift in his arms but he gently rubs her pink flannel back until she settles down. "Okay buddy, gotta go, I'll see you soon."

He hands me the phone without taking his eyes off my niece. When he looks at me he has a sheepish look on his handsome green-eyed face.

"They're amazing when they're asleep, aren't they?" he whispers, serious in his question." "I have a niece about their age but I can't imagine dealing with more than one at a time. Now I understand what my sister Inez is talking about. They're exhaustive when they're awake."

"Yes, they are," I agree. "Help me get them upstairs to the tower room where the roll-away bed is already set up."

Gently I pick up Cassie from his lap and together we take all three girls upstairs accompanied by the dogs. The sisters remain sound asleep but Cassie wakes up when I set her down on the mattress.

"Good night Aunt Harper," she whispers, "I love you… you too Mr. Wiley," she rolls over on her side and falls back asleep.

"Good God," he whispers throwing his heavy arm around my shoulders, "that is a powerful phrase when you hear it from a little angel, isn't it?"

"You mean instead of during the throes of a hot and rowdy tumble?" I tease him.

He tightens his arm playfully around my neck and we walk out of the room, closing the door after the dogs' lope downstairs in front of us.

"The guest room is always made up so please stay the night," I tell him. "You're being here with us tonight means the world to me, and to Pax."

"Don't sweat it little sister," he jokes but I can tell he's touched by my gratitude. "I'm sorry for how I treated you before," he says walking over to the fridge and taking out another beer and pulling the cork on the wine bottle as I hold out the balloon glass for a refill. "I intend to spend many a weekend out here, rusticating in the country, drinking your fine dark lager, eating you out of house and home, especially during football season… and then there's the beach parties you'll want to plan."

We spend several more minutes sipping our drinks at the counter before York and Kirby run to the side door just before a pair of head lights turn into the drive.

"That's our boy," Wiley chuckles, "to be greeted by such loyalty, amazing… and you're not so bad yourself."

"Wiley just when I start to think you've got a

sensitive side, you open your mouth and I know, you're all Neanderthal," I tell him pinching his trim waist as I walk past him.

Walking to the side door I can see Pax grab his suitcase out of the back seat and walk up to the porch. The boys wag their tails in greeting and after he scratches them and coos at them he looks up at me with such a look of longing in his eyes I can barely shut the door before he drops his bag, picks me up in his arms and kisses me, long and deeply. I wrap my legs around his waist and he carries me into the kitchen and sets me on the island counter, steps between my legs and hugs me again.

"Hey brother, don't start anything until I leave the room," Wiley teases and hands Pax a long neck bottle of beer. "You made good time," he says touching his bottle to his best friends before taking a swig. "The little woman and I were just discussing all the great parties she'll be throwing here, after you're married of course."

Pax smiles and shakes his head at the two of us.

"Where are the girls?" he asks petting York then Kirby on their broad heads as they gather at his feet.

"Sound asleep," Wiley says making me smile at the memory of him surrounded by pink and purple flannel night gowns and pajamas. "Don't say it," he warns me and pulls me into a hard hug. "I'm going to bed, keep it down. Me and the girls are going to want a big breakfast tomorrow Mommy, so don't stay up too late."

I bite his thickly muscled shoulder making him laugh and push me into Pax's waiting arms.

"She's mean Pax," he whispers and thumps me on the back of my head. "Goodnight."

When it's just the four of us I rest my head on his shoulder and inhale his scent, absorbing his presence and feel a thousand times better knowing he's home.

"I love you," I tell him making him lean his head back on my shoulder and smile.

"Prove it," he growls creating a deep surge of desire swell inside me until I need him like I need oxygen. "Let's go to bed." He steps out from between my legs and puts his empty bottle on the countertop.

"We're still thinking alike," I tell him and drop down off the counter and turn off the lights before we climb the stairs to our room and shut the door.

"I'm exhausted," he says kicking off his shoes and pulling his black t-shirt over his head. "If you want any tonight, you're doing the work."

Smiling I push him backwards onto the mattress and remove his socks and work my way up to his low riding jeans.

"Lift up one time then I'll do the rest," I purr against his naked belly.

A shiver of desire races down his body then he's naked, propped up against the headboard with all four pillows behind him as he lies there spread eagle, arms out to his side in supplication.

"Have at it," he whispers and then groans when I leave a trail of wet kisses up and down his chest ending at the junction of his thighs and the massive erection waiting on me.

"With pleasure," I breathe over his sensitive flesh.

Holding his member with one hand at the base of his shaft I kiss the length of him, once, twice, and on the third pass I take him deeply into my mouth, loving the feel of his hot, silky flesh on my tongue. The breath he is holding tells me he's fighting the urge, the desire, the need to take me quickly so I tease him for a while longer until I can't stand it any longer.

"Either let go or take me," I huskily demand feeling my own body on the verge of climax.

In the blink of an eye I'm flat on my back, he's positioning himself between my thighs and with one stroke he seats himself to the hilt. A hiss of breath rushes out of my mouth as he sets a quick and strong pace. With one hand, he tugs on my hypersensitive nipples and catching the moans and groans I can't keep still with his hot, wet mouth.

"Hold on baby," he groans into my neck as he quickens. "Give it to me Harper," he says nipping the delicate flesh and then our finely tuned bodies spiral out of control as he slams into me releasing his spirit to coat my womb. A thin sharp flick of lightning courses through my veins as I find that profound spot in my mind where everything is in alignment, the moon, the stars, the planets… and I damn near pass out from the complex trip he takes me on.

"Yes-s-s-s," he hisses as he continues to pump his hips, filling me with every drop of his semen before he rolls us over onto our sides and tries to calm his breathing. "I am always drained after being with you, mind, body and soul… I love you Harpo."

Stroking his damp shoulder, I love the sound of his hoarse, thick voice after we make love.

"I love you too," I whisper feeling like I've touched a live wire and received the shock of my life. After a couple minutes of deep breathing I remember the girls upstairs.

"We better put some pajamas on," I tell him while my brain is still functioning. "Just in case…"

"In case of what?" he asks and I smile at him being clueless about having kids underfoot.

"In case one or all of those sweet little girls comes crashing in on us," I explain and hand him a pair of his black and white plaid cotton pajama bottoms and a clean white T-shirt. He quickly slides into the sleep wear and sighs.

"Ah, the midnight caller," he says nodding his head. "I heard the girls wake up in the middle of the night a time or two when they were staying at my place with me. Thanks for the reminder."

I slip my white cotton gown over my head and climb back into our bed, snuggling down into his side and soon I'm fast asleep only to be woken a couple hours later at the sound of six then fourteen feet on the stairs and stopping outside my bedroom door. The baseboard night lights Marc installed throughout the place keep the house from being too dark so there's no need to worry about anyone tripping down the stairs.

"Aunt Harper?" Cassie whispers on the other side of the door, "Can we sleep with you?"

I hear the homesickness in her voice, which is unusual since she's stayed with me before, but she's always slept in my bed too… Making sure not to disturb Pax I climb out of bed and open the door letting in a host of dogs and girls into the room.

"Shhh," I tell them leaving the door open and getting them settled in the queen-sized bed. "Don't wake Uncle Pax," I warn and once they're situated and I hear the dogs settle on their bed in the corner. I cover us up with the blankets and then fall into a deep, almost coma-like sleep.

29

Smiling as I watch Wiley walk down the stairs wearing only the jeans he had on last night I can appreciate the fine specimen of a man he represents, too bad his mouth overrides his good looks, at least where I'm concerned. He walks over to the coffee maker and fills one of the two remaining white mug I set out before he walks over and kisses me on the mouth.

"Good morning dear," he says like we're an old married couple, plops his behind on the stool next to me, resting his head on my shoulder and asks, "What's for breakfast?"

Laughing at the big loon I tell him, "Cold cereal, banana, and a yogurt cup."

He scoffs at my menu then says, "No really, what are you fixing for breakfast?"

I nudge his head off my shoulder and say, "biscuits, gravy, and sausage links."

He grabs a hold of both sides of my face and kisses me on the forehead.

"I love you, leave that bum with the three ladies and run away with me," he jokes. Picking up his coffee mug he laughs and shakes his head before taking a sip. "I peeked into your room and can't believe he's still on the mattress. Those little demons are lying sideways in the bed, giving him a scant twelve inches to sleep on…. poor bastard."

Laughing I stand up and prepare the sausage links on a baking sheet while I take out the milk, saved bacon grease I keep for my gravy rue, and reach for the flour bin drawer.

"I'm going to take him a starter cup, and then I'll make us a fresh pot," I tell him. "The yogurt cups are in the door of the fridge and the bananas are in the fruit bowl in front of you, help yourself."

"You better put out some biscuits and gravy little lady or I'm not leaving here, and I'm serious. That guest room bed is heavenly," He threatens making me laugh as I walk up the stairs.

I must pause when I gaze upon the denizens in my bed. Cassie is snuggled up against her Uncle Pax's back. Molly and Millie are lying across the bed pillows at the head of the bed, their feet mere inches away from Pax's head. Setting the cup of steaming coffee on the nightstand I lean over and kiss my prince charming good morning.

"Mmm," he groans licking his lips but keeping his eyes closed. "I taste coffee and sex."

Laughing at his comment I whisper in his ear, "I'd love to nibble on your…ear, but Fours Company, five's a crowd."

He grins and opens one eye, sees the coffee on the nightstand and says, "I'd love to draw on your…coffee cup but my arm is asleep, my neck is kinked, and there's feet dangerously close to my temple…help me."

Walking around to my side of the bed I pull on Cassie's legs scooting her away from Pax letting him slide out of bed before I shift each little Whitaker back into a vertical position on the mattress. They automatically roll towards one another but remain deep in sleep.

"You're amazing," he whispers then reaches for me and tugs me outside into the hall. "I want to make some of those," he says nodding at the still sleeping little girls.

Closing the bedroom door, I rub my palm over his morning erection and smile at him.

"I can postpone breakfast if you want to start on our own set," I love the twitch of his root behind the black cotton of his pajama bottoms, "But Wiley might cause a riot. He's already pissed off I told him all I was making him for breakfast was cold cereal and yogurt."

"No, feed me first..." he groans and then presses me up against the wall where he rubs his lower body into mine. "God you're a temptation."

"Thanks, but either put up or shut up," I warn him. "Those little angels are only good for another half hour, forty-five minutes at the most."

He kisses me senseless and when he raises his head he grins at the desire shining back at him from my eyes.

"That's what I want to see," he whispers kissing me softly, "you unable to think when I kiss you..."

"I'm about to implode," I tell him making him push my hips even harder.

"Let's go upstairs for a second or two..." he suggests and I reach for his hand and tug him up the steps to the watch tower room and shut the sliding barn-like door being careful not to step on any dolls and their accessories. I close the roll-a-way bed covers sticking out from the middle and push it out of the way as I walk over to the cushioned window seat.

"Take me fast and hard," I tell him shucking his pajama

bottoms and lifting my robe and nightgown. "I need you Pax, now..."

That last statement was almost a cry when I hear him set his coffee mug on the deep window seal and position himself behind me.

"Bend over the window seat," he says forcing my legs further apart, "I'm going to be swift so brace your arms Harpo." He slides his warm open palm between my legs and brushes my vulnerable exposed flesh with the edge of his hand.

Just the thought of making love with three kids in our bed, a guest downstairs and two dogs outside the door makes me finely tuned to his musk, his breathing, and the fact he's more aroused at this moment than he was last night.

"Open up baby, let me feel how much you want me, all of me," he groans in my ear. "I need to be inside you, feel you grip me tightly, squeeze me dry."

He caresses my sex front and back with both hands until I'm a quivering mass of jelly, then he swats my bottom, making me shiver in delight.

"That's it," he growls running his hard shaft between my cheeks, "cover me with your dew baby; Get wet for me... yes-s-s-s, just like that."

He places his hand at the base of my neck and forces my face into the cushions then I feel him stretch my opening, making me wait for his entry inch by incredible inch until he fills me beyond what I can handle.

"Relax Harper, feel me stretch you, making you take all of me... that's what I want, what I crave...God, I'm ready to come...hold on sweetheart," he groans and I feel his marauding member rake over my ultra-sensitive tissue.

A scream is working its way up my throat when he flicks the small nubbin hiding in my folds. Pressing on my nerve center and slamming into my channel is too much and I immediately climax, screaming into the blue green cushion as he grips my hips in a bruising hold, pummeling me with his hungry body, eating up my flesh until he too groans out his release, jettisoning his life force between my thighs then resting his hot cheek between my shoulder blades. When he can stand, he hugs my back to his chest and bites my neck.

"I love you so much Harper it scares me," he says with such emotion and conviction I twist out of his hold and throw myself into his arms biting and sucking on his neck and chest.

"You make me come alive," I tell him between frantic kisses, "I can't get enough of you."

"Damn, rein it in baby girl because I hear footsteps going down the stairs," he laughs and breathes deeply of our sex lingering in the air. "I love that scent, you and me... what a fragrance."

He laughs as I straighten my gown and robe while he puts his flaccid member back into his bottoms then reaches for my hand.

"Let's start the day and remember this room for later in the evening," he chuckles and opens the sliding door. Hand in hand we make our way downstairs to find Wiley pulling the cooked sausage out of the oven, and sliding the biscuits he arranged on a baking sheet into their place.

"There they are girls," he assures his worrisome trio with a hint of disgust in his voice. "I told you they'd be right down after putting away the bed and covers right guys," he says frowning at the two of us un-repentant sinners.

"What's the matter ladies not enough room in my bed?" Pax asks making the girls giggle. "I'll have you know the dogs wouldn't take up that much room."

"But Uncle Pax you're fun to snuggle with," Cassie says in all her innocence.

"I agree with the girl," I smile and make Wiley roll his eyes and Pax wink at me. "What have you got going here Uncle Wiley?" I ask bumping my hip to his.

"What I got is well done sausages, no gravy to go with those frozen biscuits I found in the freezer. "What do you two have going?"

"The best cup of coffee served with a smile," Pax says making me laugh at Wiley's snarly face.

"Uncle Wiley was afraid you went back to sleep," Molly says making Pax laugh out loud.

"Well, now that you mention I could use another hour, maybe two...How about you Aunt Harper?" he teases.

"I'd love to lie down for a while," I begin but take mercy on Wiley, his face looking beyond angry. "But I promised our babysitter a good breakfast so scoot out of the kitchen, all of you." Picking up a wooden spoon I point at Pax, "Go ahead and take your shower, girls run upstairs and put on some fresh clothes, and Wiley, the boys need to run on beach for a good fifteen to twenty minutes, do you mind?"

"Do you intend to lie down once I leave?" he smugly asks crossing his arms over his bare chest.

"No... I'll have breakfast on the table in twenty minutes, satisfied?" I ask.

"Not as satisfied as Uncle Pax," he complains, "but I guess it will do, come on boys let's hit the beach."

The pups follow him outside while the girls and Pax head upstairs leaving me alone to fix the promised meal... I've never felt like whistling before, but suddenly I could break out in song... but maybe a whistle is good enough.

30

As breakfast is served I enjoy the sounds around me. Pax and Wiley are softly speaking about the girls' father, mentioning no names; Millie and Cassie are talking about the movie we promised to take them to see this evening; and Molly is slowly feeding York and Kirby her sausages which I guess I should have asked if everybody liked them. She devoured enough biscuits and gravy to feed a small horse so I know she's not going hungry. Getting up to refill our coffee cups I catch the tail end of what Pax is saying.

"… fired from his job and he was evicted from his apartment two weeks ago,. He's in the wind," he says holding out his empty cup for me to replenish.

"Nobody knows where he's at?" I whisper suddenly feeling more anxious now than I did speaking to the despondent man last night.

"Don't worry Harper," Wiley says waiting on more coffee. "When he failed to comply with the judge's directives a bench warrant was issued so they're on the lookout for him."

"How diligently are they looking? Is there one of those APB's out there or will this be a traffic stop for a burned-out taillight kind of hunt?" I ask feeling a sense of panic building inside me.

Pax scoots his chair out, takes the near empty carafe out of my hand and sets it on the wood planked table before he wraps his arm around my waist and presses me down onto his lap. His chin rests on my shoulder and he whispers in my ear, "Watch your tone of voice Harpo, those little girls are sharp. Trust me, he's not going to get anywhere near them, or you for that matter."

I feel some of the tension ease up and nod my head at his assurance. Wiley covers my hand with his and softly says, "Candace and the girls are heading to Buffalo to spend a couple weeks, after the spring issue meeting Wednesday. Molly is only in kindergarten so it won't be that big of a deal her missing school. I spoke with Candace this morning and I'll drive her upstate and she'll work off her laptop and through you... it will be alright Harper, stop worrying."

Nodding my head in understanding I look over at the girls and pray the man is apprehended before he does something horrible. Pax kisses my cheek and says, "Let's get married Wednesday, that way we'll be gone and won't have to worry about him trying to get us to lead him to his girls, Candace is safe upstate, and Wiley can stay out here with the boys, right?"

"Right, a pack of hounds running about the place," he says in a dramatic voice and then howls making the dogs join in.

"Just be sure you're the leader of the pack," Pax jokes and waits on me to respond.

Leaning over my shoulder I kiss his lips and say, "I'd love to marry you on Wednesday, shall we say three o'clock?"

"Works for me," Wiley chimes in making the two of us laugh as he scratches his new best buds behind their ears. The Mastiffs flank him on both sides and start drooling at his attention.

"That's perfect," my fiancé tells me, "I need to make some phone calls, call in a few favors, and get the office squared away and make reservations... man I wish Liza was here right now. I hate doing all this stuff...wait a sec, you're a personal assistant, assist me personally."

Laughing I look over at Wiley and we're both thinking the same thing but he's quicker to respond than I am.

"She already assisted you this morning, and trust me, you can't get any more personal than what she did... or at least I assume what she did from the moaning and groaning I heard all the way down here where I was slaving over a hot stove, answering a jillion questions, and trying not to step on the two small ponies you insist on having inside the house," He huffs and reaches for the last biscuit from the napkin lined basket and adds butter and jelly.

"God, you're such a nagging old woman," Pax says to his friend. "Besides, we were both very quiet but I agree, she did the best assist I've ever had."

"Stop it," I laugh placing my hand over Pax's mouth to prevent further details from slipping out. "I'll make the reservations, and get with Liza and see what I can do to help clear your calendar, but first we need to see about cleaning up the kitchen, and then speak with our parents about Wednesday, then..."

Pax pushes me off his lap and just after he kisses me laughs and says, "Gotta make a couple phone calls, come on Wiley, let's get out of here before we end up doing dishes and mopping the floor."

"Right behind you brother," he says and kisses the top of my head as he crams the biscuit into his mouth. "Sorry, but Pax needs me," he says at least I think that's what came out of his full mouth.

Turning around I see the dogs follow them outside and then hear them bark when Pax hollers the word 'Frisbee'. So much for making calls and getting things 'squared away'. Looking over at the three little angels playing with their Barbie dolls I find it hard to believe we're actually having to hide the sisters from their deranged father, but after last night's conversation I know he's not fit to be around them. Gathering up the dirty dishes I clean up the kitchen. It's amazing how much faster cleaning can be done when you don't have two dogs under foot.

"I'm going to take a shower," I tell them. "Why don't you girls come upstairs to the watch tower where you can get all your dolls out, okay?"

"Aunt Harper, are we going to Aunt Becky's house?" Molly asks letting me know she was listening to parts of our conversation.

"Yes, you're going to your Aunt Becky's house and see your cousins for a couple of weeks," I tell her in an excited tone of voice, which works because Millie tells Cassie about the log cabin her aunt and uncle live in somewhere in some mountains.

The four of us walk upstairs and in the ten minutes I'm indisposed they set off a doll and clothing bomb. Walking into the Watch Tower room I must be careful not to step on any loose body parts, cars, furniture, and tiny sharp little shoes. Smiling at the intensity of their play I watch the kids for a couple seconds, imagining my own children playing up here... Pax said he'd like three, that's the magic number.

"Girls, how about we see if the movie you want to watch is playing as a matinee?" I ask then doubt they know what that means. "We can go into town, see the movie, and eat pizza but be back here before dark, how does that sound?"

"Yeah!" they shout together.

"What time?"

"Can I wear what I had on last night?"

"Do they still make popcorn in the daytime?"

"Will Uncle Pax and Uncle Wiley come with us?"

Laughing at their questions I tickle them making them giggle and squeal as they pile on top of me bringing me down to the floor, lying on what feels like screws and glass I continue to wrangle with them. That's how the guys find us, flushed and out of breath.

"Honey you sound like you did this morning," Pax teases from his position of leaning in the door jamb. "What happened in here? It didn't look like this when we played in here."

Wiley laughs and reiterates his request from last night, "Godsons, not daughters please."

The three girls look at me and I nod my head and we run over towards the men and pull them into the room where they let us bring them to the floor but they tickle, lift the squealing and squirming children over their heads and bringing the dogs up the stairs to see what all the noise is about. Both hounds bark their heads off at such play, showing their concern for the kids. The guys set the girls back down and try to assure the dogs everything is all right but they're riled. Grabbing their collars, I take the dogs with me as I leave the room. Shocked but pleased they're instincts were to protect the kids. Suddenly I feel safer out here than in town. I reward the boys with a couple treats and wait for the men to come back downstairs. They join us in the kitchen where the dogs act like nothing happened, walking over to place their muzzles in Pax's open hands, and then letting Wiley scratch behind their ears. Pax and I look at each other and shrug our shoulders, perplexed at the workings of a canine mind.

The rest of the morning and early afternoon flies by with Wiley leaving after a lunch of turkey sandwiches, chips, and ice tea. Pax agreed going to a matinee would be best. He also spoke with Candace earlier letting her speak to the girls and even Cassie. Vic called and I told him what was going on and he suggested we bring the kids over to his place and let them stay the night there, they loved the idea from the sound of all the squealing they did so now, Pax and I are free this evening. My brother said he'd be at the courthouse on Wednesday with his girls. But if Pax was a no-show he'd bring out the shotgun this time. I kept that last part to myself when I told Pax about the change of plans...

We're back home, alone...except for the boys by six o'clock, both mentally and physically drained from having spent two hours with three little magpies all chirping and flitting about in the theatre. During the animated movie, Pax called the girls down, telling them to hush or no pizza... their eyes got as round as quarters but they minded him and the rest of the movie was watched in enjoyable quiet. He's going to be a natural father, I can tell by the way the kids respond to him… as I do it seems, well when we're not arguing…

"I'm bushed," he says sitting next to me on the sectional. "I'm going up after I take the boys out for a run. Finish your program," he says bending down and kissing me. "I had a great time with the girls, but I'm starting to lean towards Wiley's request…keep that in mind."

Laughing at him I hear the back door close and a couple barks in the distance. Settling back into the sofa I get involved with the detectives on TV. At the end of the show Pax returns with a dog-tired pair of pups and he waves as he walks upstairs, York and Kirby following closely behind him. Just as I turn off the lamp at the end of the sofa my phone rings. Reaching behind me where I left it charging on the white-washed sofa table I see the phrase 'unknown caller' on the screen and pick it up.

"Hello?" I answer.

"Hi Harper," Cody Whitaker's voice whispers "How's my girls doing?"

Apparently, he's unaware of the change of plans, which reassures me he hasn't been watching us today. Walking upstairs I want Pax to hear this conversation.

"They're fine," I assure him. "We saw a movie this evening; you know the one with the talking animals?"

He laughs and talks about how much his girls love those movies. Walking into the dark bedroom I turn on the bedside lamp and touch Pax's naked shoulder. The dogs raise their head, see it's me and go back to their slumber. Pax smiles when he rolls over but quickly sits up when I place my finger to my lips and then hit speaker on my phone.

"… too scary or they won't sleep in their own beds, you

know?" the girls' father is saying with great concern in his voice.

"Kids need to know they're safe, right?" I ask him watching Pax's face as he watches me.

"That and to know they're loved, that their father would do anything to keep them from being hurt. Harper, today I drove past my apartment building and saw a squad car pulled up at the curb…why are they after me? Did that bitch call them and make up lies against me?"

Pax nods his head for me to answer.

"Did you attend those meetings and classes like the judge told you to?" I ask knowing he didn't.

"Hell yes I went to all of them, drove around town and attended six in one night," he lies then says, "I even got a certificate of completion on the anger management class."

"You did? Maybe you should show that to the judge," I suggest hoping he'll turn himself in, even unwittingly just to end this craziness but he flips out like he did the last time.

"They'd say I made it up," he snaps. "Who the hell are they to tell me I've got a drinking problem? Has that prissy old man ever seen me drunk? No! I'm never drunk around people, hell I'm never drunk…and that anger management class is probably just a bunch of bitchy old women complaining about their husbands. 'He doesn't make enough money' or 'he says I'm too fat' or 'I want a divorce but he won't give me one'…that's all women ever talk about."

"Cody, you need to get help, please for your daughters' sake stop fighting Candace, get your life back together and then I'm sure she'll work out a visitation plan for you to see the girls…" I tell him but I know from the look on Pax's face I said too much and he's right.

"You're on her side, aren't you? You're a sniveling, whiney ass secretary that will do anything you're told, all for the mighty dollar. A lackey willing to let your own boyfriend sleep with my wife…" he rants. "Well guess what sunshine; I'm not going to take this lying down. That woman is going to know sorrow, and I mean biblical proportion sorrow." He shouts. "Once I've got the girls I won't need her then it's sayonara baby…I'll start over somewhere else, maybe Mexico or in the northwestern parts of Canada…"

Pax covers the phone microphone and whispers in my ear, "ask him if he knows people that might be willing to help him out."

Nodding my head in understanding I do as he asks.

"That's probably a good idea; you know make a fresh start. I have family in Penticton British Columbia, do you know anyone up there you can call?" I ask hoping he hears concern in my voice.

"Yeah, a college roommate of mine lives in Vancouver said I could come out for a fishing trip some time. I think he works for some shipping agency… I'll have to look Dale up when I get off the phone…Harper can I speak with the girls?"

He seems calmer now and I pray he remains that way after I deny his request.

"Oh Cody, the girls are sacked out upstairs," I tell him with a hint of regret. "The dogs have run those girls rampant, I'd hate to wake them this late in the evening… you know they need to be on a tight schedule, you always told Candace that, remember?"

"You're right; I always made sure they were in bed by nine, no matter what. I was a good father to the girls Harper, I swear I always looked after their needs, not like their 'career oriented' mother," he snaps the last part so I try to end the call on an upbeat.

"I'm sure you're a great dad, no matter what anyone else says, the girls' opinion of you is all that matters, right?" I ask shifting my legs over the side of the bed.

"Right and I won't disturb their sleep, tell them I love them and think about them constantly. Oh, and tell them we'll be together real soon." He says trying to think of anything to stay on the line with me.

"Cody, I've got to let the dogs out so I'll talk to you later, try to think about getting some help in those stressful areas of your life, okay?" I ask scooting off the bed and walking over towards the window.

"Okay, go on to sleep and you'll be hearing from me soon, and thanks Harper for believing I'm a good dad, goodnight," and he ends the call.

Pax joins me at the window, checking to see if the man was close like I thought he might be but I see no taillights or headlamps outside, plus the dogs aren't reacting like someone is outside so I hug my lover and let him lead me back towards the bed where he takes my phone and check's the last call received number, but shakes his head when no number flashes on the screen.

"Dammit where the hell is he at?" he mumbles to himself. "I'll call Candace and warn her he's still plotting to snatch the girls. She wouldn't tell me where she was at when I spoke to her earlier so I think she might have a new... friend."

Smiling at him I nod my head and say, "she received a lovely floral arrangement last week with a personal note in them, but she never told me who they were from," I yawn and lean my head on his chest.

"Come on to bed," he says placing my phone on the nightstand and lifting my t-shirt over my head.

Once I'm under the covers, snuggled into his side I wonder how Cody is planning on reaching the girls when Pax rolls over on top of me, makes a place between my legs and swiftly enters my not-quite-ready for visitors' channel.

"What?" I ask when he continues to slide past my protesting inner muscles. "Give me a minute," I tell him but he shakes his head at my request.

"Stop thinking about him," he whispers as he slowly retreats, then presses forward letting my body get used to the intrusion and once I see his smile I relax and let nature take over. "That's more like it," he says kissing me softly on my eyelids, then the tip of my nose as he braces his weight on his forearms. "Only think about me, how I make you feel when we're joined like this…now you're getting the message," he laughs when his body meets with no resistance.

He rocks us to orgasm and even though it was no way near as powerful as this morning's joining, the slow and steady build to climax is what I need. Later as I drift off to sleep I know Pax will protect me, but will we be able to protect those little girls if their father finds them…

31

Tuesday I jot down the information Candace was requesting as I hang up the phone. She's looking for a realtor in the Massena area; must be where the mysterious new man is from. I spent all day yesterday on the phone with corporate putting out fires and answering their questions on why Candace is out of the office, again. I don't recall the main office ever questioning Star Bridges when she worked from home so I think something is brewing there; I just hope Cody Whitaker isn't behind it. I managed to meet Pax at the clerk's office to request a marriage license, which was the highlight of the day. We ate lunch together and then went back to our separate hectic schedules until we drove home together only to start the same routine again today.

Ginger, who I haven't spoken to in several days sent me an email reminding me we have had no girl time lately. She and Marc are getting serious, spending as much time at his place as hers. I left her a voice mail letting her know Wednesday at three o'clock I would be getting married and could she come to the courthouse, her reply is typical Ginger.

'Will the groom be there? Of course, I will and Marc

too, see you there, and hopefully that overgrown baby you're so attached to will stay to the end of the ceremony, love you, Ginger.'

I email her back, 'he assures me he will be there with bells on…I'd pay to see that. Love you too Harper.'

Beth called me again this morning trying to talk me into waiting on the wedding so she can have the ceremony again in her back yard but this time, the landscapers have her lawn torn up as they're installing an in-ground pool… the perfect excuse not to wait because this time around, there is no way in hell Pax would postpone the ceremony, especially just so his mother can throw a party. My parents invited Pax and me over to their house for supper tonight but Pax is working late so I plan to go alone and have him meet me there later. My workload is still full but I keep my head above water. At four o'clock Shawna calls needing a favor.

"I hate to ask but could you pick up Cassie from the sitters on your way over to your folk's house? Vic's car is in the shop, your mother won't get back from her meeting in Troy in time, and I'm stuck here at work until six," she explains "The sitter wants all the kids picked by five today, she needs to close the daycare early. Can you make it?"

"No problem," I assure her missing my chatterbox niece since I haven't seen or heard from her since Saturday. The thing about having kids around is you get used to the chaos they provide. She gives me the address and says the sitter knows I'll be picking up my niece. The rest of the afternoon is peaceful except I have about six voicemails from Cody, all saying the same thing.

"Where is she Harper? I need to speak with her."

"You're keeping me from seeing my kids!"

"I thought you were my friend…"

"Fine, if this is how you want it, I'm giving you fair warning. I'll run you down just like I would if you were my ex-wife!"

The last message was shouted so loudly Tara comes into my office with a look of concern but I assure her everything is fine and she goes about her business but I decide not to erase the messages, as insurance if he tries something. I leave a message with Pax's voice mail telling him where I'll be and then finish the rest of the reports and send them to Candace's new email address. At a quarter after four I close my office and smile as I walk past Tara's desk.

"Have a nice evening," I tell her and she nods her head as she's listening to her phone call.

Walking out the building I smile at the darkening sky. It looks like we will have some rain before the end of the day. Hailing a cab, I walk over to the curb and give the address of the sitter to the driver and send a text to Poppy.

'Arriving separately but count on both of us for dinner, HMM.'

He replies, 'good, don't forget Angel. POP'

We arrive at the Tiny Tot's Daycare Center to find the two providers in the fenced in yard with only three remaining children waiting to be picked up. I wave at the attendant and Cassie who is wearing an adorable red jacket, blue jeans, and white sneakers with red laces. The sprite runs over towards the gate, turns to tell the woman goodbye, allows the helper to open the gate for her and runs over to me, hugging me tightly.

"Hey there Angel," I tell her picking her up, twirl her

around, and carrying her to the cab. "We're going to Poppy's for supper. I'm starving, how about you?"

She fills me in on what she had for her afternoon snack as I strap her inside the vehicle and then we're on our way across town. Cassie has me giggling with her when out of nowhere a thunderous noise drowns out my niece when a vehicle runs a stop sign, crashing into the cab and crushing my side of the car, sending our cab into a tailspin. My niece is pushed up against me as I'm slammed backward and forced into the door. My surroundings become surreal and I lose my perspective as the inertia presses me back into the seat. Once we stop spinning I feel blood running down my face, a sharp pain in my arm, and a dead weight across my legs besides tiny pricks of pain that feel like hundreds of bee stings on my face, arms, and neck and wonder if this is how little Joey felt when he was attacked by yellow jackets. I hear him crying in my head but know that can't be It must be Cassie...Where is she? My only concern is my niece.

"Cassie? Baby it's okay, look at me," I call out but the little girl is silent and I can't see through the blood covering my eyes. Trying to turn in the seat I notice she's slumped over but still belted in then I hear her crying for me. Thank God she's alive.

"Aunt Cassie my arms got blood on it!" she screams in fear but it sounds far away.

"Miss, can you hear me? Are you alright?" the older man driving the cab asks trying to turn in his seat but the crumpled metal and steel keep him in place, "I'm trapped behind the wheel but I've called dispatch, they're sending the police and emergency responders immediately. Just hold on ladies."

I hear him from a distance, and his voice is soft and soothing, his accent pure New York and music to my ears telling me we're all still alive. My head is pounding or is that my heart I'm hearing? Everything around me keeps spinning so I close my eyes still gripping my little Angel's tightly clasped and sticky hand. The next sensation I have is of somebody making a heck of a lot of racket but I can't open my eyes to see what's going on. Suddenly Cassie's hand is no longer in mine so I force my eyes to open only to see a group of people hovering over me through a veil of red. Blinking several times my vision clears for a second then pain shoots through my brain so I close them again.

"Can you hear me?" a deep rumble of a voice says above my head. "She's coming around guys."

"Is that you God?" I ask and then I hear several people chuckle and say no in unison.

"Cover her face and body," another voice says. "Start the jaws but be careful, she's pinned in there good and tight by the door and the post."

A horrible crunching sound begins and it's so loud my tortured nerves are shot, making tears run down my cheeks from the pain of enduring the ruckus, but minutes later the heavy pressure on my lower body is lifted and then a pain shoots up my leg making me cry out.

"It's okay Ma'am," a softer voice assures me, "you've got a pretty good gash on your thigh but nothing they can't stitch up. Do you know what day it is?"

"Tuesday I think, where's Cassie; My niece, Cassie who's got her?" I ask frantically trying to remove a thick gauze bandage someone placed over my face but a purple, latex covered hand pushes my fingers away.

"She's over in the ambulance being cared for by Blue and Patsy," the woman says as she presses the bandage back across my face and I try to calm down.

"Good thing that pick-up truck was too damaged to drive," a deep voice is saying from a distance. "Son of a bitch ran off though. Jake said the cabbie told him the truck was stopped at the crosswalk and then gunned his vehicle into the cab, on purpose…"

Fear as cold as the dead of winter races down my spine… Cody Whitaker did this, on purpose. I must speak up but someone keeps swatting my hand away as I try to remove the thick gauze pad now covering half of my face.

"Listen to me," I say to no one in particular but I need to make them realize the danger Cassie and I am in, "the man that did this, his name is Cody Whitaker…do you hear me?" I ask the EMT, blindly reaching for her arm. "Please, do not let anyone take that little girl…that man is demented."

"Honey I'm almost done here and once you're in the bus I'll tell the police officer to come speak to you okay? Now let go of my arm so I get you ready to be removed from the wreck, okay?" she asks in a gentle but firm voice. She slips a brace around my neck and secures it in place.

"Can you have someone call my fiancé Pax? His number is in my phone, in my purse, please tell him what happened," I start to cry then thankfully I pass out when they begin to ease me out of the wreckage only to awaken inside the ambulance where they're hooking an IV into my hand, a blood pressure cup on my arm, and electrodes to my chest.

"Hey look whose back," a cheerful male voice says but

the hard-plastic collar prevents me from turning my head to see his face.

"Where's Cassie?" I ask and he leans over me so his face appears upside down. He's Hispanic with a broad-face, near black eyes, around thirty something with a scar over his left eyebrow, a crooked incisor I see as he grins and the gentlest touch I've ever experienced. His take charge manner and charming smile ease my mind about my own condition but I must know who is taking care of Cassie. "The little girl that was with me, where's she at? Please tell me she's safe."

"She's with some man over in the next vehicle," he says fidgeting with the heart monitoring device. His thick but nimble fingers slide an oxygen tube around my head and into my nostrils, "this is just to keep you from feeling queasy, okay? Are you on any medication?"

He asks me a barrage of questions but doesn't answer me only jotting down my stats as his partner calls them out.

"Who is with my niece? Tell me!" I shout at him and finally my fear registers with him and he says, "Her uncle Paul I think she called him. He's very anxious to see you but we told him to follow us to the hospital. Your niece latched onto him and refused to let go so he's riding with her...now let me finish so we can get you to the ER."

I release a sigh of relief closing my eyes knowing Pax will protect that child with his life. The next time I wake up I'm being wheeled down a long corridor with lights rolling past my head, reminding me of mile markers along the side of the highway as I drive the 'Vette' along the Lake Sinclaire highway but instead of making me feel free I keep swallowing so I don't throw up on my husky attendant. I close my eyes and drift off to sleep but get jostled awake as a group of technicians lift me up on a sheet and gently place me on a hospital gurney. The bright overhead lights blind me so I keep my eyes closed, but even the thick bandage doesn't keep the spikes of lightning from flashing behind my eyelids. I can hear people working around me, but so far no one is talking directly at me. They hook up the machines, twists my arm around to check my pulse and cover my shivering body with a warmed blanket, mercifully soothing my nerves until a different voice is directly over my head.

"Ma'am, I know you're in pain and the doctor here wants to get you stitched up but I need to ask you a couple questions, if you're up to it," the gravelly voice says. "I'm Harley Graves, a detective with the APD. Do you know who was driving that blue pick-up truck?"

Licking my dry, cracked lips I whisper, "I think it was Cody Whitaker but I didn't see him."

"Is he the father of the little girl that was with you?" he asks and I hear him writing my response down probably in a small spiral notebook just like my favorite TV detectives carry and I can almost hear the next question before he says it out loud.

"No Detective, he's not the father, nor am I the mother or have I ever been in a relationship with the man," I reply making him chuckle.

"Am I that transparent?" he teases making me smile, then flinch when a sharp pain makes me stop moving. "Sorry, why do you think it was Mr. Whitaker?"

"Because he threatened to hurt me for helping his wife, who happens to be my employer, keep his kids from him. There's a bench warrant out for his arrest, he's left me several threatening voice mails plus he's been following me trying to locate his estranged wife," I relay to him and I can hear his pen fly across the paper again but still I keep my eyes closed.

"Excellent, you're doing great," he whispers to me. "Did you see anything before the impact?"

"No I was talking with my niece and then it felt like I'd been…" I smile when he finishes my sentence.

"… Run over by a truck, you had but you're lucky you were in one of the old, large taxis. Those things were built like tanks. I'll let the good doctor patch you up so that man pacing in the hall can see that you're alright, okay?" he asks and pats my arm. "I'll be in touch."

For the next two hours, the medical team is cleaning me up, sticking needles in my arm, waiting for the drugs to take effect then sewing up my leg, and pulling bits of glass from my scalp, face, and neck. I hurt all over and just want to sleep for a month. Finally, the crew leaves the room and I can rest, until I hear Pax out in the hall.

"Tomorrow I'll be her next of kin," he argues and then says, "her father and mother are right here, ask them but I'm going inside there, now move it."

Smiling at the ruckus he's making I try to open one eye but the overhead surgical lamp is glaring at me, then suddenly it's gone and when I open my eyes I see the most handsome face I've ever seen. Paxton Joseph Barrett is leaning over me, with tears glistening in his near black eyes he takes my tubed hand in his and kisses the tips of my fingers.

"Oh Baby," he sighs at me. "Are you in pain? Do you need more pain killers?"

"Just kiss me," I whisper needing to feel his lips more than my next breath.

He lightly touches his mouth to mine and if I could, I'd wrap my arms around his neck and beg him to take me home. Instead I begin to cry in relief, making him worry even more.

"Shhh, I've got you Harper, you're safe I swear on my life you're safe," he whispers as he keeps pressing small kisses to my mouth and eyes. "I'll kill him for doing this," he vows then moves the stainless-steel stool on rollers over to the side of the gurney, sits down and lowers his head to my breast.

"How's Cassie?" I ask running my scratched up fingers through his thick brown hair offering him comfort.

"She's fine, shaken up and asking for you but Vic and Shawna took her home about an hour ago, they said they'd call you later to see how you're doing," he says gently stroking my arm.

"Did you call Candace?" I ask praying she and girls are safe.

"Yes, she wanted to come over but I insisted she stay far away," he tells me. "Wiley is driving them to Buffalo," he says looking at his silver dress watch then says, "They should be arriving at her sister's place late this evening. Wiley said to take care and get well," he smiles and with his thumb gently wipes away the tears that won't stop rolling out of the corner of my eyes. "It's okay Harper, they're not even going to keep you, seems like their biggest concern was to see if you hit your head but the cat scan came back clear. So once your parents can see you're okay, I'll drive you home, put you to bed, and watch over you...for the rest of my life, deal?"

"Deal," I reply and nod off to sleep feeling safe in his presence.

How long I napped I'm unsure but his moist breath on

my cheek stirs me from my slumber making me forget where we're at for a second or two.

"Harper, babe your folks are here," He whispers in my ear. "Wake up, talk to them for a second then we're going back to Lake Sinclaire."

"Princess, how're you feeling?" my father asks leaning over and kissing my nicked-up forehead. "Can I get you anything?" he asks hating his child is in pain, no matter I'm an adult, he still needs to take care of me, make everything better… I guess that parent – child relationship never goes away.

"No Poppy, I'm just tired and hurt like a son of a bitch, but once I've taken some painkillers, lie down in my soft bed, and am able to get out of these clothes I'll be right as rain," I assure him.

"Speaking of sons of bitches," my mother says stepping up to the side rail of my gurney, "where is that bastard Whitaker," she asks to no one but I can see and hear the fierce lioness in her and suddenly I'm glad not to be on the receiving end of that verbal gun.

Pax answers her question, "They're searching the area for him right now, but he left the scene on foot so he could be anywhere. But I spoke to a Detective Graves a little while ago and he assured me they have more information on him coming in, should only be a matter of time…"

I doze off when my father bends down and kisses my closed eyes.

"We'll talk to you tomorrow Princess, rest easy and let your man do everything for you, okay?" he asks making me smile at the first time my father acknowledged Pax as my man. "I love you baby girl."

"I will Poppy," I reply, "I love you too," then I smell my mother's cologne and wait for her lips to touch my skin and two seconds later she presses a soft kiss to my temple.

"Harper, we're only a phone call away," she says stroking my tear stained cheek with her soft index finger. "Get some rest and we'll check in on you later, okay?"

"Thanks Mom, I love you both," I tell them and then the room is empty again except for Pax.

He steps outside when the nurse comes in and removes my IV. She gives me a list of instructions both verbally and printed on how to take care of my stitches and hands me a prescription for several drugs when an orderly brings me a wheelchair. Because of hospital policy I leave the ER being chauffeured to the exit where Pax is waiting with my coat, laptop, and purse making an image flash in my head of the night I miscarried and the next morning Pax wheeled me out of this very Emergency Room. That seems so long ago...

Gently he helps me into the Jaguar and stows my gear with his own laptop behind the seat and drives us to the nearest drug store, fills my prescriptions for me, picks up bottled water and gets back behind the wheel with great efficiency. He opens the pill bottles, doles out one tablet from each amber container, twists off the bottle cap of the water and holds everything out to me.

"Take these and I'll have you home in less than forty minutes," he says making me smile.

"You're one hell of a nurse maid," I tease him making him wink.

"Wait until I get to give you a sponge bath," he says raising and lowering his eyebrows in a lecherous manner then he growls and leans over to kiss me. "I'm so glad you're alright," he whispers and I know it will be some time before he no longer worries about losing me.

"Take me home to the boys," I tell him and lean my back against the headrest and close my eyes.

"Go to sleep and I'll wake you when we're there," he says putting my favorite Sade CD in the player and the soulful sounds lull me to sleep…

32

Last night all I remember is Pax carrying me inside the house and upstairs to our bedroom, stripping me down, sliding a nightgown over my head, careful not to move my arm and putting me to bed. He kept doping me like clockwork. He even brought me a cup of Poppy's homemade chicken noodle soup he must have found in the freezer and a handful of crackers. The boys never left my side sensing something was wrong and even when Pax tried to get them to leave they went into protective mode and wouldn't go.

As the evening slipped into night I heard Pax's phone ring several times and even heard his deep voice carrying up through the stair well, letting me know he was pacing, but he never disturbed me. He handled all the get well wishes, the police calls, and the office inquiries too. He could always fall back on his organization skills if the bottom falls out of advertising. But today has slipped by me, since all I want to do is sleep. He brought me some toast late this morning with juice, my traveler cup filled with coffee, and a handful of my pills. Then he left me alone to sleep until it was time for more medication and something to eat, which was another bowl of Poppy's soup. Now it's after six, the room is dark and I'm still so tired but I hear the dogs' woof and know someone is here.

"Harper?" Pax whispers from the doorway as he pokes his head into the room. "Ginger is insisting on seeing you, are you up to it?"

"Sure," I reply in a scratchy voice. "Can I have a glass of water?" I ask suddenly feeling parched noticing his worn jeans, black T-shirt and bare feet…if all male nurses could look like that.

"Coming right up," he says walking over and taking the empty glass from the night stand and kissing me on the lips. "I'm timing her visit, so don't get upset when I kick that smart ass out of here."

Laughing at the stern look on his face I nod my head just as she breezes into the room.

"That jerk wasn't going to let me see you," she snaps as he walks past her, looking gorgeous but frazzled as well wearing a man's white dress shirt over a pair of black leggings. Her hair is scraped back into a ponytail and she is sans make-up. Tired but happy she makes a face at him when he taps the crystal on his wrist watch, "yeah, yeah, yeah fifteen minutes I heard you. Geesh he's going to be impossible when you have a baby."

"Leave him alone Ginger," I sigh accepting her careful hug, "he's doing a great job."

"I know, but if I'm nice to him in times of crises he'll expect it the rest of the time," she explains making me laugh then hiss at the pain in my side. "What the hell happened?"

Shaking my head I tell her, "I don't know the details but Cody Whitaker, Candace's estranged husband thought I had one of the girls I guess."

"So... he rammed his truck into the cab you were in? Who the hell does stunts like that?" she demands not expecting an answer but needing to vent. "How bad are you hurt?"

"According to the list Pax made I have a deep six inch gash on my left thigh, he told me how many stitches but I forget, a dislocated shoulder, two bruised not broken ribs, a gash in my hairline, a shitload of scratches, nicks, dings, and cuts from the broken window and soon two black eyes, a myriad of contusions across my legs, and one hell of a headache," I list off my ailments making her shake her head and laugh.

"I'd hate to be that man once Pax locates him," she whispers in awe. "He's fiercely protective of you now," she grins and says, "I had to show two forms of personal identification just to make it inside the screened in porch. Poor Marc and Fabian didn't make it that far."

Wanting to see my Godson I ask, "Is Fabian downstairs? Bring him up, Marc too." I tell her, "I haven't seen Fabe in so long. Are things still going well for the three of you?"

"Better than well," she smiles and stands up. "We're going to look at some property he's thinking about buying on the other side of Lake Sinclaire. We could be neighbors!" she squeals making me laugh and hold my side. York and Kirby both stand up and bark which brings in the wrath of Paxton.

"What the hell are you doing?" Pax says running into the room like I was on fire or something worse as he tries to shush the excitable pair of dogs. "God dammit Simmons I told you to make it quick and don't tire her; here you are doing cheerleading crap. Your time is up, hit the road." He sets the fresh glass of water within my reach on the nightstand then puts his hands on his hips and glares at the redhead.

"Pax!" I hiss at him. "Don't blame her she's excited," I tell him knowing he will hate the news of her moving up here so I let her tell him.

"Just to make your day a little brighter Pax-my-man," my spitfire of a best friend says walking over to stand between him and the bed, she pats his cheek and says, "I'm buying property on the east end of the lake, we're going to be neighbors."

The look on his face is priceless and I can't stop the giggles that slip past my tender lips. He pushes her out of the way and lies down on his side of the bed then turns his head and says, "I can still get my apartment back in Ottawa, just say the word and she'll never find us."

A full-blown belly laugh makes me cringe in pain but I can't seem to stop.

"Both of you get out," I groan loving the playful banter they share. "Tell Fabian I want to see him but get rid of his mother."

The wicked grin on his face is filled with such retaliation I feel the need to rephrase my request as he eases himself off the mattress and turns to his nemesis.

"Pax, don't 'get rid' of her, simply walk her downstairs, are we clear on that," I ask making him drop his chin on his chest; hold out his arms to his side.

"Okay, we'll do it your way," he says leering over at her, "for now."

The two walk out of the room to be replaced with Fabian and Marc who are both super quiet so as not to disturb me. I smile at them both, hold out my arms and Fabian rushes to my side. The dogs settle down at the foot of the bed but keep a close watch on me.

"Are you alright?" he whispers when he sees my bandaged leg propped up on one of the bed pillows, the scrapes and scratches on my face and neck, plus the fact he's never seen me sick or hurt.

"Yes Fabe, Uncle Pax is taking good care of me," I kiss his cheek before he steps back to pet the dogs and sits on the rustic bench at the foot of the bed. Marc bends down, his arms braced on either side of my pillow and kisses my forehead.

"Poor baby," he coos and pulls up the wicker chair from the corner of the room and sits down. "Pax said they know who did this and that it was intentional?"

"Yes, but now that they know his name, they'll have him in custody in no time," I mimic Detective Graves words and I feel better just hearing myself say that out loud.

"Can we bring you anything? I'm sure now that I have security clearance I'll be allowed back indoors," he teases and glances over at the doorway where Pax is leaning against the frame.

"Next time come alone," he growls and then jumps when Ginger pokes him in the rib as she tries to get around the human barrier blocking her entry into the bedroom. "God, you're a menace. Marc, get her out of here," he says walking into the room and joining Fabian on the wooden bench. "Bring Fabe anytime, just ditch the girl."

He and Fabian laugh at the back and forth verbal sparring my fiancé and best friend subject us to but soon I'm yawning and I can feel the pain medicine kicking in so they carefully hug and kiss me goodbye promising to help anyway Pax will let them. Once they're gone he comes back upstairs and lies beside me, staring at me for so long I wonder if I'm a hideous mess until he leans over and rests his head on my right shoulder.

"I died a thousand times yesterday," he whispers on my skin, "First when I got a call from some policeman telling me you were in an accident but they'd give me no details, then when I arrive on the scene but you were already in the ambulance and Cassie was freaking out, then waiting for hours to see you in the hospital...my God Harper if anything would have happened to you..."

I feel him shiver in dread so I kiss the top of his head and tell him again how much I love him.

"You're the world to me Paxton; I know how I'd feel if anything happened to you, I'd die. I guess we'll just have to watch out for each other for the next sixty years, okay?" I smile down at him and feel the love he has for me shining out of his beautiful black diamond eyes.

"Ginger's right, though," he says rolling over onto his back and covering his face with his arm. "I'm going to freak out when you go into labor, won't I?"

Laughing at him I nod my head and can't stop the laughter when he nods his head in agreement.

"But until that time," he says leaning over and kissing me, "I'm going to make sure you're happy, healthy, and safe, no matter what."

He stands up and checks on the dogs resting on their bed in the corner then turns off all the lights except the bathroom light and wishes me a good night sleep.

"I'll be up later, but if you need anything just holler," he says and walks down the hall and I hear his heavy tread on the stairs but then blessed sleep covers me and I hear nothing until morning.

33

Five days later I've had enough of Pax's bedside manner. I'm in the process of escaping his well-meaning but totally suffocating rule.

"You're not going and that's final," Pax laughs, his hands on his hips glaring down at me as I slide my foot into a pair of leather driving moccasins completing my outfit of dark jeans, royal blue and white striped sweater over a white button down shirt.

Today I'm going to Sunday brunch, my family's usual get together and I told Pax I spoke with Mom Friday and she said they were all looking forward to seeing me and my colorful bruised body. But the man is throwing a fit at the notion we're going into the city.

"Pax, be reasonable," I begin for the third time since I woke up this morning. "I'm sore but mobile. You've done a brilliant job of getting me back on my feet, but you're smothering me baby, I've got cabin fever and I'm going to visit my family before one of us gets hurt."

He stares at me for a couple seconds then turns around and walks back downstairs without saying a word. I put some makeup on to hide the fuchsia half-moons under my eyes and a touch of petroleum jelly on my still healing lips. After putting my hair into a messy top knot I head downstairs. I can see my angry nurse out on the back deck talking on his cell phone while York and Kirby are playing in the yard. I pick up my purse and search for my keys but they're not in my bag. Looking over at the small wooden keyboard Fabian and Ginger got me as a housewarming gift I notice the spare set is missing too. Pax took my keys? He is diabolical when he wants his way. The key thief opens the French door and steps inside.

"…thanks so much, we'll see you then… okay, thanks again, bye," he says into the phone then walks over to stand in front of me.

"Where are my keys?" I ask getting angry at his manipulation.

"In my pocket," he smiles; thrusting his hips towards me and says, "Feel free to try for them."

Eyeing his low riding jeans, I know there's no way he will let me get them out of his pocket so I drop my bag on the island and storm into the living, frustrated beyond belief.

"Dammit Pax all I want is to see my family," I raise my voice making the dogs walk over to sit down on either side of me. At least they're on my side and make me smile when they press their muzzles in my palms.

"Fine, you'll see them in an hour since they're driving over here, food and all," he grins before crossing his arms over his chest and leaning against the edge of the counter. He's so smug and proud of himself but I can't resist the man, even when he's pulling my chain.

"Thank you," I tell him tilting my chin up at him and crossing my arms lightly over my still tender ribs.

"That's it? Thank you is all I get for moving mountains, re-arranging five schedules all to accommodate you?" he softly purrs walking over to stand in front of me in a sexy, threatening kind of swagger.

"You did all that to accommodate yourself," I laugh at his pretending to be affronted at my lack of gratitude. "I was willing to go to them, you're the one with the issues, changing their plans not me," I smile up at him then stand on tip toe and kiss his lips. "There, is that better?"

"Better, but not the best you can do," he growls then pulls me to his body and gently wraps his arms around me as I absorb the rightness of being in his embrace.

It's been six days since we've made love and both of us are showing signs of withdrawal. He's been by my side every minute of the day, but he's kept his caresses and kisses mild. Right now, I recognize the sexual tension whipping through his body because I feel it too.

"Promise to make love to me later," I whisper against his lips. "I miss you Pax."

"God I've missed you," he replies pressing his palms to my denim covered hips and pulling me closer. "I'm about to go up in smoke, but I don't want to hurt you."

"Six days and counting Pax," I remind him and he smiles counting the days in his head too.

"I was going to wait until they removed your stitches… but I'm sure we can come up with a different position, so as not to put any pressure on your thigh," he offers making me get excited thinking about finally making love with him again.

"Oh, I forgot to ask," I tell him as I push out of his arms and walk into the kitchen and get ready for brunch, "What did Detective Graves say when he called yesterday?" I was shocked the man was working on a Saturday.

He runs his fingers through his thick sable hair and says, "Same old story; they're looking for Whitaker at all his old haunts and even checked with the police in Vancouver. But so far Whitaker's friend hasn't heard from him." Pax is tensing up so I drop the subject and reach for plates to feed the crew.

"What are you doing?" he demands walking up behind me and taking the stack of white plates from me. "You're not supposed to strain your ribs or your shoulder Harper," he admonishes me and places the dishes behind him on the island. "What else do you want," he says cupping my face in his hands before kissing me softly. "Just tell me what needs done and I'll take care of it. Hey, where's your shoulder sling?"

Smiling at his accommodating manner I kiss him back and wish he'd take care of my most pressing need… Before I can say anything his cell phone rings. Removing it from his back pocket he recognizes the number then smiles before he answers his phone.

"Hey you're back," he says into the phone. "How were your folks? Did Candace and the girls get settled…? That sounds great; I'll see you fifteen minutes. You're in luck, Draper is bringing the brunch out here so you'll be well fed." He laughs at something his friend says and then ends the call with, "She's doing a lot better, looks wonderful…very colorful." Pax laughs again looking over at me and winking then says, "I'll let you tell her that, see you soon, bye."

He's laughing when he walks over to me and pulls me into his chest.

"Wiley says Candace and the girls send their love and hope you recover quickly," he relays the message but doesn't repeat what his friend said about me being colorful.

"Better get another plate and glass down," I say into the collar of his shirt. "I didn't know his parents lived in Buffalo, but then again I didn't know he even had parents, I always assumed he was spawned."

Pax laughs and says, "They live in Rochester, so since he was that close he decided to spend a couple days with them. They're very nice people."

"Wiley was adopted?" I tease making Pax laugh and shake his head.

"Good one," he says turning to take down a couple more glasses for me and we set the table for eight.

The dogs greet Wiley with their usual bark and shuffle over to the door. Pax's best friend pets the guys on the head, chest bumps his friend then walks directly over to stand in front of me. He spreads his long arms wide open and I find myself gravitating over to him, loving the warmth and friendship he's offering me.

"Honey I think you missed your eyelids with that pinkish purple eye shadow," he teases making me chuckle. "It's too much for daytime anyway." I pinch his trim waist in retaliation. "Ow, hey no fair attacking me until you're fit enough to receive my return volley."

"You're a nut," I tell him reaching up and kissing his scruffy bearded cheek. "How have you been?" I ask and smile when he goes into a diatribe on why he only visits his parents a couple times a year.

"I had two blind dates in the four days I was visiting with them," he shakes his head in amazement. "One wasn't half bad, but she and Mom are bridge partners so she might be a bit too 'mature' for me."

Pax laughs as he hands Wiley a cup of fresh coffee.

"Brother, Candace's girls are a bit too mature for you," he teases making him frown at the slam.

"Very funny," he sneers. "So, fill me in on what you found out about Whitaker."

"Detective Graves is very stingy on the news, either that or they have no idea where Whitaker's at, which personally is what I believe to be the case." Pax has that edge to his voice again letting me know he's still worried about my safety.

While they rehash old news, I grab my bright orange windbreaker and take my glass of juice outside to walk the dogs. They head towards the shoreline, noses to the ground having caught an intriguing scent of something. Watching York and Kirby sniff out the large rocks they wander out of my sight. The lake is so calm and peaceful I lose track of time and the pups. I put the empty glass in my pocket and go in search of the boys. They must have found something because they bark their heads off in excitement. Walking around a couple large boulders I still don't see the dogs. I whistle for them when a male arm steals around my waist pressing my ribs painfully. Before I can call out a sweaty palm covers my lips and a harsh voice whispers in my ear.

"Don't make a sound or I'll let the dog drown," Cody Whitaker growls. "Damn mutt almost took my arm off before I could get the leash attached to his collar. The stockier one ran back to the house after I dazed him with my fist, so we need to move, now!"

Looking around for York I hear him before I see the wet angry dog, pulling against a heavy chain wedged between tight crevices in the rock, keeping him against one large boulder. Thankfully he doesn't appear hurt, just riled. His barking is ferocious sounding and hopefully Pax and Wiley will hear his distress before I'm too far away. They'll be alarmed when Kirby arrives back at the house alone.

"Cody what are you doing?" I ask holding his wiry arm from cutting off my air supply. I try to keep the fear out of my voice and stall for time. "The cops are looking for you, why didn't you just disappear to Canada like you said?"

He keeps tugging on my arm sending a shooting pain through my recently dislocated shoulder but turn to get a good look at his face. His eyes are bloodshot as if he's been on a bender or hasn't slept in a week. His hair is oily and his bangs are whipping across his face from the wind cutting through the cliff rocks. Cody's dressed in a dirty flannel shirt and stained jeans with rips in the pant legs. The hand holding my arm is dirty and bleeding around the knuckles giving testament to the difficult time he had holding my dogs.

"Because you told some detective about my friend, who almost lost his job when he was questioned by the local police, that's why," he snarls at me flexing his arm and sending another jolt of pain down my side. "You've really made a mess of my life Candace... I mean Harper."

"You nearly killed my niece and me in that taxi cab," I snap tired of being manhandled. "Let go of me Cody, there's no need for any of this," I remind him. "Nobody knows you're here, just leave and I promise not to tell anyone your whereabouts."

He laughs and pushes me down hard in the gravel where I land on the fragile juice glass in my pocket; I feel the stem snap.

"Like I'd believe any thing you'd tell me to be the truth!" he screams, froth forming around his tightly clenched lips.

From the look on his face he's crossed some invisible boundary and I know if I don't do something and soon I won't see Pax or my family again, and that's just not an option.

"Get up!" he shouts at me forgetting how well sound travels across water.

Since the lake is empty I pray nothing absorbs our conversation but it carries over the placid surface. He continues to scream and shout how all women are untrustworthy and how he will do his part by eliminating the two vilest ones he knows, namely me and Candace.

I just sit there, winded when he hollers, "Move bitch or you'll regret it!"

"Fine," I sigh as if I've given up, "but where are you taking me?"

"I rented one of those small log cabins three houses down," he says visibly calming down when I cooperate … his mood swings are mercurial, he's so unbalanced right now. "I've been watching you for the better part of two weeks, your comings and goings… You really should think about getting curtains installed throughout the house," he laughs. "You never know who might be scoping you out."

The thought of him spying on me and Pax threatens to send my stomach in revolt but I stand up and shuffle my feet through the deep pea gravel size pebbles leaving tracks sliding my hand into the coat pocket and gripping the broken stemware in my hand. He leads me around the boulders where my sweet York is still fighting to break free. I walk towards the laboring dog but Cody grabs a handful of my hair and hauls me back against his side. I pretend to lose my balance and together we fall to the beach.

"God dammit!" he shouts when I pull out my makeshift weapon and drag the jagged piece of glass across his forearm before I quickly pick myself up and kick him in the ribs. The stitches in my leg pull but I keep kicking him hard, first in his stomach, then his groin.

"Stop it!" he cries trying to protect his body, his left arm bleeding profusely from the wound I gave him but I refuse to stop until I hear Pax calling my name.

"Hang on Harper!" he shouts and I hear Kirby barking his head off, excited to be playing this game. "Where you are baby, shout out for me!"

"Pax! Over here," I scream as I turn to run towards his voice but my damaged leg gives out from the strain and I slide across the wet rocks and go down on one knee.

That's all the opening Cody needs and he pounces on me rolling me over and straddling my hips. The madman wraps his wet, bloody hands around my throat and strangles me, cutting off my cry for help before it leaves my throat. Both dogs arrive barking frantically, grasping Cody's pant leg, trying to get the man off me but he keeps kicking at them, connecting his foot to their ribs, but they give no ground. York bites the man's forearm, making him break his hold.

"I'll kill you for that," he screams at the dog then let's

loose of a stream of horrible things he'll do when he gets me back to his cabin. Spittle streams out of his mouth as he slaps me across my cheek dazing me from the beating he continues to inflict upon me. A horrible cry of rage rips through the air, startling me and my attacker before Cody's weight is lifted off my body. Unsure what is happening I try to scramble out of the way but strong hands slip under my arms and haul me to my feet.

"I've got you Harper," Wiley says holding me in his arms, shielding me from the colossal beating my fiancé is doling out to Whitaker. "Don't kill him brother, we need something left to prosecute," he warns Pax as he folds me into his protective embrace.

The dogs are circling around me, barking and growling, blood on their muzzles. Looking around Wiley's broad shoulder I see Pax driving his fists into Cody Whitaker's stomach, repeatedly he pounds on my attacker until the weaker man drops to his knees giving Pax an opening for a hard-right upper cut to Cody's jaw. Whitaker falls over backward but Pax is beyond the realm and kicks my abductor in the ribs and would have continued to beat the man senseless if my brother, father, and Detective Graves hadn't pulled him away. Pax is beside himself, a berserker struggling to get close enough to inflict more damage but my father wraps his strong arm around the younger man's heaving chest and points with his free hand over towards me and Wiley who is holding me up.

"It's over son," Poppy says. "Go help Harper while we take care of this piece of trash."

Pax's eyes are glazed over in rage but when he focuses on me he settles down. Nodding his head for the guys to release him he runs over to me picks me up in his arms, lifts me off the ground and holds me like he'll never let go.

"Paxton!" I cry when he presses his wet face in my neck.

His heart is pounding, his lungs bellowing, and there are tears running down his dirty cheeks. Ignoring the pain coursing through my body I cling to him, kiss his cheek, his ear, any place I can touch, trying to absorb his pain, the fear, and his wrath at finding Whitaker trying to kill me. Looking over his shoulder I watch as the guys get Whitaker to his feet but Pax has incapacitated him making Detective Graves hand cuff his prisoner's hands behind his back and then put him in a fireman carry position so he can transport him back to our house.

"Pax, come on, you're about to break her in two," Wiley whispers to his best friend tapping on my lover's arm to ease his hold on me. "Let's get her back to the house and cleaned up. Her Mom's going to have a fit when she sees the mess her Princess is in."

Pax nods his head and scoops me into his arms, jostling my ribs and shoulder even more. I cry out in pain even though he's being as careful as he can. I rest my head on his shoulder as he starts forward.

"Hold on baby," he whispers his lips pressing into my forehead. "I'll have you back home in a second. Wiley, go check on York and Kirby please," he says nodding his head at the two Mastiffs that are running around in frenzy. "York scraped his neck clean of fur trying to get to Harper so be careful, Kirby is just being Kirby, running amuck."

Our motley crew arrives back at the house a couple minutes later and Wiley's right, my mother has a conniption fit over my condition.

"Where is that son of a bitch?" she shouts when Pax sets me down on the deck chair. "I'll kill him," she growls and Poppy actually holds her back when Detective Graves walks past with the unconscious man over his broad shoulder and waits on Victor to open the back door of the cop car.

"Don't worry Dee," Poppy tells her, "our son almost did the job for real," he smiles at the look of pride and satisfaction that crosses the usually unflappable woman.

"Thank you, Pax," she says and stands on tip toe to plant a kiss on his cheek. "I know she's in good hands but let me check her over, see if we need to take her to the ER."

He carries me upstairs and helps my Mother and Shawna, who hands over a worried Cassie to her father and helps undress and clean me up. The stitches in my thigh held but just barely. Mom almost faints when she sees the dark, angry looking bruises that formed across my left ribcage from the wreck. Hopefully she won't see Whitaker's handiwork.

"Oh Harper," she cries. "I'm so sorry you had to go through that nightmare."

Hugging me gently to her breast she releases me only when Pax hands me a fistful of painkillers and a glass of water. His knuckles are scraped and bloody but they're the most beautiful hands I've ever seen. Looking at him tears start to well up at what he went through.

"Shhh," he whispers sitting down on the side of the bed, holding out the pills, "I'm not hurt at all baby, I promise. Take these tablets and let them ease you into sleep."

Nodding my head in agreement I swallow the medication and relax against my pillows. Mom kisses my forehead while Shawna strokes my bare arm. Pax stands up as if to leave and

I feel a sense of panic. He turns back towards me and smiles that lopsided grin I love.

"Don't worry Harpo I'm not going anywhere," he assures me. "Ladies I'm about to strip down and get out of these wet clothes so for your sake I suggest you close the door on your way out. I'll stay with her until she falls asleep."

"I love you Paxton," my mother tells him making him grin from ear to ear. "Thanks for rescuing my baby; I'll save you a heaping plate of everything, ready when you are, how's that?"

He hugs her and kisses her cheek, "sounds like a plan, send Wiley up here if you would, please."

"Sure, get some rest dear," Mom says and Shawna waves her fingers at me smiling when Pax removes his shirt over his head before she closes the door.

Closing my eyes, I hear him moving about the room, and then he's pulling back the covers and sliding naked across the mattress to carefully gather me in his arms.

"Go to sleep baby," he whispers and the steady rhythm of his heart with the powerful painkillers he gave me lures me into a deep, healing sleep, barely aware of the man that walks into the room and helps Pax with some plan, but I'm too close to oblivion to understand any of what they're saying so I let Morpheus embrace me and then I'm out.

34

Waking up from a dreamless sleep the first thing I notice is it's still day time. I feel like I've slept around the clock but glancing over at the bedside clock I see I've only been out for four hours. Tentatively stretching my aching arms and legs I notice Pax's side of the bed is cool, he's been gone for a while. I can hear hushed voices downstairs and the sound of muffled laughter making me smile; my family is still here.

Sitting up I swing my legs off the side of the bed when a sharp pain shoots up my stitched thigh. Glancing down I'm grateful the stitches are holding but I guess I'll be walking with a light step until that wound is healed. My ribs hurt like crazy and my throat is sore but other than that I'm sound. Carefully I make my way to the bathroom and get my first real look at myself since this morning. My hair is no longer in a cute bun but all tousled and sticking out the side of my head, the mascara from my lashes transferred to black half-moons on my cheeks joining the pink and purple rings under my eyes; I look like a hung-over raccoon with my bloodshot eyes. Stretching my neck, I can see Cody Whitaker's individual finger shaped bruises where he tried to strangle me... that will set Pax off again. I pull my wild hair back into a ponytail and gently wipe the mascara residue away with a tissue.

Turning away from my frightening reflection I pull my white terry cloth robe off the back of the door and wrap it around me, grateful for its comfort and the fact it hides my battered body from view. Now to get downstairs…standing on the landing I whistle for the dogs and in seconds they come running up the stairs with Pax and Wiley closely behind them. Wiley is grinning over Pax's shoulder but my man isn't happy to see me out of bed. He looks amazing in dark jeans, a brown flannel shirt, and those grungy boots he loves. But the look in his dark eyes makes me glad I'm not alone with him now.

"Get back in bed," he tells me climbing the stairs with an intimidating look on his handsome face. "Harper, you need to rest." He stops a step or two below me, his arms spread between both railings and blocking my path, waiting on me to comply with his order.

"I need to be with you and my family," I counter taking a couple tentative steps towards him, hoping he doesn't see my legs tremble from the exertion.

"Come on Pax," Wiley cajoles his friend. "After what she's been through cut her some slack." He leans around Pax and offers me his hand, "Come on little sister, I'll help you down; looks like your hero is failing you already."

Pax quickly turns his head and glares at Wiley shoving his best friend's outstretched hand out of the way before he loses his temper.

"Back off Wiley," he hisses, "I want her to stay in bed because of what she went through today, you idiot. But if she wants to be bull-headed and risk falling I'll be the one to carry her so get out of my way," He snaps then looks up at me and says, "Turn around and wait on me at the top of the stairs while Wiley grabs the dogs. They're likely to trample you to death when you roll down the steps."

Trying not to smile I can't stop the giggle that escapes from between my lips. But Pax looks down at me when he reaches the landing and leans in to kiss my mouth.

"I love you Harper," he whispers before he melds his lips with mine. "But you suck at taking orders. Will you let me know when you get tired?"

I nod my head in compliance as he joins his lips to mine again, only he deepens the kiss, much to my delight. Just the warm taste of him makes me light headed but when I hug him he scoops me up into his arms and smiles down at me.

"Your smile is a sight for sore eyes," he says making me feel tingly all over until he finishes with, "the rest of you appears thrashed."

Wiley can barely hold York and Kirby back as Pax brings me into the living room filled with our family and friends. My parents are in the kitchen with Marc who smiles at me while he tosses a salad; the aroma of Poppy's baked ziti hits me and my stomach growls. Mom is holding two heavy baking sheets of garlic toast that could heal the sick and dying. Shawna and Cassie with Fabian are setting the wide planked dining room table as Ginger opens a couple bottles of my favorite Merlot.

"Look who decided to join us," Stanley Carmichael says accepting the tall stemware half full of the dark wine from my dear friend. "How are you feeling honey?"

"Oh, Harper…" Pax's mother Beth dressed in her usual gray slacks and white blouse holds out her hands and gently takes my left hand in both of hers. "You poor baby, Pax put her over on the sofa, Wiley stop playing with those animals and bring that afghan over here," the woman barks out orders. "Can she have wine? No, wait, she's on painkillers, right? Better give her a glass of milk; she needs to build up her strength…"

Pax sets me down gently in the corner and pulls away but I grab ahold of his wrist and whisper in his ear, "Don't you dare leave me alone with your mother in this mood. She'll have me wrapped in cotton and stuck on a shelf somewhere."

He laughs and kisses me hard then steps back and grins, "get used to it Princess," he says using my father's nickname for me. "Oh, by the way, I caved."

"What? Pax what are you talking about?" I ask then Beth sits down beside me and grins looking so much like her son it's frightening. The woman is practically beaming over something.

"So, let's talk about the wedding and what we'll do differently this time," she begins, making sense of Pax's comment about caving. Apparently, she's under the assumption I'm willing to go through the entire big wedding ordeal again. Before I can set her straight my brother joins us holding his sleepy eyed little girl. She leans down and lightly touches the cuts on my forehead from the wreck and then smiles at me… such an angel.

"Does that hurt?" she asks making me grin up at her concern so I take her hand in mine.

"Not now," I tell her and kiss her plump little fingers. Victor shifts the little girl in his arms and he leans down and presses a kiss on my forehead, then grins down at me with a mischievous look on his face, he offers a slight change from the last non-wedding.

"How about the groom stays to the finish?" he teases making everybody in the two rooms laugh, including Pax who picks up an orange from the fruit bowl sitting on the coffee table in front of me and lobs the naval grenade at my brother who deftly catches the citrus missile and hands it to me. "Have some orange juice instead of milk."

I try holding my ribs but the laughter must come out and it hurts so badly. Cassie whispers to her father and he sets her down. My niece walks over and climbs onto Beth's lap surprising my future mother-in-law. The cherub smiles and says to the older woman, "I want a different dress and new shoes and flowers 'cause Mommy threw the others away, and I want a kitty."

Beth hugs the little angel and says, "Whatever you want, you get when you're at Aunt Bethy's house, except the kitten okay?" Looking down at the small blonde she says, "Now describe to me what kind of new dress you'd like."

"Hey Aunt Bethy," Wiley interrupts, munching a crust of garlic toast he pilfered from the cloth lined basket now sitting on the food-filled island. "I want a different gal to walk down the aisle with; Ginger Snap over there is mean, plus she always has to be touching me." He shudders in feigned revulsion making Marc and my father laugh. She sticks out her tongue at him in silent retaliation.

The easy bantering and ribbing goes on even after we're sitting down at the lovely table my mom set. Poppy's two large pans of hearty baked ziti are surrounded by a lovely antipasto tray, a cheese and grape platter with an assortment of crackers, figs and tangerines nestled beside ripe pears. The guys filled my plate so I wouldn't have to stand in the buffet line and I think they gave me a man-sized portion of everything; Stuffed pasta shells with crab and ricotta cheese; Italian sausages in bowtie pasta with peppers, onions, and tomatoes; cheese stuffed tortellini, and a scoop of Poppy's ziti. Pax filled a bowl of salad and set it between us to share… There is no way I will be able to eat all this, especially since Pax is holding my hand in his lap, feeding me bites of garlic toast and offering me small sips of wine from his glass but refusing to give me my own due to the medication his mother reminded him about. Poppy is smiling at something Vic and Wiley are arguing about, Cassie is going over her hastily made list of all the items she wants from Beth and Stan, my mother and Shawna are talking about dresses, Marc and Ginger are making come-hither stares with one another while Fabian is slipping pieces of hard salami from the antipasto tray to the boys stretched out beneath the table. It's a perfect family get together.

35

Half-way through the meal the dogs jump up and nearly push Fabian's chair over trying to get to the side porch door. Their barking resonates off the exposed beamed ceiling startling me and the others at the urgent alarm they're sending to whomever the unfortunate soul is about to be welcomed by the two dogs.

"I'll see who it is," Pax says wiping his mouth on his linen napkin motioning for the others to stay seated. "Come on boys, let's go outside for a bit," he tells the duo circling his long legs. Standing on the screened in porch he looks over his shoulder and smiles back at the table. "It's Detective Graves, Wiley get another plate, Vic grab a beer from the fridge and Fabian, you can have my chair and we'll give him yours okay?"

"I'm done anyway, may I be excused?" my Godson asks his Uncle Pax who nods his head.

"Sure, we'll call you when we're ready for dessert," my dad says after the boy grabs his backpack I know from experience is filled to the rim with toys.

"I'll be up in the watch tower Poppy," he informs my father who smiles at the child's use of my nickname for

325

him. "Don't forget, I want a big brownie with a scoop of chocolate ice cream," he says turning towards the stairs then remembers the manners his mother and father drummed into his head and walks back over towards my father and says, "please."

Poppy hugs my Godson and kisses the top of his head, "Go and play; I promise not to forget young man."

Fabian smiles and races up the stairs just as Pax holds the door open for the policeman who keeps looking behind his back at the two big dogs.

"Hello Detective," I greet him pushing my half-eaten plate to the center of the table. "Come join us for a bite to eat."

"Well, normally I'd decline such a gracious offer but I could smell this food down by the driveway," he grins and takes the seat Wiley offers him before the cold beer bottle touches his hand. "Thanks, this is what I'd call the supreme Sunday family get-together."

Poppy loves to watch people tuck into one of his dinners. Once everyone is seated again we finish our meal while I fend off questions about am I too tired? Am I in pain? Would I like to lie down? Marc and Ginger clear the dirty dishes, which in no way disturbs the cop still shoveling every bite of food on his plate into his mouth. Pax sets the coffee pot in the center of the table while Victor gets the out-of-this-world brownies my father makes.

"Cassie, are you ready for dessert?" her mother asks but the little one is looking sleepy resting across Beth's lap.

"Can I just have ice cream?" she asks her grandfather who smiles and nods his head. "Maybe Mister Graveyard would like my brownie?"

Detective Graves laugh at his new last name and says, "Why don't you and your family all call me Harley, okay? Oh, and I'd love to have your brownie if you're sure you don't want it?"

"No," she yawns and accepts the single scoop of chocolate ice cream in one of my antique dessert dishes her grandfather sets in front of her. "I'll just finish this."

Beth hands her over to sit on Stan's lap while she walks over to the bottom of the stairs and calls for Fabian.

"Brownie and ice cream," she shouts making the rest of us laugh at her. "Come and get it!"

Fabian flies down the stairs and runs smack into the older woman then apologizes and walks sedately over to sit on Marc's lap. Once we're enjoying the hedonistic chocolate fest Pax brings up this morning's drama.

"What happened after you went back to the city?" he asks dipping his spoon into my bowl since his is already gone. "Did you arrest him and throw him in jail?"

Harley grins and picks up his coffee cup, takes a sip of the rich brew and shakes his head.

"Oh, I arrested him, read him his rights, and let him call his attorney, all from the hospital bed he's lying in now." The police man drops his smile and sets his coffee cup down into the saucer. "Son you just about killed that man…"

"Don't bother trying to make me feel bad Graves," Pax interrupts the cop. "The bastard's lucky I didn't weight his body down and row him out to the center of the lake."

"Paxton Joseph Barrett!" his mother hisses at her son's statement as she looks around the table appalled at the simmering violence in him. "Don't say things like that."

His mother's face is shocked at the hatred pouring off

Pax but my mother offers her own brand of humor to the situation.

"Your mother's right Pax," she says picking up her wineglass and upending it before setting it down on the table, "at least don't make plans like that while there's a cop sitting across from you."

The crowd laughs and Harley Graves is holding his sides like I'm doing. He finishes his dessert and looks over at me, staring into my eyes.

"Honey, I'm glad your man put the hurt on that son of a ... gun," he says changing what he was about to say due to small ears in the vicinity. "As a father of a teenaged daughter I can tell you there's nothing I wouldn't do to protect her but as a cop, your future mother-in-law is right, don't say things like that when I'm working a case, got it?"

"I thought you were working your way through a free meal," Ginger says taking offense at our guest's reprimand. "Did you know he rented a place here on the lake?" Marc squeezes her tense shoulder reminding her who she's snapping at.

"Yes," he replies looking directly at me and making Pax drop his spoon into his empty bowl and rise out of his chair. Graves holds out his hands to calm my fiancé but it's too late, Pax is fired up.

"Do you mean to tell me you knew where he was? That he was three houses down from us this entire time and you didn't think to tell us... Get the fuck out of here!" he snarls pointing his extended arm at the cop who is remaining seated.

Wiley scoots his chair out and makes his way over to Pax's side, the dogs stand up, a low growl in their throats at the tension that fills the room. Poppy nods his head at me silently warning me to deal with Pax's temper.

"Baby, don't do this," I whisper to him as I grab on to his wrist, feeling the incredible fury emanating from his body, coiled like a cobra ready to strike. "I'm sure Detective Graves was following procedure, right?" I ask looking across the table at the man of authority. "Surely you wouldn't have used me as bait…"

"Son of a bitch," Pax swears under his breath. "That's exactly what he did. Mother, take Cassie upstairs for me please," he says intending to have it out with the unperturbed officer.

"No Pax," I tell him trying to stand but my muscles have tightened up and I fall back down in my seat. Instantly Pax is hovering over me, checking to see that I'm not hurt.

"Are you alright?" Pax asks bending down to make sure I'm fine when I take advantage of his nearness and kiss him long and hard in front of our audience.

When we break apart I see the anger still glittering in his eyes but he has himself under control. He smiles at me and nods his head agreeing with my silent plea to remain calm. He scoops me up and sets me down on his lap resting his chin on my shoulder and picking up his wine glass offering me a sip before he takes one. A collective sigh rings around the table as Pax calms down and a new crisis has been averted. York and Kirby lie down at our feet but keep watching the policeman, just in case.

"Tell me Detective Graves," my mother speaks up and those of us that grew up hearing that direct tone of voice knows the man is in for an ear full. "Are my children correct? Did you use them to lure that psycho out into the open? Keep in mind I'll be wearing your badge as my brooch if you tell me a lie."

Graves laughs and finishes his beer before he replies, "I couldn't tell your daughter or Paxton about an ongoing investigation. Keep in mind I was working with the local county sheriff's office but they're shorthanded like most rural area departments. I've been staking out this side of the lake from the Hutchins' place. I was on the other side of the lake questioning the old man that lives on the right side of Whitaker's cabin when I saw his truck fly past. He's been gone for almost a week and I only had authorization to be up here until this evening, so even though I'm sorry he attacked you, at least we nailed him, well at least your fiancé nailed him." He leans back in his chair and softly says, "We found letters he had written to his wife, to you, and to his attorney… let's just say you're lucky he never got around to doing those things he wrote about."

"See, everything worked out for the best," Beth says trying to smooth things over but Pax is still fuming over me being set up, probably always will be a sore spot with him. They're right; it's over, at least for now. Candace and the girls are safe from that man.

"Pax let's forget about this morning," I whisper in his ear. "You saved me, now you're responsible for me…all the rest of your life."

He laughs and gently hugs me to his back.

"Sorry for losing my cool," Pax says to the room, even though he's not sorry in the least. "Wiley, it's okay we're not hiding any bodies in the lake today, go sit down and finish your dessert before Vic does."

Resting back against Pax's shoulder I glance around the

table once more, glad to be alive, surrounded by friends, and relieved there will be no suspicious trips across the lake tonight. As the sun sets in the darkening October sky my family puts away leftovers, loads the dishwasher, and picks up sleeping children. I hug them goodbye and all but Wiley and the detective are heading back to the city. Following behind Pax I lie down into his side as we crash on the sectional, kicking off our shoes and snuggling under the afghan, the dogs are on their bed in the corner, everybody but me has a fresh beer his hand and they rehash today's events.

Later Pax lifts me up in his arms and carries me upstairs to bed. Removing my robe, he hands me a couple pain pills with my antibiotic and a glass of water.

"Come on sleeping beauty let's get some rest," he smiles stripping down and sliding under the covers. I snuggle up to his side, careful of my bruised ribs and rest my head on his bare chest. "I can't believe Graves has been staying across the yard for almost two weeks and we had no idea."

Laughing I reply, "I can't believe you and Wiley were going to start a fight with the cop."

He laughs with me and says, "You'd have bailed me out of jail, right?"

"You, Wiley, my mother..." I tease and once we settle down he lets out a big sigh.

"This is the second time in less than a week I almost lost you," he shudders rolling over onto his side and spooning his front to my back. "I need you Harper," he whispers. "I'll be extra careful but I need to be with you, inside you..." he groans as I arch my back, pressing my bottom to his aroused flesh.

"I'm waiting on you," I whisper over my shoulder. "Make my dreams come true Pax, let's end this day on the best positive side possible, you and I joined at the hip and beyond."

He chuckles as he slips into his favorite position, gently rocking us to the first orgasm either of us has had in almost a week. Our joining is sweet, pure magic and sends us both gliding into a blissful place where we'll spend the next fifty or sixty years… our voices sing out together in perfect harmony, telling me we're both living the same dream.

36

"Harper, hurry up or you'll be late for your wedding," my mother calls up the stairs.

Giving myself one last look in the floor length mirror on my closet door I nod in approval at the white boucle wool skirt and jacket I chose for my wedding outfit. Pax and I finally convinced our parents we would not do the 'over the top' wedding ceremony, and since the clerk's office is closed on the weekend we decided to say our vows in the small church here in Lake Sinclaire. Pastor Phelps and his wife looked like they stepped out of a nineteen fifties TV show, suited to the small-town persona. Pax and I met them three weeks ago and they welcomed us to their congregation and were thrilled to perform a fall wedding.

"Coming Mom," I holler as I open the bedroom door only to find Pax leaning against the door frame, dressed in his good black suit, a rust colored vest and a black tie. He looks amazing as he stands there taking in my wedding finery.

"We need to talk," he says and forces me back inside the room creating a sense of déjà vu from our last non-wedding.

"Forget it," I tell him placing my palms on his broad

chest and pushing him backwards towards the door. "The only words I want to hear out of your mouth is 'til death do us part, I do; and I love you… in that order mister."

He grins and covers my hands in his lifting them to his lips and kissing my knuckles.

"Don't worry, you'll hear all that and more but something's happened and I don't want you to hear about it later," he says making me even more nervous than I was before his reassurance.

"What?" I ask staring into the eyes of the only man I'll ever love. "Don't keep me waiting Pax, tell me."

He takes a deep breath and says, "Cody Whitaker was released yesterday due to a technicality, mainly me. Apparently, he's pressing charges against me, you, Harley, the Lake County Sheriff's Department, and the Albany Police Department too."

"Why? He's the one that nearly killed me, twice all because he thought I was keeping Candace and the girls away from him," I rant, hating the injustice of the criminal's rights superseding the victims.

"Don't worry, the restraining order you have on him should keep him in the eyes of the sheriff's department, but they had to drop some of the charges against him due to mitigating circumstances, mainly the dog bites on his arms and legs, the swollen groin from your foot, and the concussion, broken ribs, and two missing teeth courtesy of yours truly," he smiles as he lists off the bastard's injuries.

"What happens next?" I ask dreading having to go to court and seeing him again.

"We get married, go to Tahiti, and avoid the press that is going to be surrounding this case thanks to him and his family who apparently have a bit more money and influence than any of us realized. They're a big to do back in Vancouver, or so Harley informs me." He hugs me to his chest and says, "But all that must wait as you and I are getting married no matter what."

I kiss his lips and wipe off the small trace of berry lip gloss on his smiling lips.

"I'm ready when you are," I tell him and he nods his head in approval.

"This time no body is running out of the church, but... your father has already itemized the food and drink then given me a copy, just in case..." he laughs as we walk down the stairs and join our parents waiting patiently in our kitchen.

Poppy's favorite staff members will stay behind and prepare the tables to be set up outside in the back yard facing the lake and the lovely fall foliage along the banks and since it's been unseasonably mild the weather seems to cooperate with our outdoor plans. There will only be about forty guests this time, and we'll know everyone here.

"Son, I'm happy to give my Princess away and I know this time you're ready to be that man she deserves," my father says holding out his hand to Pax who immediately accepts it with his own.

"Just so you know," Pax says smiling over at me and our folks, "I'll never give her back, she belongs to me no matter what, right babe?"

I kiss his cheek and smile at him.

"This time when you leave the ceremony I'll be right beside you, forever."

"Great, let's go get these kids married before they

change their minds," Stan says ushering his wife out the door. "We'll be expecting you to be expecting real soon too."

"Yes sir, so will we," Pax says linking our fingers together and walking out to the jag. "Who knows, nine months from now we may give them what they want, right?"

My mother and Beth clasp their hands together and make baby shower plans as they head towards the door.

"Hey, another dream come true plus it will keep them out of trouble for the next couple of months, so let's get this show on the road," Poppy laughs and closes the side door waving at the Mastiffs waiting like sentinels on the other side of the screened in porch door.

Forty minutes later Mr. and Mrs. Paxton Barrett walk out the front double doors of Lake Sinclaire Church of Christ grinning from ear to ear, being dowsed with bird seed and well wishes. By the time we get into the car we're covered with the tiny pellets but laughing so hard we don't notice the soft pings of the seed falling out of our hair and clothes.

"I love you Mr. Barrett," I tell him wrapping my arms around his broad shoulders and kiss his smiling lips.

"I love you too Mrs. Barrett," he replies hugging me back before he turns the key in the ignition. "Let's go home."

"I'm always home when I'm in your arms," I tell him.

I know our life together won't always be perfect, but our love makes living the dream possible.

Printed in the United States
By Bookmasters